A would-be battle—with a very real zombie.

The boys from Texas don't stand around and talk when there's trouble, and they especially never hide from a fight. So five of them, with various bloody wounds, wrestled with the slimy, charcoal gray corpse of Mrs. Barnaby, who was tossing them around like she was a mad bull just out of a pen.

I yanked the lid off my Tupperware and waited to glimpse some body part of hers, the swampy smell of decay choking me. Then her gnarled black hand thrust out and grabbed Stucky Clark's beefy arm.

I propelled myself forward, raising my voice. "Go now and peace do keep. Return at once to your sleep." I tossed the passion-flower potion, splashing it on the pile.

The room sucked all the air from my lungs, and I dropped to my knees, gasping, trying to pull some breath back in. I couldn't. I was dying, suffocating for real. My mouth moved, screaming soundlessly for help, then everything went black.

Would-Be Witch

KIMBERLY FROST

BERKLEY BOOKS, NEW YORK

THE BERKLEY PUBLISHING GROUP
Published by the Penguin Group
Penguin Group (USA) Inc.
375 Hudson Street, New York, New York 10014, USA
Penguin Group (Canada), 90 Eglinton Avenue East, Suite 700, Toronto, Ontario M4P 2Y3, Canada
(a division of Pearson Penguin Canada Inc.)
Penguin Books Ltd., 80 Strand, London WC2R 0RL, England
Penguin Group Ireland, 25 St. Stephen's Green, Dublin 2, Ireland (a division of Penguin Books Ltd.)
Penguin Group (Australia), 250 Camberwell Road, Camberwell, Victoria 3124, Australia
(a division of Pearson Australia Group Pty. Ltd.)
Penguin Books India Pvt. Ltd., 11 Community Centre, Panchsheel Park, New Delhi—110 017, India
Penguin Group (NZ), 67 Apollo Drive, Rosedale, North Shore 0632, New Zealand
(a division of Pearson New Zealand Ltd.)
Penguin Books (South Africa) (Pty.) Ltd., 24 Sturdee Avenue, Rosebank, Johannesburg 2196, South Africa

Penguin Books Ltd., Registered Offices: 80 Strand, London WC2R 0RL, England

This is an original publication of The Berkley Publishing Group.

Cover art by Kimberly Schamber.
Cover design by Rita Frangie.
Text design by Laura K. Corless.

First edition: February 2009

Library of Congress Cataloging-in-Publication Data

Frost, Kimberly.
Would-be witch / Kimberly Frost.—1st ed.
p. cm.
ISBN 978-0-425-22577-6
1. Witches—Fiction. 2. Heirlooms—Fiction. 3. Texas—Fiction. I. Title.

PS3606.R655W68 2009
813'.6—dc22

2008044758

PRINTED IN THE UNITED STATES OF AMERICA

10 9 8 7 6 5 4 3 2 1

Acknowledgments

I would like to thank the following people:

My parents, Chris and Audrey, who listened indulgently to my endless childhood monologues. It turns out you were building an author. My closest childhood friend, Sandy, who read my writing before it was fit to print. Thanks for being an audience of one for many years.

Members of the Houston Fiction Cartel, especially Gene and Bethe, who taught me how to critique. All my charismatic and witty friends from WRW, especially Lorin, Brenda, Roman, John, Jason, Donna, Christine, Susan, Dennis, and Beth. Nancy Pickard for the first encouragement I ever got from a published novelist. My new friends at the Houston-area chapters of RWA for providing me with a great writing community in my own backyard.

All my family and friends, too numerous to mention here, who have encouraged me along the way, especially Michael, Vincent, Diane, Melissa, Sherry, Sandy and Dan, Stephanie, Rick H., John S., and Mrs. Millie Mohan. My wonderful and numerous friends from the medical community, especially Margaret, Brent, Larry and Jane, Sally, Shelley Halley, and Elizabeth Jones Cochran.

My agent, Elizabeth Winick, for your faith and guidance. It was a fortunate day for me when we met. My editor, Leis Pederson, for your wonderful insights. Books are very lucky to find themselves in your hands.

My best friends and critique partners, David Mohan and Bonnie Johnston. I am grateful to you for far too many things to mention here. I'll just say . . . Thank you for everything.

Chapter 1

*　*　*　*　*

Jenna Reitgarten is awfully lucky that my witch genes are dormant, or I'd have hexed her with hiccups for the rest of her natural-born life. She stared at me across the cake that had taken me thirty-six hours to make, a cake that was Disney on Icing, and shook her head.

"Well, it's a really pretty cake and all, Tammy Jo, but it's got too much blue and gray. It might be good for a little boy, but Lindsey *just loves* pink—"

"The castle stones are gray and blue, but the princess on the drawbridge is wearing pink. The flower border is all pink," I said, tucking a loose strand of hair behind my ear.

"Uh-huh. I'll tell you what. I'll take this one for the playroom. I'll put the other cake, the one with the picture of Lindsey on it, in the dining room. And I can't pay two hundred thirty dollars for the castle, since, after all, it'll be a spare."

"Why don't I just sell you the sheet cake?" I asked, glancing at the flat cake with the picture of her three-year-old decked out in her Halloween costume. Lindsey was dressed, rather unimaginatively, in a pink Sleeping Beauty dress.

"And what would you do with this one, honey?" Jenna asked, pointing at the multistory castle, complete with lakefront and shrubbery.

"Maybe I'll just eat it."

She laughed. "Don't be silly. Now, you'll sell it to me for a hundred thirty dollars or I'll have to complain to Cookie that you didn't follow my instructions, and then—"

"I followed your instructions," I said, fuming. "You said 'think fairy-tale princess.' Well, here she is." I flicked the head of the sugar-sculpted princess, knocking her over on the blue bridge.

Jenna gasped. "I've had just about enough from you," she said, standing the princess back up. "You know we order once a week from this bakery for our Junior League meetings. Cookie will have your hide if you lose my business."

Cookie Olsen is my boss, and "Cookie" fits her like "Snuggles" fits a Doberman. As a general rule, I don't want Cookie mad at me, but I was in the middle of remembering all the reasons I don't like Jenna, which date back to high school, and I really couldn't concentrate on two annoying women at the same time.

"You can buy the sheet cake, but you can't have the castle cake."

She huffed impatiently. "A hundred seventy for the castle cake, and that is final, missy."

I'd never noticed before how small Jenna's eyes were. If she were a shape-shifter, she'd be some kind of were-rodent. Not that I'd seen any shape-shifters except in books, but I knew they were out there. Aunt Mel's favorite ex-husband had been eaten by one.

I come from a line of witches that's fifteen generations old.

They've drawn power from the earth for over three hundred years. Somehow I didn't think Jenna would be impressed to hear that though.

Jenna flipped open her cell phone and called Miss Cookie. She explained her version of the story and then handed the phone to me.

"Yes?" I asked.

"Sell her the cake, Tammy Jo."

"No, ma'am."

"I'm not losing her business. Sell her the cake, or you're fired."

"Yes, ma'am," I said.

"Good girl," Cookie said.

I handed the phone back to a very smug Jenna Reitgarten.

"Bye-bye," she said to Miss Cookie and flipped the phone shut. She dug through her wallet while I put the castle cake into the box I'd created for its transport. I took out the sheet cake, which was already boxed, and set it on the counter.

"That'll be forty dollars," I said.

"What?"

"Cookie said I could either sell you the castle cake or get fired, and I'm going with option B. A cake this size will feed me for a month," I said. "Longer if I act like you and starve myself."

Jenna turned a shade of bright pink that her daughter Lindsey would have *just loved*. Then she tried to reason with me, and then she threatened me, waving her stick arms around a lot.

"Sheet cake, forty dollars," I said.

Her complexion was splotchy with fury as she thrust two twenty-dollar bills at me. "Lloyd won't hire you. Daddy uses him to cater meetings and lunches. And there are only two bakeries in this town. You'll have to move," she said.

"Well, I'll cross that drawbridge when I come to it," I said, but I knew she was right. Pride's more expensive than a designer purse, and I can't afford one of those either.

Jenna stalked out with her sheet cake as I calculated how long I could survive without a job. I'm not great at math, but I knew I wouldn't last long. *Oh, to heck with it. Maybe I will just leave town.* If Momma and Aunt Melanie came back and found me gone, it would be their fault. I hadn't even gotten a postcard from either of them in a couple months, and the cards that came were always so darn vague. They never said what they were doing or where they were. I really hoped they weren't in some other dimension since I might need to track them down for a loan in the very near future.

* * *

Like most ghosts, Edie arrives with the worst kind of timing. It's like getting a bad haircut on your wedding day, making you wonder what you did to deserve it.

There was a strange traffic jam on Main Street, and as I was trying to get around Mrs. Schnitzer's Cadillac, Edie materialized out of mist in the seat next to me. It certainly wasn't my fault that it startled me. I rammed the curb and then Mrs. Schnitzer's rather substantial back bumper.

I held my head, wishing for an ice pack or a vacation in Acapulco. Then I got my wits together and moved my car into the drive of Floyd's gas station and out of traffic. I grimaced at the grinding sound I heard when I turned the wheel too far left. I hoped the problem wouldn't be expensive to fix, given my new unemployed status. With my luck, it would be. Maybe I could just avoid left turns.

Mrs. Schnitzer didn't bother to get her Caddy out of people's way. She slid out from behind the wheel of her big car and sidled up to mine. She wore a lime green polyester skirt that showed off her own substantial back bumper, which, except for the dent, matched her car's perfectly.

She asked me a series of questions, like what was wrong with my eyes (plenty, since I can see Edie, my great-great-grandmother's dead twin sister), was I on drugs (not unless you count dark cocoa), and what did I think Zach would say when he found out (which I decided not to think about).

Edie was decidedly silent in the copilot's seat. She was dressed in a black-sequined flapper dress, which is a bit much for daytime, but I guess ghosts can get away with some eccentric fashions, being invisible to most people and all.

"Here Zach comes now," Mrs. Schnitzer said, beaming.

"Great," I mumbled and checked my rearview mirror. Sure enough, a broad chest of hard muscle covered by a tight, white T-shirt was approaching.

Mrs. Schnitzer said, "Tammy Jo ran right into the back of my car. And I've got to get home to get ready for the mayor's party. I don't have time for this nonsense today, Zach."

In other words, "Deputy Zach, straighten out your flaky ex-wife." I clenched my teeth, resenting the implication.

He played right along with her. "Y'all go on, Miss Lorraine. I'll deal with this."

She wiggled back to her car and drove her dented bumper off into the sunset. Zach tipped his Stetson back, showing off dark blond curls and a face that incites catfights.

"Girl, you're lucky your lips are sweeter than those cakes you bake, or I'd have revoked your license a long time ago."

I'd had a fender bender or two in the past. Mostly, they weren't my fault.

"Edie showed up—"

"Tammy Jo, don't start that. It still chaps my ass that I paid that quack Chulley sixteen hundred bucks to get your head shrunk, and all I got for my trouble was a headache."

"I told you it wouldn't work."

"Then you shouldn't have gone and wasted my money. Now listen, I'm busy. You go on home and get ready for Georgia Sue's party, and I'll talk to you there."

"We're driving separate?" I asked. Zach and I have an on-again, off-again relationship, but we were supposed to be on-again at the moment, as evidenced by the fact that he'd slept over the night before last and I'd made him eggs and bacon for breakfast.

"Yeah, I'll be late," he said. "I was at T.J.'s house when they called me to give them a hand with this. Longhorns were on the thirty-yard line. You believe I'm out here today?"

On game day? Frankly no. If there's no ESPN in heaven, Zach will probably pack up and move to hell. The fact that he forgets our anniversary and everybody's birthday every year, but has the Longhorn and Cowboy football schedules memorized as soon as they come out is just one of the reasons our marriage didn't survive. Another small problem was the fact that I still believe in the ghost sitting silently in my passenger seat, and he felt a psychiatrist should have been able to shrink her out of my mind with a pill or stern talking-to.

I looked around at the traffic jam as Zach examined my front end. "So what's going on here?" I asked. He didn't answer, which is kind of typical. "What's happened?" I repeated.

He looked at me. "What's happened is you crashed your car,

which means I'll have to call in another favor to get it fixed. Unless you've got the money to pay for it this time?"

Now didn't seem the right moment to mention I'd gotten fired. "I'm going home," I announced.

"You think you can handle it?" he asked, his lips finally curving into that sexy smile that could melt concrete.

"Yes."

"Good. Gimme some sugar." He didn't wait before stealing a wet kiss and then sauntered off just as quick.

"Hi, Edie," I said, as I maneuvered back into traffic. "I really wish you wouldn't visit me in the car."

"He still has quite a good body."

"Yes."

"Are you together?"

"Kind of." Like oil and vinegar. Mix us up real good and we'll work together, but sooner or later, we always separate.

"So it's just sex," she said, voice cool as a snow cone.

I sighed. "You shouldn't talk like that."

"He is forever preoccupied and yet often overbearing, an odd and terrible combination in a man. It wouldn't matter so much if he could afford lovely make-up gifts, like diamonds."

"Can we not talk about this please? I've had a rough day."

"I heard you quit your job. Well-done."

"I didn't quit. I can't afford to quit. I was fired."

"That's not what I heard."

"Well, what did you hear? And who from?" It unnerved me that there were ghosts that I couldn't see strolling around spying on me. Did they watch me in the shower? Did they watch when Zach parked his boots under my bed? I blushed. Edie noticed and laughed.

I stole a glance at her exquisite face. With porcelain skin and high cheekbones, she was prettier than a china doll. She wore her sleek black hair bobbed, either straight or waved, depending on her mood and her outfit. Her lips were painted a provocative cherry red today. Rumor had it that Edie had inspired men to diamonds—and suicide. It was generally accepted in my family that one of her jilted beaus had murdered her, but she never shared the details of the unsolved 1926 New York homicide of which she'd been the star.

"How are you?" I asked.

"I'm dead. How would you be?"

I opened my mouth and closed it again. I had no idea. Was it hard being a ghost? Was it boring? She was very secretive about her life, er, afterlife.

"What made you visit today?" I asked, still trying for polite small talk.

"I heard you showed some backbone. I decided to visit in the vain hope that you might be turning interesting."

I frowned. Edie could be as sweet as honey on toast or as nasty as a bee sting. "I'm so sorry," I said. "For a minute I forgot that this isn't my life. It's your entertainment."

Her peridot eyes sparkled, and she favored me with a breathtaking smile. "Maybe not so vain after all. Did I ever tell you about the time I stole a Baccarat vase from the editor in chief of *Vanity Fair* and gave it as a present to Dorothy Parker? I liked the irony. He fired her, you know."

"Who was the editor?"

"Exactly," she said with a smile. "Getting fired isn't such a bad thing. You just need a present to cheer you up. As luck would have it, one is on the way."

"One what?" I asked, peering at her out of the corner of my eye.

She couldn't take a corporeal form, so there was no way she could pick something up from a shop or even call into the Home Shopping Network, which was really a very good thing. From what I knew of Edie, she had very expensive tastes. There was no way in the world I would have been able to pay for any "presents" she sent me.

"What's this?" Edie asked as she moved through the passenger seat to the back.

"A cake," I said.

"It's a Scottish castle. Eilean Donan. Robert the Bruce still visits there. You're such a clever, clever girl. Only you have the bridge a bit wrong."

"I've never been to Scotland. It's just a castle I made up."

In the rearview mirror, I saw her tilt her head and smile. "Did you see it in a dream perhaps?"

"A daydream," I said hesitantly.

"It's about time, isn't it?"

"About time for what?"

"I'll see you later." She faded to mist and then to a pale green orb of light that passed out of the car and was gone.

I was happy that she'd liked my cake, but troubled by what she'd said. I was afraid she was thinking, as she had before, that I was finally "coming into my powers." She'd proclaimed as much on other occasions and had always been disappointed. No one in the history of the line had ever had their talents appear after the age of seventeen. Here I was twenty-three years old now; I knew I was never going to be a witch. In a lot of ways, it was a relief. Magic had always tempted my mother. She'd mixed a potion to help her track down a lost love, and she hadn't made it home to Duvall in more than a year. Finally her twin sister, Aunt Melanie, had gotten worried and had gone after her. Now who knew where they were? And what about Edie? She was said to have had remarkable powers, but they hadn't saved her life, had they? They may even have drawn something evil to her. Magic was dangerous, and I was glad I didn't have it. Really, I was.

* * *

Like a lot of things about our family, our home is more than it seems to be. From the street, it's a Victorian cottage that yuppie couples find quaint and offer us lots of money for. But that's because they can't see over the big wooden fence. The backyard hides a darkly shaded Gothic alcove with a collection of brooding gargoyle statues and a garden of poisonous plants and plenty of stuff for potion-making. It's the kind of place where Edgar Allan Poe would have felt right at home but that I try to avoid except for an occasional round of fertilizing. You'd be surprised how well witch's herbs respond to Miracle-Gro.

I was relieved to find a package on the front step. My friend Georgia Sue had remembered to drop off my Halloween costume for me. I was going to be Robin Hood this year, and had already been practicing getting my long red hair squished down under a short brown wig. I scooped up the box and went inside, only to remember I had left the cake in the car.

I zipped back out and retrieved the cake. As I set it on the countertop, I noticed that the light on the answering machine was flashing and pressed the message button.

"Tammy Jo, it's me. I dropped off your costume. I thought you were going to be Robin Hood, honey? Well, at least it's blue and green, and those are good colors for you with your hair. But hoo-yah, I don't know what Momma's going to say. And Miss Cookie. Tongues will be wagging. You know how the ladies of First Methodist are.

Katie Dousselberg still hasn't lived down singing that Britney Spears song on Talent Night . . ."

I scrunched my eyebrows together, advancing on the box suspiciously. Georgia Sue's voice kept going. I love her dearly, but she's the sort of person who can't see why anyone would say in one sentence what could be said just as well in three.

"Did you hear about the sheriff's house? There was a crazy traffic jam on Main, Tommy Hilliard said. If Zach told you anything, you better call me up. I want to have the best gossip tonight. I am the hostess, after all. Don't hold out, sugar. Call me up."

I pulled the wide cellophane plastic tape off the box and peeked inside, blinded for a moment by the reflection of a million little sequins.

I pulled out the gown, which had some sort of stiff-spined train and a plunging neckline that would embarrass a Vegas showgirl.

"What in the Sam Houston?"

I shook out the dress and realized that the back was a plume. In this costume I would be something of a pornographic peacock. I tilted my head and wondered how I'd gone from a sprightly Robin Hood to this. Then I remembered Edie's comment from the car. She'd sent me a present.

Our town, Duvall, Texas, prides itself on having all the things that the big cities have (on a slightly smaller, but still significant scale), and one of our residents, Johnny Nguyen Ho, had created diversity for Duvall in several ways. He was our Vietnamese resident, our community theater director, and our not-so-secretly gay hair salon owner. Recognizing his talent for costume-making during his early play productions, most people in town sent him orders starting in February for their Halloween costumes.

Johnny Nguyen, in addition to his other considerable talents, fancied himself a psychic. And crazily enough, Edie had found a way to be partially channeled into his séance room, a spare bedroom he intermittently converted for this purpose by using a lot of midnight blue velvet and a bunch of scented candles from Bath & Body Works.

As I looked at the dress, I clenched my fists. There was no time to get a new costume, and I could not skip my best friend's Halloween party.

"Edie!" I called, wanting to give the little poltergucci a piece of my mind. But Edie is not the sort of ghost to come when called.

"Edie!" I snapped, as a new thought occurred to me: Liberace had had less beadwork on some of his costumes—how much would this upgrade cost me? I didn't need to be psychic to have a premonition of myself living on peanut butter and Ramen noodles.

If Edie could hear me, she ignored me. "Typical," I grumbled. One of these days all the people and poltergeists who didn't take me seriously were going to need me for something, and I just wasn't going to be there—or at least I wasn't going to be there right away.

Of course, my day of vindication would likely be sometime after Sheriff Hobbs, a serious churchgoing man, arrested me for indecent exposure. He'd probably give me a stern lecture on how short the path could be from poultry to prostitution.

Chapter 2

*   *   *   *   *

I had done my best with strategically placed safety pins and double-sided tape to restrain my boobs from making any unscheduled appearances, but I still wasn't making any sudden moves as I walked into Georgia Sue's annual Halloween party.

I was sure my face blushed as red as my hair when people turned to stare at my outfit.

"Hey, y'all!" I said with a cheerful wave.

"Hey there," Zach's brother TJ said, looking me up and down with a grin, while Mrs. Tabacki pursed her lips so tightly they turned white.

Hellfire and biscuits. I am never going to live this down. I wondered how many of them had heard I'd been fired. Maybe I could chalk it all up to temporary insanity. I put my hand over Edie's locket, which hung down the expansive front plunge of the dress. The starburst of diamonds under my palm was familiar and reassuring. I walked a little taller. I wasn't going to let anything rattle me,

I decided, and pushed through people as I tried to get to the kitchen, where someone would hopefully be making frozen margaritas or pouring tequila shots.

Georgia Sue intercepted me before I could find a drink. She swooped in, pecked me on the cheek, and started right into things.

"Well, you know what the traffic jam on Main Street was all about, don't you?" Georgia Sue asked, her dark brown corkscrew curls bouncing.

"Something to do with the sheriff. He's okay, isn't he? No heart attack or anything?" I asked.

"No heart attack, though with all the steak and cheese the man eats it's a minor miracle he got through the day without one. I've told Miss Marlene she really needs to watch his diet better. You just can't let a man eat whatever he wants. You know Kenny would eat bacon with every meal if I—"

"Georgia Sue! What happened?"

"Well," she exhaled, giving me a whiff of her crème de menthe breath. She'd had a grasshopper or two in the past hour. "Apparently while Miss Marlene was at her Friends of Texas Fish and Fowl fund-raiser lunch, burglars robbed their house in broad daylight."

"Someone broke into the sheriff's house?" I asked, with a slight smile at the irony.

"Yes, can you believe it? Waltzed right in, bold as brass, and stole that nearly original Thomas Kinkade painting they have, which is worth almost two thousand dollars. And they got into the safe hidden in the floor and took everything in there."

"What was in the hidden safe?"

"The sheriff hasn't said so far. But the thieves found it, so what does that tell you?" she asked in an urgent whisper.

"That they've chosen the right line of work?"

She giggled. "That too maybe, and the sheriff's spitting mad. But how could they have found it? Unless they knew it was there? This was an inside job."

The use of the word *job* made me feel like we were in a 1970s movie like *The Getaway* with Steve McQueen. I just love old movies.

I cocked my head. " 'Inside job' means inside the house. You're saying you think the sheriff or Miss Marlene set up a fake robbery?"

"What? Oh, of course not! No more liquor for you—"

"I haven't had any," I protested.

"By 'inside,' I mean inside the town. Must have been."

"Hmm," I said, chewing on the thought. The sheriff and his deputies were considered a pretty competent outfit. They didn't always arrest people for causing trouble, but they always knew who deserved arresting. No one in town would be hot to tangle with the sheriff once he was good and pissed off.

"Why would someone from town steal the painting? Not like you can hang it or pawn it around here without someone knowing," I said.

"That's right. You're absolutely right. See what good it did you being married to Zach? You guys should get remarried. You're already sleeping with him again, for pete's sake."

"I don't like being married to him. When we start fighting, I have to stay over at someone's house, carting my pots and pans all over town, people shaking their heads at me like they saw it coming again. This way when he starts bossing me around too much, I can just throw his clothes on the front lawn and be done with it," I said.

She giggled. "You know you love that man."

"Love is most definitely beside the point," I said. Married and divorced before we were twenty, Zach and I had probably set some kind of Duvall record.

I needed to stop messing around with him, but old habits die hard, and I'd been crazy in love with him since I was ten. Emphasis on crazy. I looked around, wondering if the reason he hadn't shown up yet was because he was still busy with the case at the sheriff's house.

I froze in place when I saw Edie. She was sitting on top of the armoire next to Georgia Sue and Kenny's big-screen TV. She was wearing a large black-and-white hat and a drop-waist dress. She held a martini in one hand, looking flawless and elegant, and not at all out of place among the pinstripe-clad gangsters with plastic tommy guns hovering near the buffet table. She waved with her free hand, and I wondered: where did she get gin and olives in the afterlife?

". . . and there's going to be a big surprise later," Georgia Sue was saying, giving my arm a squeeze.

I wondered if the party would turn into a murder mystery. She'd done that one year, and it had been fun. I'd gotten to play a gumshoe.

". . . mingle and have a good time before Zach gets here and has a fit about that dress."

I pursed my lips defiantly. "Zach can't tell me what to wear. I'll wear what I want to." *Or whatever I'm forced to by a manipulative ghost and her sequin-sewing sidekick.*

"Uh-huh," she said, not sounding convinced. Then she was off to greet some more people.

"Hello, Tamara."

The hair on the back of my neck rose, and I shivered. Very few people call me Tamara, and only one of them has a deep voice that's sexy as sin and smooth as molasses. I turned to find Bryn Lyons. With his black hair, cobalt-colored eyes, and Edie's martini as a prop, he could have passed for the real James Bond. Tonight, he was dressed as Zorro.

"Hi," I said, crossing my arms over my chest, trying to cover up as gooseflesh rippled over my arms. "I'm surprised you're not at the mayor's party."

"Care for a drink?" he asked, handing me one of Georgia Sue's fancy wineglasses with magnolias hand-painted on the side. "Chambord margarita."

I took a sip. Delicious raspberry flavor burst over my tongue, and then I felt a strange reverberation coming from Bryn's direction. *Magic.* He'd been using tonight. I was surprised that I could tell since, as a nonpractitioner, I can't usually detect magical energy.

"What have you been doing?" I said.

"Why do you ask?"

"Well—" I paused, leaning closer to him. He inclined his head, which I suppose was to let me whisper in his ear rather than to get closer to my barely covered body. Still, my heart hammered with sexual heat. Bryn had always been dangerously gorgeous, but he'd never sought me out. He tended to import his girlfriends in from Dallas. They were often tall, tan, and too perfect to have been born looking the way they did. I don't think he worked any glamour on them, but maybe he paid for their plastic surgeons. He was certainly rich enough to afford it.

"I didn't know you were active," I said.

"Active in what way?" he asked. His teasing voice had that faint Irish lilt that I sometimes detected. I wondered again where he was from. He and his father had moved to Duvall when Bryn was around thirteen. Being six years younger, I didn't meet him right off. Our paths crossed by accident for the first time when I was sixteen, and I'd been curious about him ever since. Momma, Aunt Mel, and Edie had immediately shut down my questions though and forbid me from talking to him, but I always listened with interest to anything they said about him and his father, Lennox.

I raised my eyebrows. "Never mind," I said. "I really can't talk to you."

"Why is that?"

I took a gulp of my margarita to stall. I couldn't tell the truth: that for reasons I didn't understand, I'd been made to memorize Lenore McKenna's List of Nine. Lenore was my great-great-grandma and Edie's twin sister, and she'd written down nine last names that a McKenna girl was never supposed to associate with. Something to do with the family being destroyed for all eternity. On Lenore's list, Lyons was smack-dab in the middle at number five. But since the list was a secret, I didn't know what to say to Bryn about why I couldn't talk to him.

I guess I could have blamed it on Zach, saying he'd get jealous, but Bryn would probably think my getting involved with Zach again was as stupid an idea as, well, it was.

"I can't really say, but it was nice seeing you."

"Why can't you say?" he asked.

"Beautiful and deadly," Edie said. I turned my head to find her standing next to me. "He's a Lyons. Off-limits, and you know it. Too bad, too. I wouldn't have minded the show. He's spectacular out of those clothes."

I gasped. How did she know what he looked like out of his clothes? Did she have Superman X-ray vision? Or had she haunted his house for fun?

I could forgive Edie being a ghost voyeur. After all, what was there to do after death besides people watch—and, apparently, drink martinis? But I did *not* want to hear about it if she watched me making love. And if she'd been kinky before she died, that was her own business and not mine.

Bryn's cobalt blue eyes narrowed, and his gaze focused on the spot where Edie stood staring back at him. She smiled and blew him a kiss. He didn't respond, but he didn't look away either.

"What's wrong?" I asked him, wondering if he could see her.

"There's something here. Do you feel it?" he asked.

Uh-oh. "No."

He mumbled something. *A spell!* I felt his magic and a sudden rush as Edie slammed her way back into the locket. The only remnant of her was a faint bluish afterglow near my shoulder. I wondered if his spell had hurt her, and it upset me to think so.

"Well, if you'll excuse me," I said, backing up.

His eyes moved up one of the twin slits that kept showing flashes of thigh when I walked. "That dress suits you."

"Oh, I hope not," I said, escaping to the screened porch.

* * *

There were a dozen of us in the back room when Georgia's surprise started: two guys dressed as old-timey bandits walked around collecting loot from everyone. I hoped I'd get to be part of the posse to hunt them down during the game.

I noticed that Elmer Fudd—Mr. Deutch—hesitated to let his wife, a cross-dressing Bugs Bunny, put her big canary diamond ring into the pillowcase the bandits were using as a sack.

"C'mon, Pops, get with the program," the bandit with a red bandana over his face said as he grabbed Mrs. Deutch's hand. He wrestled the ring off her finger and dropped it in the case.

Then he moved in front of me. I dropped my little beaded clutch purse into the sack.

"I'll take that too," he said, nodding to the locket.

"Oh, no," I said. "I can't take it off here."

"This is a stickup, Birdie. Everything goes into the bag."

"No." I put my hand over the locket, pressing it against my chest.

Old-timey Red pointed his old pistol at the mounted head of a moose, which had already been shot once in Alaska by Kenny in 2003, and pulled the trigger. The pistol's report startled us all into silence, and then Red pointed it at my head. "Put the necklace in the bag," he said.

"A loaded gun? The sheriff will kill Georgia Sue," I muttered.

The second bandit, who wore a green bandana over his face caught my arm and yanked it down. The locket pulled out of my hand, and Red snatched it and dragged it up and over my head.

"Wait," I yelled and grabbed Red as he turned to leave. Red broke free, and both bandits waved their guns menacingly as they ran toward the door. "No," I shouted, stumbling after them. Mr. Deutch grabbed me around the waist to stop me.

"Let go! They've got Edie," I snapped.

"You named your locket?" Mrs. Deutch asked.

I jerked free of Mr. Deutch's hold and rushed out of the room. The bandits had left the front door wide open, and I hurled myself through it. They were actually leaving, actually stealing the locket!

"Hey!" I sprinted toward the driveway, coming right out of my shoes when the heels got stuck in the lawn. "I'll pay you for the locket. I'll pay a lot!" I screamed as they peeled out in Councilwoman Faber's brown Jaguar.

I ran after the car, pounding the pavement with my bare feet until it turned a corner and I lost sight of it.

"Oh no," I whimpered, holding my head as I panted for breath. *How could you have let them get it? Why didn't you hide it when you saw them taking things? You were supposed to keep her safe,* I shouted at myself in my head.

"I thought it was a game. Another murder mystery game," I whispered to no one. "Oh, this is bad. This is so bad," I mumbled. October twenty-fourth was only six days away. I had to get Edie back by then or she'd be destroyed forever. And what if she came out before that? What if she came out again tonight? She'd be lost without someone from the family to connect to and then she'd get sucked into whatever darkness had almost gotten her twenty years ago.

I turned and ran back to the house. Everyone was in an uproar. People were yelling at Georgia that she'd gone too far with this game, that letting the actors carry real guns was madness. I rubbed the tears off my cheeks with the heel of my hand, hoping the others were right: that it was a game, and that the bandits would bring the locket directly back.

"Just shut up!" Georgia Sue snapped in a voice that could've pierced armor. "I did not hire them! My surprise was a magician. Those men with the sack must be the same ones who robbed the sheriff. It's a crime spree is what it is."

"Oh dear Lord," Mrs. Deutch wailed.

"They took my Jaguar. I've got to get it back," Mrs. Faber said, her patrician nose turned up.

I stood numbly in the corner. I hung my head, looking at my pale pink toenails. I needed to do something, but I didn't know what.

"Tamara, your feet," Bryn said. "Come and sit down."

I didn't resist as he led me to a wingback chair at the edge of the foyer.

"They took my locket. It's a family heirloom. It means the world to us," I mumbled, sinking down. "Has someone called the sheriff?"

"Yes, the police are on the way," he said, shaking his head as he looked at the bottom of my feet, which were dirty and skinned.

"Did they take anything of yours?"

"My Rolex. My fault. Zorro didn't wear a wristwatch. I should have left it at home."

"I'm sorry about your watch," I said, but I didn't really mean it. I was so preoccupied with my own trouble that I didn't have a bit of sadness to share for someone else's.

"Oh, don't worry. I'll be compensated when they're found."

I looked at him suddenly. Bryn Lyons knew magic and was rich. That combination meant he usually got whatever he wanted. If anyone could make sure the thieves were caught quickly, he could.

"I need my locket back as soon as possible. If you find them will you make sure that I get it? It can't be stored in evidence or anything like that."

"If I find them before the police, you'll have it back immediately."

"Thank you," I said, clutching his arm. He was on one knee in front of me and looked suave enough for celluloid.

He smiled.

We heard sirens and both looked toward the door. "The cavalry," he said.

"I should rinse my feet and put my shoes on."

"I'll get your shoes." He stood. "It'll be all right," he added.

I nodded with a weak smile and limped off to the bathroom.

By the time my feet were clean, Zach and the others had arrived. The sheriff had a colicky look as he tried to calm folks down.

I grabbed Zach's arm and pulled him toward the back room.

"Easy now," he said, extracting himself. "I need to listen to the sheriff and so do you."

"They got my locket, Zach. The Edie locket."

"Well, good riddance," he said, moving back toward the people crowded around the sheriff.

I felt like he'd dumped a pitcher of ice water over my head. I stood rigid as a steel beam and stared after him.

I would wait my turn to tell him and the sheriff what I'd had taken. And, for Edie's sake, I would pester him as much as I could to get them to find the thieves, but, once I had her back, I wouldn't bother to cross the street to talk to my cold-blooded bastard of an ex-husband. Good riddance, indeed.

I looked around and saw Bryn Lyons sitting on the back porch swing, talking calmly into his cell phone. I hoped he was hiring a band of mercenaries to hunt down the criminals. I hoped his people found the loot first and made the sheriff and his deputies look like fools. And I hoped really hard that he did it all before the twenty-fourth of October.

Chapter 3

The next afternoon, I stood by the ATM machine with a receipt in my hand that told me I had insufficient funds to make a withdrawal. I'd forgotten that I'd made the mortgage payment early before I'd lost my job.

I couldn't ask Georgia Sue for money. She'd already maxed out her credit card to buy a new jukebox for the bar. And because I wasn't taking charity from Zach, I'd given him the money to get the mechanic to fix my car. I regretted that now. I would need that money to buy spellbooks to help me get the locket back. Though I don't have strong witch powers like the other women in my family, I do have a little psychic energy like most people—maybe more since I can see Edie and sometimes I can sense Bryn Lyons's magic. It was only when I tried to cast the spells that Momma taught me that nothing happened. Still, it had been a long time since I'd tried, and I can follow directions pretty well. I didn't think I'd be half bad at potions since, as a pastry maker, I've got measuring and mixing down cold.

Plus, there are spells that anyone can do, although they're a lot riskier for the average person to try than for a witch, because a real witch can control the energy that goes in and comes out. So I wasn't happy about having to try to do magic. There was a chance that things could go wrong, and I'd blow myself up or maybe create a really bad smell in the house. But with Edie's soul at stake, what choice did I have?

The trouble was that when Momma left she took half the library of family spellbooks, and when Aunt Mel left, she took the other half. At the time, I didn't object because I didn't have any powers and wasn't a witch wannabe. But now I needed them. Real spellbooks had some power in them, and that would help me. I wouldn't get any boost from a Barnes & Noble dictionary of spells that had been handled mostly by teenagers working part-time to get discounts on CDs and mochas. Besides, most of the spells in those kinds of books were written by nonpractitioners and were just plain wrong.

I needed to take a road trip to Austin to the Witch's Brew—a pagan gift and coffee shop where real witches went to get discounts on CDs and mochas—and to go into the back room to buy from the inventory of proven old spellbooks and charms. Unfortunately, those books would all cost upward of three hundred dollars. On my current budget, they might as well have been three million.

And I couldn't wait until I could get the money together to buy one. I needed to do something now. I thought about Bryn Lyons. I just bet he'd have some fancy books, but they'd probably be full of mojo as black as his hair.

Bryn and his father were the only other magical family in town besides us. Too bad I couldn't ask him for advice.

"Well, well, well."

I spun around to find Jenna Reitgarten staring at me.

Great. Just who I wanted to see in my darkest hour.

"No money in your account?" she asked with a saccharine smile.

Hiccups for life. Hiccups for life. Hiccups for life. I tried to hex her, but, of course, nothing happened.

"Well, maybe you just ought to use better judgment the next time you have a job. How long until you move?" She looked at her manicured nails while I glared at her. "I never did like y'all living here anyway. You and your aunt, divorced women, and your momma, who never even bothered to get married before she had a child? That's not the kind of family values we want to promote in this town. But yours *is* a cute little house. Maybe I'll buy it when you go and rent it out to some nice couple that's planning a family and a *normal* life."

"That's a wonderful idea," I said in my sweetest Southern belle drawl. "Except I'll burn it to the ground and collect the insurance money before I sell it to you."

"Then you'll go to jail when I report you to the sheriff."

"At least I'll have a place to live rent free, with my house gone."

She rolled her eyes, but I just smiled as she strutted off. Okay, so I wouldn't really burn down a house, but I couldn't let her walk all over me in her flowered, freaking Keds. And no normal people were going to live in my house. It was strictly for witches and women obsessed with spun-sugar sculptures.

Home was a couple of blocks away, and I headed there on foot. It was a nice sunny day, and the big Texas sky stretched out above me like a beach blanket. I waved absently at neighbors as I walked.

"Hello, Red!" Doc Barnaby called.

"Hi," I called back.

"Come sit a spell," he said.

I hesitated. Dr. Barnaby was our hearty seventy-two-year-old retired psychiatrist. He'd lost his wife in March and had been pretty lonely since. He had an excellent selection of Chinese teas, so I sometimes made pastries and dropped in to see him, although I hadn't been by lately. A year ago, I'd paid him five dollars and a strawberry cream torte to get my head shrunk for an hour. He'd have listened to me for free, of course, but I'd paid to get the doctor-patient confidentiality so I could tell him about my life. I felt like I was a disappointment to my family of witches for lacking the gift, and asked him whether he agreed that it was unfair that they didn't appreciate me for my cherries jubilee and my chocolate lava cake. Halfway through a plate of chocolate coconut drops he'd agreed completely with me. I had a rare and valuable gift he'd assured me.

"What are you doing? Come on in," he called.

I thought maybe a few minutes on his sofa and some tea might help me feel better, so I went.

Inside the sunroom, I nestled into the cream-and-yellow cushions and felt more cheerful. He had a nice tape of chirping birds playing in the background, and as I sipped tea I began to feel very relaxed. And then I began to feel sleepy. And then I began to feel dizzy.

He smiled at me and murmured some comforting words, which were so distorted that all I heard was wa, wawas, wama wa.

"Somethin's wrong," I slurred. Then I slumped over.

He got up and patted my head, still smiling. I tried to speak, but my jaw was stuck shut as if super-sticky peanut butter had glued my tongue to the roof of my mouth.

It turned dark. I struggled to get up, but my body stayed limp. What was happening? I tried to keep my eyes open, but the lids felt like they weighed twenty pounds each.

Help me. I'm schick. I'm sick.

Something bit my finger. I heard a faint garbled moan. My heart pounded, and a mosquito bit my head.

Oh, Dr. Banaslee. You poishinned me. Evilin. If I live, I'm telling Zash on you.

* * *

It was dusk when I woke up with a monstrous headache and found myself in a hammock in Doc Barnaby's backyard. I pushed the crocheted afghan off me and tried to get up. I fell out of the hammock, banging my knee.

"Kiss my behind," I said to the rotten universe.

I stumbled to my feet and wove my way to the wrought-iron gate. I didn't know why Dr. Barnaby had poisoned me, and I didn't care. I was pissed off, and it was making my head hurt worse. The gate was unlocked, and I staggered forward, stopping to get my balance. I turned toward the house for a moment and shook my fist.

"You son of a gun." It was the best I could do. I was too sick to confront him.

I marched—well, shuffled—home. I stopped near the hedge to have some dry heaves, feeling like someone was hammering "I Wish I Was in Dixie" on my skull.

I couldn't manage the three steps to my door. I didn't remember them being so steep. So I crawled up them, grabbing the door handle to hoist myself to a standing position. I panted from the exertion and fought another wave of nausea.

"Thank you, door," I mumbled, resting my forehead against the cool wood and feeling slightly better.

Several beats of a police siren sounded and then stopped.

"Now what?" I grumbled.

"Tammy Jo, I should whip your ass," Zach's voice boomed from somewhere behind me. "Where the hell have you been?"

"Poisoned."

"So I see. Where the hell were you drinkin'? I looked all over town after Doc Barnaby called. You're lucky the man didn't have a heart attack, or I'd be charging your sweet ass with manslaughter."

"Wha—?"

He pulled me aside, maneuvered my key in the lock, and then scooped me up.

"He did it."

"Who did what?" Zach said, carrying me to the couch and setting me down.

"He gave me poison tea." I held up my hand and turned it this way and that about three inches from my eyes. There was a Band-Aid on my index finger. "He poked me."

"What are you talking about?"

My arm was too darn heavy. It fell with a thud onto my chest. "I told you. He did it."

Zach squatted down next to me and sighed heavily. "Jo, we've been through a lot together, and I've got to tell you, darlin', I'm worried about you. You don't have to tell me where you been, but I wish you would. I know none of your girlfriends have seen you 'cause I talked to all of them. And I know they wouldn't dump you on your front step in this condition. Only a man, and not much of one, would leave you like this. It wasn't Doc Barnaby; you were already drunk and out of it when you called him."

My lip quivered. I could not believe this.

"He's a liar," I slurred.

Zach stroked my hair. "C'mon, Tammy Jo, you're on somethin'. Whyn't you just tell me what? You know I'm not going to arrest my ex-wife. Just tell me who gave it to you."

"Barnaby."

"Uh-huh. Remember that time June got you to try pot in high school and you thought Earl was Skeletor from the *He-man* cartoon? You almost drowned trying to get away from him, and yours truly had to fish you out of the lake. Next day, even you said that you can't take any of that stuff. Some genetic thing that makes you hallucinate, you told me. Your momma was the same way."

I squinched my eyes shut and tried to keep the tears from escaping. Doc Barnaby had poisoned me and made me look like a fool and a drug addict. He wasn't going to get me to cry, too.

"It's one of two reasons that you aren't telling me who you were with. Either you can't remember because you were too messed up, or you're protecting whoever it was because you're worried about what I'll do. Well, I'm here to tell you, I'm gonna find out. And when I figure out who it was, I'm going to kick the ever-lovin' shit out of him."

I felt him kiss me on the forehead.

"Anybody leaves my baby like this *is* going to answer to me," he said, picking me back up. He carried me to the bedroom and tucked me into bed.

The tears dripped from my eyes. Not because I was mad at

Barnaby, the finger-stabbing, poison-pushing bastard, but because Zach's country boy, he-man routine does it for me every time.

* * *

To find Zach when I woke up, I followed the sound of Toby Keith singing. Zach was on the phone but hung up when he saw me. A yellow legal pad of notes sat next to a half-eaten pizza and empty Bud bottle.

"How you feelin'?"

"Like a cement smoother rolled over my head." My stomach grumbled. I took that as a sign that, despite the poison, I wouldn't be staring up at a tombstone or living in a locket any time soon.

"Wanna tell me who you were with?"

"I did," I said, pulling a slice of pizza free and taking a big bite.

"Uh-huh."

"Barnaby poisoned me."

"Why would he do that?"

"I don't know. I'm a pastry chef. Detecting is your job."

"You *were* a pastry chef. Miss Cookie told me you quit."

"Miss Cookie fired me for not letting Jenna Reitgarten serve me my pride on a cake plate."

"Jenna again? I thought you were over that."

"I am," I said, pulling the legal pad to me. At the top, there was a list of the stolen items and their estimated values. I realized that they were listed in terms of importance, and my locket was at the bottom of the list.

The yellow diamond ring and Mrs. Faber's Jag were at the top. Two pendant necklaces, a pair of earrings, and Bryn's Rolex were next. Then Edie.

"Where's all the other stuff? Everybody was putting stuff in the bag," I said.

"Yeah, but most of the stuff was fake jewelry for their costumes. Not really valuable."

"Oh. Did they take money?"

"They got a few wallets and purses. Not too much cash from any one person."

"They were trying to pretend it was a show for the party by wearing those costumes. As Georgia would say, an inside job. Inside the town, that is."

"Mmm-hmm. We did think of that, but thanks for the help," he said, sliding the pad back over to him.

I frowned. I wasn't in the mood for sarcasm. In fact, I wasn't in the mood for much of anything, except, it seemed, pizza. I devoured another slice.

"I've got to get back to the station."

"Any new information? Do you have any idea who did it?"

"Nope," he said, getting up. He leaned over me and stole a kiss. "Stay out of trouble."

Nope. I planned to get right back into trouble the minute he left.

Chapter 4

* * * * *

There are some spells that I know pretty well from having seen my momma and Aunt Mel do them. They were always losing their keys and things and scrying for them instead of looking around.

I sat for nearly an hour with my face over a bowl of water trying to scry for the locket, but I could only make out watery shadows. It's an advanced technique that requires deep energy and concentration, which, let's face it, I don't have. My head was back to throbbing, so I put a cold washcloth over my eyes for fifteen minutes and ate a handful of Hershey's Kisses to fortify me. Then I got up and collected some odds and ends from around the house that I needed for my next try at a spell.

Though I didn't hold out much hope for them working, I had to try something. And Edie and I were connected mystically through the magical line. Now if I could just remember the details of the spells.

When I was little I used to read Momma and Aunt Mel's spellbooks all the time, thinking I'd be coming into my own big powers one day. When I finally realized I wouldn't be a real witch, I gave up on the books, favoring cookbooks and brides' magazines. After I married Zach at eighteen, I'd had other things on my mind. I'd moved on to a normal life and hadn't looked back. Now it had been five years since I'd looked at a spell.

I found a picture of Momma wearing the locket, so I cut out just the locket, then snipped a strand of my hair and a couple pieces of twine. I set myself up at the kitchen counter with an incense stick, some matches, and a pair of small white envelopes. I stood the stick in a faded "Kiss the Blarney Stone" coffee cup and lit the stick. The smell of pine wafted through the air. I passed the locket picture, my hair, and the twine three times through the smoke to purify them of anyone else's energy. I concentrated hard on the items as I used the twine to bind the locket photo to the strand of my hair.

"Thanks to the person who brings the locket back to me. Thanks to the person who brings the locket back to me. Thanks to the person who brings the locket back to me at least before October twenty-fourth."

I put the hair-locket wrap into one of the envelopes and sealed it. The other important thing that I needed to do was to prevent Edie from coming out of the locket while someone else had it. I never saw Momma or Aunt Mel do a spell to bind a spirit, so I didn't really know what to do. But since it wasn't likely to work anyway, I decided to keep things as simple as possible.

I took a photo of Edie and passed it through the pine smoke, then rolled it into a small tube. I used a bit more of the purified twine to tie the picture up that way.

"You are happy in the locket, Edie. You stay in the locket. You are at peace in the locket, Edie."

I put the rolled picture into the other envelope and sealed it. I took the two envelopes into the bedroom and placed them in the bottom drawer of the jewelry box, which Aunt Mel had always kept empty for the products of meaningful actions. I didn't want anyone to open the envelopes or mess with them before the locket-return spell came true.

I closed the doors of the jewelry box and hugged it. I hoped a little of Momma's and Aunt Mel's power was still around to help me.

Afterward, I lay down with a cold pack over my eyes and had just gotten comfortable when the doorbell rang. I waited, hoping whoever it was would leave. The doorbell rang again insistently, and I got up and went to see who it was. I paused when I looked out. Bryn Lyons stood just outside, looking tasty even through the smudged peephole. I opened the door.

He held a large cage that was covered with a swath of deep brown satin. The smell of sandalwood was strong, and the faint reverberation of magic hummed over my skin. I was surprised again that I could sense his magic so well.

"What can I do for you?"

He smiled. "What did you have in mind?"

I thought about great-great-grandma's list. "I can't invite you in."

His smile faded, and he cocked his head. "I wish you'd tell me why you won't associate with me. Have you had some sort of premonition you're worried about?"

I just smiled and shrugged.

"How about a short ride? We'll go to a neutral place like Magnolia Park. I need to talk to you."

I eyed the cage. "What do you have there? Canary?"

"A gift for you. And before you say no, hear me out. You need it."

"I'll meet you in the park in half an hour."

"You want me to sit around for thirty minutes waiting for you?" he asked skeptically. "Maybe I'll just forget that I was going to help you and go home."

"My car is in the shop. It'll take me a while to walk there."

"And there's no way that you'd just get in my car and drive over with me?"

"No, I really can't, but thank you for the offer," I said, glancing at his black Mercedes with tinted windows.

"Thirty minutes then."

When I got to the park, I found him sitting at a picnic table. He looked out of place in his dark designer suit. His shirt probably cost more than the park's monthly landscaping budget.

The covered cage was sitting in the center of the table and my gaze went to it more than once as I sat down on the bench across from him.

"You've been in trouble."

"I lost my great-great-grandmother's locket."

He shook his head. "I'm not talking about that. You were in danger sometime earlier today."

I narrowed my eyes. "What makes you say that?"

"I felt it. You called out for help."

"You were a little far away to hear me."

"I meant psychically."

"I know what you meant. Nobody could hear my psychic cries. They're too faint. I'd say it's more likely you heard I had trouble courtesy of Ma Bell. Zach called all my friends. They probably called all their friends and so on. My guess is that the whole town knows I went missing this afternoon and evening."

"And the reason I know you were doing magic just before I rang the doorbell?"

I raised my eyebrows. He probably thought that his knowing would give me the willies, but I took a more practical view of things. If Bryn Lyons, a known practitioner, had sensed me working, then maybe my spells might actually do their job. And that made me happier than a bee face-first in nectar.

"I'm not sure what your family told you about Duvall, but it's a tuning fork for psychic energy. Macon Hill is a tor, a ley center. Ten ley lines, conduits for the earth's heightened energy, converge at the tor. The lines travel outward for thousands of miles. If I felt you casting spells, so did others. Yours is a raw energy that's untrained, but someone experienced could exploit it."

"I don't have enough power for anyone to bother coming thousands of miles to see me."

Bryn folded his arms over his chest and stared at me.

"I don't. I've never had it. My momma and Aunt Melanie tried a bunch of times to bring it out of me when I was a teenager."

"Maybe they weren't the right people to train you. Maybe your power has different origins from theirs."

"What have you found out about the robbery? Did you hire anyone to find your Rolex?"

"I can buy another Rolex."

"But you said that you would get even with the thieves."

"I don't have to find them to get even with them. They've taken something of mine. I can cast a spell that will reach them wherever they are."

I shivered. His eyes sparkled in the bit of illumination cast by the street lamp. I'd seen him on and off for years, but I'd never been afraid of him until now.

"Well, it's been nice chatting with you." I stood up and he reached over and caught my arm.

"Wait."

"Look, I can't get involved with you. If there's any training to be done, you're not going to be the one to do it. Now let go of me."

"You don't know when or if your mother and aunt are coming back."

"They *are* coming back!"

"Tamara—"

"Stop calling me that. We're not such close friends that you get to call me different than everyone else does. It's Tammy or Tammy Jo, period."

He let go of my arm. "When you need help, you know where I live."

Yeah, he lived in Shoreside Oaks, along with most of the wealthiest folks in Duvall. His back acreage looked out onto the Amanos River. He probably even had a view of Cider Falls. Nice land if you could afford it.

Bryn got up and walked toward his car.

"Hey, what about this?" I asked, motioning to the cage.

"He's yours. If you don't want to take him home, just open the cage and turn him loose. He and Angus wouldn't get along."

"Who's Angus?"

"My dog," he said, climbing into his car. He left me sitting in the darkness with the cage. I pulled the satin cover off. A pair of big, dark eyes reflected the lamplight and stared back at me. The cat was tawny and beautiful, spotted like a leopard.

"Hey there."

He purred.

"I can't keep you. The gorgeous wizard probably wants to use you to spy on me or something. I'm pretty sure he's into the dark arts, which my family tries to avoid. The only thing I like really dark is chocolate." I put my finger in the cage, and he licked it. "It's not personal against you or anything. I just know he can't be trusted. After all, he's a lawyer."

The cat went on licking my fingers. "I don't think you'll starve. Mario's throws out a lot of seafood each night. You like shrimp fettuccini Alfredo?"

What am I doing talking to a cat?

"I'm going to let you out." I opened the front of the cage and he sprang out, landing with a thump on my lap and then using his claws to pull himself up onto two paws.

"Ouch, ouch, ouch," I said, pulling him off my chest. His claws were like needles.

"Okay, go on. Live long and prosper," I said, dropping him on the grass.

I got up and turned toward home. I didn't look back, afraid if he seemed disappointed, I'd suddenly be a cat owner. I hurried down the sidewalk. I wondered if he was following me. I checked left and right, using my peripheral vision. No felines.

I turned my head side to side. Nope. Finally, I looked over my shoulder. Definitely gone. I sighed but told myself I shouldn't be sad about it. I couldn't accept a present from Bryn Lyons. Still, I wouldn't have minded a little company for the walk home, and it's not like the kitty cat had somewhere else to be.

* * *

I took a long bath, ate a few Special Dark miniatures, and settled into bed. I must have fallen asleep quickly, but suddenly I was startled awake. The clock read five forty-five in the morning.

Someone with a small flashlight was in the bedroom. I stayed stone-still, afraid the person would know I was awake. He was dressed in black with a black mask, like all the psycho killers wear. His back was to me as he rifled through the jewelry box. *Great, take my stuff. I don't need it.*

Maybe he was just a burglar. Maybe he'd just leave me alone.

There was a rattling outside and then a wailing sound somewhere in the distance. I felt it as well as heard it. The burglar must have heard it too because he turned out the light. I couldn't see him, which was scarier.

Oh, God. Go away. Please go away.

I didn't want him to come near the bed or to figure out that I was awake. My breath came in short pants that I tried to keep quiet. Sweat trickled down my neck. I didn't have a weapon. *Oh, why did I divorce Zach? So he forgot our anniversary and went out drinking with the boys. So he never took me seriously and sent me to a psychiatrist over Edie. No relationship is perfect, and he had such a big gun.*

Chapter 5

The burglar's soft footfalls moved toward the door. *Yes, you slimy bastard, get the heck out of my house.*

As soon as he left the bedroom, I was out of bed. I got on the floor and crawled on my hands and knees to the door. I wanted to get a glimpse of him, but it was too dark. My heart thumped in my chest, my fingers stiff with fear. If I went out of the bedroom and he was lurking, he might get me. I felt for the handle and slammed the door shut. I locked it, stumbled to my feet, and ran to the phone. Footsteps pounded down the stairs.

I yanked the phone off the hook, but there was no dial tone. *No!*

My cell phone was downstairs on the counter. I ran to the window and looked down. The burglar tore out the front door but tripped over a small shadow that darted toward him. The man fought with the shadow, then got up and ran, limping on one leg.

He disappeared around the corner, and I looked back to see the shadow moving slowly, like it might be hurt.

I ran down and found the cat from the park sitting on the top porch step with his back to the open front door.

"Hey," I said.

He made some sort of kitty sound of acknowledgment. He looked around for another moment and hissed at the darkness. Then he stood, turned around, and padded into the house. I closed and dead-bolted the door.

There was a small trail of blood on the wood floor. "You're hurt! Oh, no."

He looked at me with big eyes and then licked at his right shoulder. I lay down on the floor on my belly near him. I didn't want to scare him.

"Let me see," I whispered. I touched his shoulder gently. My fingertip slipped into a small hole. "Ouch," I said since he couldn't. "That nasty jerk stabbed you. I'll take you to the vet. But wait, I don't have my car." I tilted my head. "I'll call Zach. He can drive us, and I'll make a police report."

I turned on every downstairs light and the stereo. I found the phone that was off the hook and set it back on its cradle, then lifted it again.

The phone rang five times before I slammed it back down. *Damn him. Never around when I want him.*

"I called my ex-husband. He's out doing heaven knows what, so we'll go without him. I'll wake up Jolene next door, and she can drive us," I said, putting on my shoes.

I walked to the door, but he didn't move. "Come on." I waved a hand toward him, but he ignored me and instead hopped up onto a chair and then onto the countertop. He padded over to the sink, made an unpleasant sound and then hopped into the sink basin.

"You want a bath? Cats don't like water."

I looked at the blood on the floor. Cleaning the wound was a sound idea. Good thinking for a kitty.

I went to the sink and turned on the water. He wailed loudly enough to wake the dead in two counties. It was the same sound that I'd heard earlier, the one that had interrupted the burglar at work.

I washed him with some orange Palmolive antibacterial dishwashing liquid. He didn't like it, but he didn't hop out of the sink until I was finished rinsing him. He shook vigorously, spraying me and the counter, with water. Then he sat down and licked himself. His paws were huge. I'd thought he was full grown, but from the look of things, he wasn't nearly done.

A gold disc hung from a gold chain collar around his neck. I lifted the disc. *Mercutio* was engraved on the front. And his birthday on the back. Mercutio was seven months old.

I petted his damp fur. "You're very impressive. At seven months all I could do was hold my head up."

He meowed.

Boy, he was cute. And courageous. And cute.

Maybe I'd keep him for a little while or forever.

"Let's go see what he took. Then I'll call the sheriff." Mercutio watched me walk toward the stairs, then bounded up them ahead of me, favoring his left side a little. The burglar had limped worse, I thought with a satisfied smile. *My kitty cat kicks ass.*

The doors of the jewelry chest were open, but the drawers were closed. I opened them one by one. My earrings and my class ring from high school were still in the top drawer. The string of pearls from my grandmother was untouched in the second drawer, but Aunt Melanie's magic gemstones and crystals from the third drawer were gone, and the bottom drawer was empty. The bastard had taken my spells. Now how the hell was I going to tell the sheriff about this?

* * *

I spoke to the sheriff, who was strangely quiet, like too much crime had happened in too short a time and he'd had to leave a zombie in his place while he took a Mexican vacation. When he wasn't looking I checked out the pulse in his neck. Yep, beating. Not a zombie then, just playing one in Duvall.

I didn't tell him about the spells. I just said some gems and crystals and some important paperwork was taken. He grunted that he understood and said he'd look into it when he got a chance.

"You know, if you were still married to Zach, this never would've happened."

"Why not, Sheriff? They broke into your house. Doesn't seem like having a lawman around helps all that much," I said, giving him a wide-eyed and innocent look.

He scowled. "I wasn't home when they showed up. You can bet things would've been different if I had been. Now, you lock all your doors behind me."

It was clear that he wasn't going to be a lot of help anytime soon, and his deputies were all out doing their thing, so I was still on my own.

What a way to start a Monday morning. I made a snack and

discussed the case with Mercutio. He ate every bit of his ham and eggs and was more attentive than Zach had been for most of our thirteen-month marriage.

Some country whoop-ass music came on, and Mercutio skidded around me in circles while I danced in the middle of the hardwood floor where I'd rolled the rug back. Dancing cheers me up, and Mercutio seemed to like it, too. For Zach to dance like that would have taken a court order or drinkin' half a bottle of Glenfiddle at a wedding. Mercutio, I decided, was nearly the perfect male, and I wondered what kind of spell it would take to turn him into a man. As I ran out of steam, I collapsed on the couch, giggling as Mercutio played a game of attacking the glass coffee table.

That night I slept with the lights on until Zach woke me up at eleven thirty in the morning by pounding on the door like he planned to knock it down. My hair hung in my eyes, which I'm sure is part of the reason why I didn't spot Merc on top of the tall bureau that stands next to the door.

When Zach came in, Mercutio sprung Hollywood-stuntman-style and landed on Zach's head and shoulder, making a vicious one-pawed swipe across the back of Zach's neck.

Zach howled and flung Merc across the entryway, but Mercutio landed light-pawed and unfazed. He swiveled to face Zach. I blinked, openmouthed with surprise. Mercutio's the size of a tabby cat, but he doesn't seem to know that. And he's a baby and impressionable, so I didn't think it was a good idea to encourage him, especially since Zach can be pretty ornery.

"Not nice," I said to Mercutio, but was drowned out by Zach.

"What the fuck?"

Zach ran a hand over his neck and came away with a smear of red. "Whose is that? I'm gonna skin him alive."

I walked over and took a look at Zach's neck. The wound wasn't deep, but I bet it stung. "No, you're not. He's mine," I said. "It's just a scratch. I'll get the peroxide."

Zach growled at Mercutio, who hissed back.

"Hey, cut that out," I said to them. "Settle down, Zach. He only jumped on you 'cause he doesn't know you." *I think.* "And you come banging on the door like you're going to kick it in. You woke him up."

"He's going back to wherever you got him."

That clinched it. Now I was a permanent cat owner. I put my fists on my hips. "He stays."

"You don't even like cats."

"He's not a cat."

"Oh, no?" Zach asked, narrowing his eyes suspiciously.

"He's a superhero in a cat suit. He protects me. He's in disguise."

"Well, I hope he's faster than a speeding bullet 'cause he jumps on me again, and I'm gonna introduce him to one."

I rolled my eyes. "Come on to the sink so I can clean that."

"He better have all his shots."

I nodded, wondering what shots cats need.

"He does, right?"

"Uh-huh." *Probably.* As far as I knew, Bryn Lyons wouldn't give me a cat full of diseases, but then he was on that list of nine. Hmm. I'd be really pissed if people started dying of distemper.

Zach took off his shirt and stood bare-chested with his police belt hanging around his narrow hips and looking like the opening scene of a pornographic video, or what I imagined would be the opening scene of one since I've never actually had the nerve to rent one.

Zach leaned over the sink, and I washed the back of his neck gently while he grumbled.

"All right," I said. "Done."

"Now, where the hell were you last night?" Zach demanded.

"Why?"

"Just answer the question."

"I guess you didn't talk to your boss then?"

" 'Bout what?" he asked, rubbing the water off his shoulders with a dish towel.

"For your information, I was home, getting my house broken into while you were probably out drinking with your brothers."

"Tammy Jo—"

"I don't want to hear it," I snapped. "Mercutio was here and probably saved me from getting raped and murdered in my bed. Now, I want to know what you're doing to catch the guy who stole my locket and broke in here last night."

"What makes you think it was the same guy?"

"Well, it doesn't take a genius to know that it's the same crook. I don't think all this breaking and entering is unrelated. Do you?"

He grinned. "No, I don't suppose I do, but we've still got to look at the facts. What was taken?"

"Just some crystals from the jewelry cabinet. He might have thought they were gemstones. He got scared off before he got a chance to do anything else."

Zach nodded, serious again. "And you didn't go out last night before or after it happened? You didn't go by Doc Barnaby's?"

"No, I didn't. You couldn't drag me there. Why? Did someone else he poisoned throw a rock through his window?"

"Not exactly."

"Well, what then?"

"Come take a ride with me. We can pick up your car when we're done. The bumper's fixed."

I slipped on my flip-flops with the orange silk roses and glanced at Mercutio. My house didn't feel totally safe, and I didn't want to leave him behind to face things alone. "C'mon, Mercutio."

"Hell no," Zach said, buttoning his shirt back up.

"He'll sit with me," I said, opening the front door. Mercutio, who had been reclining on the countertop, hopped down and streaked past. I smiled, knowing Zach wasn't going to chase him down.

"What kind of cat is that? I've never seen a house cat with that many spots," Zach said suspiciously.

Hmm. Neither had I. "Oh, I can't remember exactly what the lady said." I didn't think it would be a good idea to tell Zach I'd gotten Mercutio from Bryn Lyons. Zach wouldn't be keen on my getting presents from another man.

"What lady? Where did you get him?"

"Never you mind about my cat." I climbed into the squad car, and Merc hopped onto my lap and curled into a sleek ball, closing his eyes.

Zach got in, still eyeing Merc suspiciously. He started the car. "How old is he?"

"Um, seven months, I think. I'm sorry about the scratch. We didn't get much sleep, and I don't think he's a morning cat."

We rode down the block to Dr. Barnaby's, and Zach led me to

the backyard. The hammock I'd slept in was shredded and had been ripped from one tree, a hunk of bark missing from where it had been anchored.

"What in the world?" I mumbled and looked at Zach, who was watching me closely like he thought I might have had a lot of spare time and an ax and a straight razor for company the night before. "It wasn't me."

Merc slinked over to the tatters and hissed. He pawed the canvas and backed away.

"It wasn't Mercutio either. As you can tell, he doesn't approve."

We walked to the back door of the house, which was splintered and gaping. A wave of dread rose up inside me. It tasted a lot like bile.

"My gosh! Is Doc Barnaby okay?"

Zach nodded. "He wasn't home when it happened. He was visiting his wife's grave. Lucky for him or today he'd be getting buried with her."

I followed Zach inside. The house was wrecked. Furniture and papers had been tossed about, glass and china smashed.

I walked to the overturned dining room table. It probably weighed more than a hundred pounds. I glanced at it and then at Zach. "And you wanted to know if I did this? You think I maybe drank a few steroid mochas and went crazy?"

"Dr. Barnaby thought you might have been involved. And I asked him why you would be if he hadn't done anything to you."

"Exactly."

"He didn't have a good answer. I thought we could all sit down and sort things out."

I passed Zach, exploring the house until I found Dr. Barnaby in the guest room, sitting on the torn mattress of a daybed. The stuffing from a shredded cotton comforter covered the room like snow. The remnants of Mrs. Barnaby's doll collection were scattered over the floor, and Dr. Barnaby looked as shell-shocked as the sheriff had. What would happen to Duvall if its men all went to pieces?

I noticed Dr. Barnaby's face was streaked with dried tears, and I'll be damned if I didn't feel sorry for him. When he saw me, he shook his head.

"I deserved it. I know I did, but did you have to mess with her things?"

"I didn't do this. How could I do this?" I asked, stepping over broken dolly parts to get to him. It was like a kiddie crime scene and somehow more sinister because of it. I sat down next to the doc and put an arm around his shoulders.

He broke down and cried. "I just wanted her back. That's all I wanted. I only took two drops of blood and four strands of your hair. You wouldn't even miss them."

"You're sure right. I don't miss them," I said and pulled off the Band-Aid and showed him my fingertip. "You can't even see where you pricked me. No harm done."

"I'm sure sorry about the tea. I hated to do it, but I didn't think you'd let me try to bring her back."

"She wouldn't come back the way you want."

"No, she didn't."

I gasped. "You did a spell already? And something happened?"

He nodded.

"Could she—Maybe she came home and was confused," I said, looking around at the destruction. I'd heard ghouls were strong, and it took a person with special powers over the dead, which Doc

Barnaby wasn't, to control one. He'd raised her, and now she was on the loose without anyone to stop her. Jiminy Freakin' Crickets! What the hell were we going to do?

"No, she ran off toward the distilleries. I drove straight home, and the house was already like this."

"Did you mix the ingredients here?"

He nodded.

"What about the incantation?"

"Part of it here and some of it in the cemetery."

"Where in the Sam Houston did you figure out what to do?"

"I read it in a book."

"Good grief," I said with a shake of my head. Most spells wouldn't work for the average person, but with some of my witch blood and in the middle of a town with a powerful tor, who the heck knew what would happen? Well, apparently now we knew exactly what could happen.

"Did you do any part of the spell in the yard?" I asked, thinking of the hammock.

"No. Tammy Jo, I need more blood, just a few drops so I can put her back."

"We'll need some help, I think. We want to do that right."

"Yes, we do," he said.

"I'll come back in a few hours. Just take it easy until then. And whatever you do, no more spells."

I got up. Zach stood with his arms folded across his chest, shaking his head.

I walked toward the door, and he fell in step with me for a few paces. "The guy's looney toons. I'm sorry as hell I didn't believe you yesterday."

"It's okay. Nobody's perfect," I said. "Least of all, you."

He barked out a laugh.

"Let's go get my car," I said.

"That'll have to wait. I've gotta arrest him and take him in. It'll probably take me an hour to get the paperwork done."

"Arrest him for what?"

"Poisoning you."

"Oh, I'm not goin' to press charges. He's sorry enough."

"Tammy Jo, the man is dangerous. He's delusional, and I'm *gonna* lock him up."

"All righty, good luck with that then. But I don't know how you'll prove anything, seein' as how I'm not going to be able to make a statement on account of my head being pretty fuzzy about what happened and all." I held my head like I was dizzy and then let my hands drop. "Now, come on. I've got things to do, and I need my car."

I walked away from Zach as he sputtered, "Girl, what has gotten into you?"

I found Mercutio stationed on an overturned table in the center of everything. His head moved side to side and those big eyes watched all the doorways.

"Will you look at that," I said to myself. I shook my head as I got to him and scooped him up. "When we're done fighting evil, I'm gonna buy you a big box of catnip."

I didn't let Zach convince me to go to the station with him. And I ignored his lecture about how I shouldn't have gone along with Dr. Barnaby's delusion by acting like he really had raised his wife from the dead. I wondered if Zach might sing a different tune when a partly decomposed Mrs. Barnaby started raiding farms. I wasn't sure what ghouls like to eat, but I think, like most undead things, they go for blood. I wasn't sure she'd be strong enough to take down a cow, but you can count on the fact that the chickens wouldn't be safe.

Chapter 6

I waited until we were alone in my car with the shiny new bumper to discuss what I suspected with Mercutio. He licked his paws thoughtfully as I talked.

"There was a lot of destruction there. Who's got that kind of strength? Vampires, but I can't see them using the energy. They're kind of like cats that way, no offense. They'll do something when it gets them what they want, but they're not known for kicking up a fuss just for the sake of it. Shape-shifters always have energy to burn, but they're not drawn to witch magic any more than vampires so far as I know. A ghoul or a zombie, but who raised it if it wasn't Mrs. Barnaby? Unless maybe Dr. Barnaby raised more than his wife." I shuddered. "If not the doc, maybe a warlock. And that might make some sense if it was the same person who broke in my house to go for the spells, the same person who got my locket. I just know that someone besides those old-timey bandits is behind the robberies. And I can't see them raising a zombie. A dust storm maybe, but not zombies."

Mercutio purred.

"You know who I bet knows more than he's telling? Bryn Lyons. He knew trouble was coming my way and gave me you. How? You think he knows who raised whatever destroyed Dr. Barnaby's house? You think we should ask him?"

Mercutio cocked his head.

"Yeah, I'm not sure either. But what do we have to lose?"

I drove to Bryn's house. I wasn't sure it was a good idea, given the list and all, to go inside, but I thought I could ask him to come out and talk to me. And maybe I'd get him to let me borrow a book or two.

I buzzed security, and the guy let me in. I drove to the mansion, got out, and rang the bell. A butler who looked like he'd been chipped from a giant fossil answered. He didn't seem magical to me, but I couldn't really rule out that he'd been raised from the dead either.

"Yes?" he asked.

I feigned tripping so I could grab his hand. It was warm enough, barely. I don't relish the circulation problems that come with old age, but at least he wouldn't be raiding any chicken farms.

"I'd like to see Mr. Lyons."

"He is not at home. Business has taken him to the city of Dallas today."

I sure liked his English accent. "When will he be home?"

"He won't be available this evening."

"Why won't he be available? What will he be doing?" *Conjuring demons and sending them out to smash doll collections?*

"He's a patron of the arts. Tonight, he's going to a fund-raiser dinner for the SWWA—Southwest Writers and Actors. Would you care to leave a message? He'll be back to change clothes between engagements."

"No, thank you," I said. I went back to the car. When I got in, Mercutio lifted his head and yawned.

"Yeah, I'm sleepy, too. Bryn Lyons is going to a charity dinner for actors. Did you know he's a patron of the arts?" I shook my head, trying to wake up. It was hot in the car. According to the weather report, Duvall and the rest of Texas were experiencing record high temperatures. I wished global warming would just quit. Summer in Texas already lasts half the year.

"He doesn't support the community theater here. Never seen him go to a play in town. Don't you think that's strange, Merc?"

Mercutio blinked.

"Yeah, me, too. There's only one type of arts that I believe him to be a patron of. You got it, black arts. What should we do? Tail him?"

Merc didn't disagree.

"All right, we'll come back. First I've got to figure out a way to put Mrs. Barnaby in her grave. Then I hope we've got time for a nap because I have to get back to trying to find my missing family locket, too." I looked over and found that, conserving his energy in a very catlike manner, Mercutio was already asleep, curled in the passenger seat with the air-conditioning blowing his whiskers back.

I decided I wouldn't mind being a cat some days.

* * *

Sometimes when Momma didn't have a spell for something, she'd make one up. That's probably the sort of thing that a very experienced witch should do, not so much a novice one, but I was in a serious pinch here.

I needed to be quick and discreet. There were only six or seven people in town that knew magic was real, which was the way I aimed to keep it.

On the whole, folks in Duvall can be pretty sweet, but you just never know when some little town's going to get it into its head that Salem had the right idea about what to do with witches. And Aunt Mel always supposed that might happen right about the time folks found out we didn't keep three hundred and eighty-two Earth candles because we like the smell of dirt.

So far, we'd had good luck keeping it a secret, which wasn't the easiest thing in a small town. Now, I'm not saying that people in Duvall are nosy, but just because I don't say it doesn't make it not true. And if it got around that someone used my blood and hair to raise the dead, we'd probably have two camps. Some people would come on over to ask me to raise all their aunt Marlenes for an occult iced-tea party, and other people would start collecting wood for a town barbeque with yours truly as the main attraction.

So time was important. Zombies are basically nocturnal, and night was in an all-fired-up hurry to take over the sky. I went in the kitchen and dug out the mortar and pestle. I knew at least two ingredients that I'd put in for certain: my blood and my hair. To undo a spell, a little of the hair of the dog, or in my case, pastry chef, seemed logical because they must have been the active ingredients, but I was pretty much stumped at the rest. I consulted the Internet, vowing never to tell Momma about this. I searched by herbs and found that passionflowers are good for peace and sleep, which was exactly what I wanted for Mrs. Barnaby. I wondered if we had any dried passionflowers in storage, but then when I checked to see what passionflowers look like, I realized that the big star-shaped violet blossoms blooming in the backyard were exactly what I needed.

"Well, fancy that," I said to Merc, who was half-asleep on the counter. "My luck is changing for the better all the time."

I didn't totally believe that, but I was trying to think and act positive, to give myself the best chance of success. I walked outside and stood looking at the green vine that had climbed all the way up the tallest tree to get out from under a shady canopy. Bursting purple in the sunlight, passionflowers beamed down at me. I kicked off my slip-on shoes and climbed up the lowest branch of the tree. It was fun, like when we were all kids and used to climb trees. It had always been a competition to see which boy could climb the highest and which girl he'd pull up with him. The first day Zach took me to a treetop was one of my happiest memories. When we were kids, Zach did all sorts of stuff to get my attention. By the time we got married, he acted like all the sweet things he'd done as a boy meant he didn't need to do anything new, like love was money in the bank that would be there if you just left it alone.

I thought about the time I'd wanted to go to Galveston for a romantic weekend. He thought it'd be a waste of money to stay in a fancy hotel, and maybe he was right about that. But it didn't hurt my feelings any less when he bought a new fishing rod and splurged on a charter with his buddies to go deep-sea fishing. When I got mad about him not spending time with me, his response was, "Hell, sweetheart, you can come fishing with us. Not like we've got kids you need to stay home with yet."

I shook my head. Like deep-sea fishing with him and the boys was any woman's idea of romantic. But I could't change his mind by talking to him. He always did what he felt like doing, except that one time I got my way. Too bad it was in divorce court.

I plucked a flower and climbed down. In the house I showed it to Merc. "Look how pretty that is," I said, and he blinked. A deep violet color, the ten petals were arranged like a pinwheel, contrasting nicely with the silvery strands that pushed out from the center. In the middle there were thick pale flower parts crisscrossed into a pattern that reminded me of a pentacle. I decided that was a good omen.

I wasn't sure if live flower parts were more or less powerful than dried herbs so I decided, better safe than sorry, I'd use the whole thing. Then I lit a match and sterilized a sewing needle and pricked my finger.

I yelped, and Merc meowed in sympathy. I dripped blood into the purple mush then ground it all together with a few strands of my bright coppery hair.

"It's too thick. I don't want to have to get close enough to smear paste on her. I need something I can splash from a goodly distance away."

Merc cocked his head.

"What do you think? Mix some water in? That's what I do when I get a batter that's too thick."

Merc licked his paw.

I poured half a cup of water into a small metal mixing bowl and dumped the mash in it. I stirred it all up then put it in Tupperware and sealed it with a rubber lid.

"We'll start at the cemetery and see if we can follow her tracks. How are you at tracking?"

Merc didn't answer, but he was more energetic after his nap, and he hopped down and headed to the door to wait for me.

"I still probably need an incantation, you know." I shook my head. Momma and Aunt Melanie's spells always sounded pretty, like song lyrics, but I'd gotten a C-minus in poetry. I'd never heard that witches had to know poetry, so I didn't think iambic pentameter was necessary for a spell, but I figured I'd better at least make it rhyme.

With my passionflower mash tucked under my arm, I let Merc out the front door and locked it.

"Merc, what rhymes with grave? How about brave? 'Now you've got to be brave, and just go on back to your grave.' "

Merc batted roughly at his whiskers in a gesture that looked suspiciously like the way Zach thunked himself in the forehead when he thought I'd done something really dumb.

I opened the passenger door, and Merc hopped in.

"What? You don't think I should mention grave? You think it'll upset her? I guess maybe she might not know she's dead. Like all those people in *The Sixth Sense*. And we don't want to upset her; she might decide to do something mean to us. Not that it'd be intentional." I closed his door and walked around the car.

I got in and glanced over at him as I turned the key in the ignition. "All right. What rhymes with 'go back to sleep'? Hmm. 'Now, no more counting sheep, it's time to go back to sleep.' Ugh. Too corny and who really counts sheep anyway?"

I drove to the Duvall cemetery. As cemeteries go, it's nice. Most everybody in town has kin in the ground there, so it's always a competition to see who keeps the family plots the prettiest. Some people literally are pushing up daisies. But plenty have roses, sunflowers, and hydrangea. My favorite area is the plumeria section where the Gaffney family is buried. It smells prettier than a bottle of perfume over there.

I walked up and down the rows looking for Mrs. Barnaby's grave. I found it at the east edge of the cemetery with all the flowers ripped loose and the ground broken open. I shivered and looked at Merc. His fur stood straight up on his back, and he hissed and backed away.

"C'mon. You're brave. Let's go," I said, marching past the grave, following clumps of dirt to the field behind the cemetery.

"We don't even need a bloodhound," I said, looking at the smashed grass. "This is going to be no problem."

Daylight faded, and the air was hot and stagnant. What was with this stupid freak heat wave? Sweat trickled down my neck and made my shirt stick to my back. I grimaced. I needed a tall glass of iced tea or a mojito. I wiped the sweat off my forehead, sighing.

"This is a fine cat on a hot tin roof, huh?" I said to Merc, trying to keep things light and positive. I looked over and realized he was gone. "Merc?" I called out. I waited, and when there was no answering meow, I scowled. He'd deserted me. "You better not be lying in the shade under a plumeria plant!"

The trail had gotten thinner and the grass taller. I picked up a switch and started to beat the brush. The last thing I wanted was to get bitten by a copperhead. I hadn't thought to put on boots. I looked sullenly at my bare legs, shaking my head. Shorts and open-toed shoes were just plain foolishness for a hike through knee-high grass. I slapped a mosquito on my thigh irritably.

"I shouldn't even be doing this. It's not my fault Mrs. Barnaby got raised from the dead. I was poisoned into unconsciousness. I should march right back to my air-conditioned car," I muttered.

I reached the edge of the field and stared at the wire fence closing off Glenfiddle Whiskey's property. Glenfiddle's one of the three main businesses in Duvall. It's owned by the Gaffney family, who came from Scotland six generations ago. At first, they only had little stills and made moonshine, but then, three generations back, they started putting fancy labels on recycled whiskey bottles and selling their homemade stuff all over the Southwest.

Maybe it says something about my hometown that the second largest business also makes booze. Armadillo Ale's owned by the workers who make it. It's only sold in Texas, and that's the way the Armadillo boys plan to keep it, although the people who smuggle it to Oklahoma and Louisiana have other ideas. I don't suppose Armadillo's going to have a choice about expanding soon.

The last big business in Duvall is one that no native Duvallan ever thought would work out. It's energy. We've got a queer amount of wind in Duvall. I'm guessing it has something to do with the tor and the magicks in the area, but nobody else knows about my theory, of course. Anyway, a retired college professor from Austin, with Bryn Lyons as a silent partner, bought a plot of land and put up a bunch of super-tall metal windmills. We power the whole town off the wind, and now we're shipping our wind power out. Professor Rubenstein's just about the smartest man anybody's ever met, although his silent partner's not shabby either. To hear rumor tell it, Bryn's investment had paid a 300 percent return so far.

I wished that Mrs. Barnaby had wandered into the windmill field. The grass there is very short, and you can see all the way across it with a glance.

I looked at the Glenfiddle distillery that was about a half mile away. It's made of pale gray stone, and, to hear Big Gaff—Joe Gaffney—tell it, it's a lot like a Highland clan's fortress. Don't ask me how he'd know that though. I'm pretty sure Big Gaff has never set a toe out of Texas.

I twisted my hair off my back and shoulders and blew out a

chokingly warm breath. Where the heck was our famous wind now? *I'd kiss a snake for a breeze,* I thought furiously.

I stomped forward, feeling more and more nervous as the sun receded from the sky. I wanted out of the field, and I was getting an increasingly uneasy feeling.

I stepped on something squishy and shrieked. I looked down and shuddered. There was a pair of dead snakes with their heads bashed to a pulp. I whimpered. *She's meaner than a snake?* I looked over my shoulder. How far back to the car?

I shook my head, muttering nervously and wishing I'd made a protection spell for myself while I was making the passionflower soup.

There was a torn-up plot of land ahead. I cocked my head. It looked like she'd maybe lain down for a while and dragged her hands through the dirt over and over.

I heard shouting. "Darn it," I spat and rushed toward Glenfiddle. *The enemy has breached the fortress.*

I smelled the mesquite woodsmoke and whiskey. My heart hammered in my chest, my lungs tight as I ran.

I got to the pair of big doors, which were open, and stood stunned at the sight inside. As a Texan, Zach's not unique. The boys from Texas don't stand around and talk when there's trouble, and they especially never hide from a fight. So five of them, with various bloody wounds, wrestled with the slimy, charcoal gray corpse of Mrs. Barnaby, who was tossing them around like she was a mad bull just out of a pen.

Women screamed and rushed forward to help their men as Mrs. Barnaby flung Red Czarszak into a wall. He went still, his neck at a crazy angle. I gasped and ran toward them. I had to stop her.

The Glenfiddle workers tackled her, piling on like a high school football team. I yanked the lid off my Tupperware and waited to glimpse some body part of hers, the swampy smell of decay choking me. Then her gnarled black hand thrust out and grabbed Stucky Clark's beefy arm. There was a bone-cracking pop, and Stucky wailed.

I propelled myself forward, raising my voice. "Go now and peace do keep. Return at once to your sleep." I tossed the passionflower potion, splashing it on the pile.

The room sucked all the air from my lungs, and I dropped to my knees, gasping, trying to pull some breath back in. I couldn't. I was dying, suffocating for real. My mouth moved, screaming soundlessly for help, then everything went black.

Chapter 7

I woke up, shaking and wet. Zach knelt over me, looking a way I've never seen him look. Scared.

"What in the holy hell?" someone behind him said.

"Talk to me, darlin'," Zach said.

"I'm all right," I croaked. I cleared my throat and shook my head, seeing an empty bucket near my feet. Someone had doused me with water.

"What happened?" I asked. "Is she . . . Did she . . ." I wanted to say "Did she go back to ground?" but I couldn't ask that. I didn't know who was listening.

I clutched Zach's arm and pulled myself up. The room spun around me, and I would have fallen backward and cracked my head on the floor if he hadn't grabbed me. He clutched me to him. His body felt warm and good against mine.

"I'm getting her out of here," Zach announced, standing up and cradling me to him.

"You are not. We've got a quarantine situation here until I hear different," the sheriff said.

"Quarantine?" I said in a raspy voice. My throat felt like I'd been gargling glass shards. I looked over Zach's shoulder and saw that the Glenfiddle workers, my friends and neighbors, were all laid out in a row.

"Oh!" I screamed. *I killed them. I'm a murderer. Oh God, I didn't mean it. Please, no.* Tears welled in my eyes. "They're all dead. Oh, no. Oh, no."

"They're not dead."

"Not dead?" I sobbed.

"No, it's some kind of fever. That damn Doc Barnaby dug up his wife, and her rotting corpse must have been infected with something. Only the good Lord knows which dumbass moved her body here, but whatever she's got, they've got, too.

"How did you get here?" I mumbled. *Did I do this? Did I give them all a sleeping fever? Sweet Jesus, how am I going to undo it?*

"Your cat showed up at the station. Tore my damn shirt, too. And then took off, and I figured I'd better see where you were at. I followed him here and found this mess. The sheriff saw me drive by the cemetery and came out to have a look. And now we're all probably infected."

"Dr. Barnaby dug her up first," I said, playing along. "He's fine. Maybe some people are immune."

"Or maybe it just ain't hit him yet."

"Well, he's been at home, walking around in his yard. If he's infected, so's my block. We could go to my house."

"I don't think so." Zach carried me to the door.

"Sutton?" the sheriff said.

"I'm just getting a little air. Not going anywhere, Sheriff," Zach said.

"What the hell's wrong with this cell phone?" the sheriff snapped, hooking it to his belt. He followed us out to the prowler.

"Try your radio again," the sheriff said.

The sky seemed to sizzle overhead. I stared up, and a fat raindrop hit me on the forehead. A buzz of dizziness swirled around me for a second and then was gone. I felt a whole lot better than when I'd first woken up. Spell-casting takes a lot out of a girl, I decided.

"What's wrong with your police radio?"

"Don't know. It went out 'bout half hour ago when the sheriff tried to use it. His isn't doing jack either."

A streak of lightning lit the sky. Zach's chest muscles tensed, then rain poured down.

"Great," Zach said, backing up to get under the silver and burgundy Glenfiddle awning. He set me down in one of the old rocking chairs that the smokers use when they take a break.

I heard a yowl and looked up as Mercutio, who had been perched on the big awning, jumped off with legs outstretched. I gasped, thinking he was going to go splat on the ground, but, at the last second, he pulled his legs in and landed sure-footed. He spun instantly and darted under the awning, shaking vigorously to rid himself of as much water as he could.

"Hey there," I said.

He hopped onto the seat of the rocking chair next to me and went to work on his fur with his tongue.

"Is that really going to dry you?" I asked.

He didn't answer. Not in the mood to be interrupted, I guess. I leaned over and pressed a kiss onto his damp head.

"We need help, Merc. Zach can't help us unspell these people. You should have gotten Bryn. Only he was gone, wasn't he? And you figured that Zach's good in a fight, huh?" I nodded to myself. "It was good thinking. Only now we've got to get out of here and find some witch help. But which witch help?"

I nodded at Zach, who was sitting in his patrol car, trying the radio. Water pounded the dirt.

"I know you don't like water. I'm not crazy about maybe getting struck by lightning either, Merc, but I've got to fix this. He said they've got a bad fever. What if their brains are cooked by the time I unspell them?

Merc looked up at me, tilting his head at the thought.

"You don't have to come with me. But maybe you could, like, make a diversion or something, 'cause Zach and the sheriff aren't just going to let me waltz off."

Merc licked his paw.

"I'm pretty sure that Zach wouldn't shoot you, but I can't vouch for the sheriff, so don't go too crazy. And whatever you do, when you run and hide, be kitty-quick. You get me?"

He stared at me with those big eyes, and I wasn't sure he did get me. *He's just a cat,* I thought. *What makes you think he can understand you? But he went and got Zach for me,* I argued with myself. *And he kept the burglar from getting me.*

Zach got out of his car, slammed the door, and then ran back to the building.

"Radio's dead. What the hell's going on here?" he said as he walked back inside.

"Now's my chance!" I announced in a fierce whisper to Merc. I darted from my chair and ran headlong into the storm, not looking back.

"Please don't let a snake bite me, God," I prayed. "You know I didn't mean to make those people get sleeping sickness. It was an honest-to-goodness mistake. I couldn't let Mrs. Barnaby's zombie rip them to pieces. And how come You let people get raised from the dead anyway? Far as I can tell, the last time it worked right was Lazarus, and Doc Barnaby's no Jesus Christ, I'll tell You that."

Thunder cracked the earth, making me jump.

"Not that I need to tell You that, Jesus being Your Son and all." Wind and rain whipped my body. The last person I wanted to piss off was God. I could afford that like I could afford a Corvette.

"And, You know, I'd be the last person to lecture You," I hollered over the storm. "So I'm just going to be quiet right now." I ran through the slippery field, squealing in pain as the grass slashed at my legs. "Only I'll just point out that if a snake bites me, it would really slow me down. And I'd think I need to hurry up and save those people on account of their brains are cooking. Plus, I need to find our family locket before Edie's immortal soul is destroyed. Okay, then. That's all I wanted to say. Amen."

I ran like a bat out of hell, which I pretty much was, except for the bat part. Bloody rainwater ran down my calves from the grass scratches, but I was just glad I'd gotten past the snakes.

I nearly jumped out of my skin when something moved on my car roof.

"Damn it, Mercutio! You scared me to death." I yanked my driver's door open. "Get in."

He dropped down and leapt to his seat. I got in and slammed the door, shivering. He rose to his paws and shook, spraying me and the whole front of the car, including the windshield.

"Thanks. I wasn't wet enough, you know," I grumbled. I wasn't really mad at Mercutio, of course. I was soaked and scared. If I couldn't unspell those people, they might die. And I didn't want multiple homicide on my record before I was even old enough to rent a car. I just know those Hertz people wouldn't understand.

I backed my car up and swung the wheel toward the exit, turning up my windshield wipers. They whipped back and forth, hardly able to keep up with the rain. I squinted and drove determinedly through water two inches deep in the streets. I passed Sycamore and turned onto Palm.

When I got to Bryn Lyons's sixteen-feet-tall gate, I wasn't at all sure I wanted to go inside, but my options weren't really all that extensive, so I pushed the security buzzer.

"Hi there. It's Tammy Jo. I was here earlier. I'd like to come up to the house again."

The security guy told me to wait. Probably going to check with the boss man. I looked down at Mercutio, who licked the scratches and water on my legs.

"I don't think that's gonna help, but thanks," I said, rubbing his head and neck.

The gate swung open, slow and steady and pretty damn ominous in the rain. I thought again about the list. I wasn't supposed to be going here. And definitely not twice in one day.

I followed the circular drive to the front of the house and got out. The sky dumped another few buckets of water on my head as I ran to get under the porch awning. The front door opened. I knew what I must look like. I was soggier than bread pudding, but nowhere near as tasty.

The butler crinkled his eyes at me, probably thinking I was going to mess up his floor if he let me in. But Bryn walked up and shouldered past him to open the door wider.

"Hi," I said, shivering.

"Jenson, get towels," Bryn ordered, and the butler shuffled off. Bryn ushered me in. The house was overly air-conditioned and colder than a meat locker. My teeth chattered.

Merc sidled in behind me. Merc wasn't shivering, but then he had the advantage of being furry.

"I n-need help," I chattered, trying not to shake as goosebumps conquered every inch of my skin.

"Come," Bryn said, leading me across his very expensive Mediterranean tile. I left dirty, wet footprints like a toddler who'd been making mud pies.

"I'm sorry about the floor."

"Don't be. Mrs. Freet, my housekeeper, has been waging a personal war against dirt for thirty years, and she's had too many easy victories in this house. Mobilizing the maids and their mops for the foyer will be the highlight of her month, I promise you."

I giggled, feeling slightly better. He opened a door and looked in.

"Closet," he said and shook his head. He opened another door. "Here," he said, and we went into a large laundry room.

Bryn slipped off his black suit coat and rolled up the sleeves of his expensive blue shirt.

"What are you doing?"

He stepped forward and pulled my tank top out of my shorts and dragged it up.

"Hey!" I squeaked, grabbing the fabric and yanking it away from him and back down over my bra.

"You're wet and cold. I wouldn't want you to catch pneumonia," he said, reaching for me again.

I slapped his hands away and stepped back. "Just a darn minute. Last I checked I could dress and undress myself."

"Sure, but wouldn't you be warmer if I helped?"

My jaw dropped open. I was in the middle of a crisis with people in a fever-coma. I was counting on Bryn Lyons to be my savior, not some normal red-blooded guy who noticed that frostbite had my nipples hard as arrowheads.

"Look, I'm in trouble."

"Clearly."

"And I didn't come here for you to put your *Urban Cowboy* moves on me."

He grinned and folded his arms across his chest. "Tamara—"

"It's still Tammy Jo!" I snapped and then blushed in embarrassment as Jenson appeared and frowned at me for yelling at the boss. Jenson held out a stack of thick white towels. I took them.

"Thank you."

Jenson then lifted a black terrycloth bathrobe that had been draped over his arm and shook it straight with all the flourish of a magician pulling a tablecloth free from under a china setting. "I took the liberty," he said, glancing at Bryn.

Bryn nodded, and Jenson hung the robe on a polished silver hook on the wall near the door. "At present, we do not have any slippers to fit you, Miss Tamara. There are socks in the pocket of the robe." Jenson gave a slight bow and then turned and left.

"Where can I get me one of those?" I mumbled, looking wistfully after the butler.

"The United Kingdom."

"Did he cost a lot?" I asked, rubbing the water from my hair.

"Less than a yacht. More than a pair of silver candlesticks."

"Hmm. That narrows it down. You—" I said, pointing at him.

"Yes?"

"Out." I pointed to the door.

"Is this your house?" he asked with mock curiosity.

I scowled at him, which made him smile.

"I'll be in the hall. Call me if there are any spots you can't reach."

I flicked him with the towel as he left.

There was no lock on the door, so the Indy 500 pit crews had nothing on me as I stripped. I wrapped myself in his plush monogrammed bathrobe and tossed my wet clothes in the oversized dryer. I pulled on the socks, feeling very vulnerable. The only other man's clothes I'd ever worn were Zach's jerseys and T-shirts. This felt a whole lot like cheating on Zach.

You're not married to him! I told myself. *You can do what you want and don't need to feel guilty.*

Except Lyons is on the list.

I opened the door and found Bryn leaning against the wall waiting for me.

"You're a lawyer, right?"

"Is this a trick question?"

"I need to hire you."

"All right." His eyes roamed over me from head to toe. "What would you like to give me as a retainer?"

About all I had left was tumbling on the high-heat cycle, and somehow I had a feeling my bra and panty set wasn't what Bryn had in mind since I wasn't in them anymore.

"We'll have to sort that out later."

"Sounds promising."

"Hey! I have a real problem here. Stop giving me the Sylvester the Cat look. I'm not Tweety. I need serious help."

"I'm listening. Unlike some of the men in your life, my intelligence doesn't disappear in the face of noncognitive pursuits."

I cocked my head.

"I can lust and think at the same time. Tell me your problem."

"Attorney-client privilege, right?"

"If you need it," he said with a nod, his black hair gleaming like patent leather when it caught the light.

I spilled the story about needing to put a zombie back in the grave and having put the Glenfiddle workers in a coma.

"Who is the zombie?"

"Not relevant," I said, thinking I ought to tell him no more than I had to, on account of the list. "What do I do?"

"You need a counterspell."

"I don't know one. And I'm afraid if I make one up, it'll go wrong."

"That's a reasonable fear."

"So?"

"You know there are rules that govern this sort of thing."

"What are you talking about?"

"I can't teach you spells unless you're bound to me as an apprentice. We have a coda of laws. I helped draft them."

"Why?"

"Because witches and wizards are not to give information out indiscriminately. Magic is dangerous in the hands of the uninitiated, as you've just seen. Young practitioners need mentors. Normally, your aunt or your mother would act as mentor."

"Well, they're not around."

"I know."

"Look, I can't bind myself to you. I'm not even supposed to associate with you. I'm only here because this is an emergency. How about if you don't tell me how to do it? What if you just cast the counterspell?"

"A normal spell wouldn't work. Your magic did the damage. I

can't counteract it unless I've already got some connection to you or to the people that have been spelled or if there is some talisman that I could destroy. You know, something physical that the magic is tied to. Or unless I want to use an extremely powerful spell that would put me personally at risk, which I'm not interested in doing."

I stamped my foot, stubbing my toe on the granite. "So what you're saying is you won't teach me how to fix it and you won't fix it yourself?"

"I can teach you if you—"

"No. I can't be your student."

"Then you're just going to have to wait and hope that the magic fades and that the spell dissipates before the people die of dehydration."

"Arrg!" I choked out a strangled cry. "Who else could teach me? Or is there someone I could talk to about breaking the rule? It's an emergency. People are dying."

He was quiet.

"What? You know something. Tell me."

He looked me over. "I'm not in favor of turning you over to another witch or wizard for an apprenticeship. They might exploit you."

"And you wouldn't?"

He smiled and shrugged. "The devil you know or the devil you don't."

"I can't bind myself to you. It'll have to be someone else. There must be someone you know who's good. Someone you trust."

"You realize that we're limited in our choices. We need someone local. If those people are as ill as you say, they won't last while we make the rounds to interview potential mentors." He glanced at his watch. "I'll tell you what, it happens that I have a meeting tonight with a group of practitioners. They're not a ruling body, so they can't vote to change the rules, but we can put it to them. If they support our breaking the law, then I'll do it. It'll improve my defense when I'm charged."

"Charged?" I echoed, drawing my eyebrows together. Just what was I getting him into?

"I don't have time to explain. If you're coming with me, you need to hurry and change. You can't go to a meeting of the Southwest Witches and Wizards Association dressed in my bathrobe."

"SWWA?" Southwest Writers and Actors, my eye.

He nodded. "Do you have a gown like the peacock one you wore to the Halloween party? The New Orleans faction hails from the French Quarter. A sexy dress will go a long way toward winning them over."

"You want me to flaunt my body to win votes?" I scoffed. "I'm not that sort of girl."

"Would you rather sell your body or your soul?"

"Does it have to be one or the other?"

"Hey, you decided to play. No one forced you to cast that spell."

I thought about the poison. I could tell them how the zombie had gotten raised in the first place and throw myself on the mercy of the court, but then what would happen to Doc Barnaby? He was an old man, a really foolish, irresponsible, tea-poisoning old man, but I couldn't just tell on him. If Bryn Lyons was afraid of whoever was in charge of the witchcraft police, I sure didn't want them coming to Duvall after a little old man.

"I don't have any hooker dresses, but I know where I can get one."

He smiled. "You don't have to put it that way."

"Hey, let's call it like it is. You want me to come back here or will you pick me up?"

"I'll pick you up."

I walked away. "I'll give you back your bathrobe when I see you," I called over my shoulder.

"No rush. I like the way it looks on you."

I sure hoped that Zach and the sheriff, afraid of exposing the rest of the town, would stay under quarantine with the sick folks until I got back with an antidote spell. And I sure hoped the witches and wizards at the meeting agreed to let Bryn help me. Well, I would have to convince them. That was all there was to it.

Merc met me at the door. He licked his lips and seemed to have some milk on his whiskers. I looked toward the hall he'd come from. Jenson was standing there.

"The feline has been fed."

"Well, lucky him," I mumbled. "Thanks for the socks and stuff, Mr. Jenson. When I get back to my regular life I'm going to bring you a real nice pie. You like pecan?"

"You have an excellent reputation as a pastry chef. I have heard that your black raspberry torte is exceptional."

I beamed. Jenson, the sneaky pete, had just ensured that he would get tortes for life. "I'll make you one. The market's got good raspberries." I waved, and Merc and I went back outside. The rain had let up and was just a slow drizzle. I walked to the car, snagging Bryn's socks on the paved, stone drive. "Well, I sure like that Jenson, but the rest of the night wasn't so hot, was it? I'm glad you had some dinner 'cause you're gonna need your strength. We just skipped out of the freezer and into the fricassee, my friend."

Chapter 8

* * * * *

Twenty minutes later, Bryn Lyons's black limousine pulled into my driveway. He usually drives a black Mercedes, but I guess the Merlin set likes to impress each other. It was almost like being in Dallas.

I put a trench coat on over Aunt Mel's 2002 "Lady of the Evening" Halloween costume that I'd borrowed. I tied the strap of my coat tight. Given that stepping outside was like getting into a sauna, only a nut or someone with something to hide would choose to wear an ankle-length coat. I was hoping that my neighbors would think I'd gone insane, but I worried they wouldn't. They were most likely going to report back to Zach that I'd gone on and become a flasher, but there was no way I could climb into a car with tinted windows wearing a borrowed streetwalker outfit. Thinking about the potential gossip made me wish I lived in a big city where women were free to wear clothes that they wouldn't want to be caught dead in.

Merc got to the car door, but stopped and hissed when it opened.

"Come on," I said.

He didn't budge.

"Get in the car, Mercutio," I said, but I took a step back, wondering why Merc hesitated.

Bryn climbed out, looking like sin in a suit.

"You're not coming with her?" Bryn asked the cat.

Mercutio looked at the door, hissed again, then circled my legs, bumping me back from the car.

"What's in there?" I asked.

"Not what. Who. My father's in the car, but I suppose Mercutio smells Angus. I let the dog in the house before we left, and my father petted him."

I narrowed my eyes suspiciously. Bryn put his arms out as if to show he wasn't hiding anything.

"See for yourself," he said.

Mercutio sauntered away.

I moved forward and peeked inside the car. Lennox Lyons, normally a handsome man like his son, looked like he'd gotten on the wrong side of a celebrity diet. He was pale and thin, his cheekbones slanted like twin shards of glass under his skin.

I straightened up and looked at Bryn. "He doesn't look well," I whispered.

"He was ill. He's recovering."

"That's recovering?" I asked with a half gasp.

Lennox spoke from inside the car. "Join us or don't, but make up your mind. I'm not interested in basting in my own juice from this freakish heat." His voice was startlingly strong.

I slid in, accidentally flashing a bunch of leg as I did. Bryn's eyes didn't miss the show.

"What color is your dress?" he asked when he sat down across from me.

"What dress?"

Lennox laughed, a rich, dark-chocolate-sauce kind of sound.

"You did say we'd get more votes if I showed off my body," I added to Bryn.

"Gets her wit from her mother," Lennox said. "Under the same instructions, her aunt Melanie would have worn a sweat suit. But Marlee would have worn a dress and then not let you see it."

I stared at Lennox, his onyx eyes glittering in the low light. As far as I had been told, Momma and Aunt Mel had never associated with him. And, as a result, I knew more about compound interest than I did about him, which, given the state of my bank balance, you can bet wasn't much.

* * *

The water poured down so hard the windshield wipers had to work overtime. The driver crept along, and Lennox rubbed his sunken eyes.

"The meeting should be postponed. Certainly, the weather witches will be out with their lightning rods. We won't have enough members to conduct business," Lennox said.

I chewed my lip nervously. I needed this meeting to happen.

"I said I would be there," Bryn said, shrugging.

I went on chewing my lip as thunder shook the car every few minutes.

The rain slowed by the time we got where we were going, a

small redbrick building in the middle of a field in the middle of nowhere. We parked on a square of gravel with a collection of other cars. I huddled under Bryn's black umbrella and followed him to the building.

We went inside and brushed the water from our clothes. The earth tones of the anteroom were warm and inviting. I slipped the coat off my shoulders, and Bryn and Lennox looked me over. The black gauze dress hugged like second skin and its halter top was nearly as skimpy as a bikini.

Lennox cleared his throat and glanced at Bryn.

I blushed. "Too much? I can put my coat back on."

"No," Bryn said, taking the coat from me. "I'd sooner put a drop cloth over a Degas."

"But after the meeting, the red-light district would like their wardrobe back," Lennox added.

"What's the red-light district?" I asked.

Lennox laughed and nodded for me to precede him through the door as he held it open for me.

I looked at Bryn, who shrugged. "Never heard of it," he said, which made Lennox laugh harder.

"Have you ever been out of Texas?" Lennox asked, as I passed him.

"Sure." To New Orleans, Nashville, and Puerto Vallarta. But I didn't need to leave Texas to find out most stuff. That's what some-one invented the Internet for. I'd know all about this Red Light county by morning.

There were five big, round tables clustered together with real pretty flower arrangements of cream roses on them. The chairs at the tables were only on the outside, so everybody would be facing everybody else when we sat down.

I picked out the Cajuns easily by their guttural French. A craggy-faced guy who looked like he'd escaped from the Rolling Stones Voodoo tour had his shirt unbuttoned to reveal a menacing green snake tattoo. A woman with wild curly black hair and sallow skin leaned close to him. Her lipstick was bark-colored and she wore a bracelet of chicken bones and eerie red-violet contact lenses. They sized me up like I was a crawfish they wanted to drop in a pot of boiling water.

I shivered and stayed clear of their table. There was a trio of old women at one table. They wore long cotton skirts and turquoise jewelry. A parakeet with them hopped from one slightly slumped shoulder to the next.

Lennox led us to a third table where there was a woman so tall and slim her chest might have been mistaken for her back. She had smooth sepia skin with a tawny glow like she'd been dipped in caramel.

"How are you, Astrid?" Lennox asked.

"*Muy bien*. And you?"

Lennox nodded and sat next to her. Bryn pulled out my chair, and I sat between him and his father.

"This is Marlee Trask's daughter," Lennox said.

"*Claro,*" Astrid said briskly. The woman extended a willowy hand with another word of Spanish, but Bryn grabbed my arm and pulled it back before our hands touched.

"She's untrained," Bryn said to Astrid, like I was an unhouse-trained puppy.

"How interesting for you both," Astrid said, lowering her hand.

"What was that about?" I whispered to Bryn after Astrid and Lennox started talking.

Bryn leaned toward me, his hand still resting on my arm. "It's common to push power from the palm during a handshake between witches and wizards, to test each other's powers."

"Sort of like dogs sniffing each other?"

He laughed. "Crude but accurate."

"So what would have happened if I'd shaken her hand?"

"Probably just a mild shock or a burning sensation. Nothing more serious, unless Astrid meant to do you harm."

"Why would she?"

"Witches suffer from the same emotions as human beings."

"Meaning?"

"She likes to be the most beautiful woman in a room."

I glanced at Astrid's supermodel cheekbones. "Well, she should be happy here then."

"It's a matter of taste, of course, but if I were the magic mirror, I'd advise you not to accept any apples in that dress."

I sighed and blew a strand of hair out of my face with a frustrated breath. "Listen, Abracanova, I'm not here to flirt with you."

He grinned.

"Or to get the Witchcraft 101 lecture. I'm here to—" I cleared my throat. "Um, okay, I am here to learn some witchcraft, but just 'cause we've got magical families in common doesn't make us compatible," I hissed at him in a whisper. "So you can just cut out all that flirting. Our names aren't Tim and Faith, and this ain't Nashville."

He laughed softly. "When you tell Zach to stop flirting with you, does he listen?"

"I don't tell him to."

"Never? Even during the divorce?"

I waved a dismissive hand. "That's none of your business."

"So you've said."

"When are we going to ask them to vote?"

"We don't have a quorum yet. The bad weather's delayed things. We'll have to wait to see if enough members come. Once the meeting is under way, there will be a point when the discussion is opened for new business."

The chicken-bone gypsy narrowed her creepy red eyes at me, and the Cajun wizard, having caught me looking at them, flexed his pecs. The snake tattoo's head jerked, and the man licked his lips with a tongue that was split like a lizard's. A forked tongue! *Yuck. Let me out of here.*

My body convulsed into a shudder, and I leaned closer to Bryn. "If it comes down to me using my body to charm the Cajun out of his vote or all those poor people staying asleep, I want you to know that I'm going to buy them all some real nice feather pillows."

Bryn laughed softly. "I don't blame you."

* * *

I sat quietly with my hands folded across my lap. I felt totally out of place, like a fly in a room full of long-legged spiders just hoping I'd make it out before they started spinning webs.

Our table fell into a discussion of the changes in the national bylaws. There was a general objection to something the wizards' council, the Conclave, had pushed through requiring witches and wizards to submit to a test called the Highcrest Challenge.

"John Barrett's way of trying to locate threats, those powerful enough to challenge his authority," Lennox said.

"And yet, he must know that the challenge is effort-based," Astrid observed.

"He's counting on egos to make us all push ourselves to the limits of our magical strength," Lennox said.

"I think Mr. Barrett misunderstands the nature of some wizards. Take Bryn, for example." She looked at Bryn, and he raised his eyebrows. "I heard you submitted to the challenge and only reached the fourth level."

"The best I could do."

"Oh, *sí*. Of course, yes," she said with mock agreement. "And yet when the Black Oyster Coven was under siege from a pack of Razak demons, you went to their aid. Lucinda said you held back the pack until she could raise the fades to drive them off."

Bryn shrugged. "The Razaks must have been worn out. Lucinda's sister had wounded them."

Astrid smiled. "Of course. Still, a fourth-level wizard couldn't have done what you did. Level five would have been more believable. Although, perhaps Barrett doesn't know of the Razak battle."

"He doesn't need to know about it. It was one wizard coming to the aid of the coven in his region. In North America, we simply want to be left alone."

"Yes, so lucky that you're American. Because with Celtic blood, a black Irish bloodline, Barrett would need to worry very much about that."

"I don't know much about the Celtic bloodlines," Bryn said.

Lennox cleared his throat and exchanged a look with his son.

"Your pretty new *chica* looks like she might," Astrid said, flicking a strand of my hair. I frowned and leaned away from her spindly fingers.

"Half-bred fae from the look of her," Lennox said with a nod.

My mouth fell open. What in the Sam Houston? "Why do you say that?" I didn't know thing one about my daddy, whoever he was, but I always assumed, given my lack of abilities, that he was a human and not magical at all. Except now I seemed to have come into some power, but maybe that was finally from Momma's line.

"Your mother was a circle groupie. She certainly spent her share of time underhill. And your bone structure, you've had that unearthly beauty for several years now," Lennox explained.

Saying I was too pretty to be all human was a backhanded compliment if I'd ever heard one, and I'd heard plenty. "What's a circle groupie?" I demanded.

"Dad," Bryn said with a small shake of his head.

Lennox smiled, and it wasn't an "I'm happy for you" smile. It was a "How come you never guessed you're a faery's bastard daughter?" smirk.

Bryn assured me, "Your mother's gorgeous. You look like her."

"Only better. Too much better," Lennox observed.

I clenched my teeth. "What's a circle groupie?"

"Here's quorum," Lennox said, nodding to the doorway, where two young blond wizards had just walked in and were shaking the rain from their jackets.

One of the grandmotherly-looking witches stood, undisturbed by the parakeet standing at attention on the crown of her head. "Let's begin."

I wanted to pay attention, but I couldn't focus. The fae live under hills, and you're supposed to be able to find the entrance in a circular patch of discolored grass. When I was little, Momma told me tales of faery knights who'd rescued humans from all sorts of peril—throat-rippers, as she called vampires, clawed beasts, demons, and all kinds of vicious predators of mankind. Had she more than admired the fae? Had she chased the knights until they caught her? Was she still chasing them?

Boom! I jumped, startled by the earth-cracking noise. It was almost as loud as the thunder, but too close. A hush fell over the room as we listened, and then something slammed against the door. *Bam!*

Witches and wizards leapt up, drawing back from the room's entry. The old witches pulled out wands. The Cajun and gypsy yanked out clawed skeleton hands. I backed up and noticed Bryn's face. He looked worried.

"Blood?" Bryn said, pulling out a small pocketknife. He glanced between Lennox and Astrid.

Lennox shook his head and pulled out an amulet from under his shirt.

"Tamara doesn't have an amulet," Bryn said.

"More's the pity for her. Her family should have trained her or stayed around to protect her instead of chasing mist."

Bryn muttered a curse under his breath and turned to Astrid. "Astrid, we'll be stronger together."

Bam! Bam! The door groaned.

"Not if you try to protect the girl, too," Astrid said, shaking her head.

Great. Whatever was outside was going to try to tear us to bits, and I was the only one on the battlefield without a weapon.

Chapter 9

"There's a spell on the door," Bryn said, taking me by the arm and leading me to the back of the room. "It's not holding. Stand here," he said, putting me in the corner. "Give me permission to cast a protection spell on you."

Bam! I shook, my eyes darting to the doorway. "What's out there?" I gasped.

"Brute force. Probably shifters or demons, and a lot of them."

The door cracked under the force of the next blow. My heart pounded just as hard. Something horrible was trying to get in, and when it did, it was going to get us.

"Give me permission!" Bryn snapped.

"Yes, okay."

Bryn opened his knife. "Stay inside the circle. Whatever happens, don't step out." Bryn scored his fingertip and blood welled. The red swirled before my eyes, and I felt dizzy.

"Don't. Don't faint." He squeezed my arm with his unwounded hand. "Promise me."

"I promise," I said, my blood draining to my toes as he knelt and marked the floor with his blood. I braced my hands against the walls. And then Bryn stood and marked the walls with stars and a crescent moon as he muttered some enchantment.

The door splintered, and I heard the most horrible sound I'd ever heard in my life. A snarling howl. A pack of huge werewolves rushed the room, long muzzles with dagger-sharp teeth bared. A couple were only partially shifted, taking the form of wolf-men covered in fur with clawed hands and feet, faces deformed and feral.

I slammed my back against the wall for support and couldn't breathe. Bryn shouted something in Latin and flung his arms out, advancing. The other witches and wizards threw spells, too.

The wolves tore through the magic, and one ate the parakeet in one gulp before they knocked down the old witches. Two pounced on the Cajun and tore his chest open. Blood splattered.

I shrieked and flung an arm across my eyes. I didn't want to see them kill me. The growls were deafening, and so were the sounds of bodies falling and witches and wizards screaming.

Finally, things went quiet, except for the wolves' growling. I opened my eyes and saw Bryn on his knees, arms outstretched. Lennox had a hand on his son's right shoulder and the amulet in the other. Astrid too had a bloody hand on Bryn's left shoulder and one hand out. Some of the beasts were dead or seriously wounded, but the ones who weren't leapt forward, blood dripping from their jowls.

An invisible barrier repelled them, but when they bounced back they recovered immediately and slammed forward again, battering the magical energy and forcing the trio back.

A huge clawed pair swiped through the barrier and Lennox fell, cracking his head on the floor.

Astrid, breathless and limp, sank down onto her hands and knees, and a wolf towered over her. I screamed as it gnashed its teeth and tried to bite her spine. Bryn kept his arms up and the wolf's mouth slid just shy of Astrid.

I could see Bryn struggling to hold them back, his arms shaking slightly. They surrounded him, looming huge and vicious. Sweat dripped from Bryn's hair and the veins on his neck popped.

Too many of them. They'll wear him down.

He was splitting his strength to shield me. And we were both going to end up dead if someone didn't help him. I needed something—a weapon. I looked at the table service. I hoped it wasn't just butter knives wrapped up in the linen napkins.

I stepped forward, and the bubble popped. Bryn gasped as the power sling-shotted into him.

"No!" he yelled, glancing back as two wolves jumped, sliding over the shield and coming straight for me.

I saw the steak knives on the buffet. I ran toward it.

"*Carpe facto!*" Bryn shouted, and I felt myself flung forward. I closed my eyes and screamed, feeling my hands close on cool, wooden knife handles.

I crouched and spun, thrusting my arms out. I fell back when they slammed into me, and I squeezed my eyes shut and pushed my fists forward as hard as I could, burying my hands in fur up to the wrists. I felt the knives plunge into the wolf-men, then they were off me.

I realized I was screaming and stopped. The room was deathly quiet. I opened my eyes, tears already flowing. Bryn bent over, gasping. Blood flowed from a wound on his side.

I stood and swayed, but caught myself by leaning against the table with my elbow. The crimson scratches on my legs stung. I dropped the steak knives; raw meat hung along the serrations. I staggered, feeling sick. I grabbed the table and bent my head to sob. I didn't want to look at the bodies, half eaten by the wolves, rank as a sewer.

"It's okay," Bryn said, sounding far away, though he couldn't have been, because I felt his hand against my head. "Let's go."

"I can't look."

"Hold on to me, and I'll lead you outside."

I shuffled along, my shoes slipping in places, and I tried not to think about the carnage. Outside the rain had made the air smell nice, and I gulped in a couple of Texas-sized breaths before I opened my eyes.

The door of the limo hung open and Lennox was slumped on the seat with his head back.

"Is he okay?" I asked, taking a step forward.

An engine roaring to life made me look up, and mud splattered as Astrid swung her white sports car around and barreled it out of the field onto the road.

I slid into the seat next to Lennox, and Bryn sat across from us. Bryn shrugged his suit coat off, and I noticed that the left lower part of his shirt was shredded and saturated with blood.

"Oh no," I gasped.

"It's all right. How are your legs?"

"Okay," I stammered, staring at the deep scratches on his side where I could see muscle and marble-size blood clots.

"It's all right. I'd feel worse if I'd lost much blood."

I turned to Lennox. "Are you awake?" I asked softly.

"Yes," Lennox said in a voice that was sandpaper rough.

"Where are you hurt?"

"I'm fine. Just tired," he said, but the upper right shoulder and chest of his suit were wet and dark.

"I'm sorry they broke through," Bryn said, brows drawn together with worry.

"If you hadn't been there, we'd all have been dead," Lennox said matter-of-factly.

"Why did they do that? Why did they come and attack you?" I asked, shaking like a vine in a hurricane.

"They must have been hunting someone. Werewolves have preternatural tracking abilities. Not only can they follow a human's scent, but also a particular witch or wizard's magical essence. Our energy has a unique signature," Bryn said. "It's unfortunate that they caught up with whoever they were looking for during the meeting. They tried to kill the rest of us just because we were there. In that form, they're basically animals."

We rode for a while in silence with only the sound of the rain for company. I looked out the window and cried for the strangers who'd died. In all my life I'd never seen anything so violent, and it had shaken me up like not much else could have.

Finally, I pulled myself together and cleared my throat. "What kind of spell can we cast to heal ourselves? 'Cause I definitely don't want to turn into a werewolf." I coughed and shivered some more before adding, "I'm real firm on staying human. I don't even like dogs, and I'm pretty sure Mercutio feels the same way."

Lennox laughed softly. "She's entertaining, this one."

Bryn smiled. "We can't be turned. The magic doesn't cross over. The power that makes us witchfolk prevents us from becoming werewolves or vampires or other types of magical creatures. We're a different species."

"I'm not much of a witch though. Not really."

"You certainly are," Bryn said. "When you came out of that blood circle, the energy I used to create it should have dissipated, but you thrust it back into me, gave me back my strength."

"I didn't give it back. I didn't cast any spells."

He shrugged. "You willed it. It happened. That's witchcraft."

"Think so?"

He nodded.

"Am I strong enough to undo my spell on those people that I put to sleep?"

"Yes, with the right ingredients for the counterspell."

"Then you're going to tell me what to use. No more asking for permission and checking with the other witches and wizards. We tried to play by the rules and almost got eaten. So, you tell me what to do, and I'll keep it a secret that you ever helped me. I can't let those people die on a technicality."

"And if he does you a favor, you'll owe him one in return," Lennox said.

I looked pointedly at Bryn.

"That does seem fair," Bryn agreed.

I could see that I was going to be trapped very neatly into associating with him more than I wanted to, but I couldn't help that. And no one in my family could actually tell what the list really warned against anyway. Maybe the name Lyons had been a mistake. Maybe it was supposed to be "lions" and meant I should never go on safari. Okay, it was a stretch, but, under the circumstances, you couldn't blame me for trying.

* * *

Bryn had the car wait while I ran into the house and dried off and found the paper with the spell on it. I put on a pair of jeans, my fastest sneakers, and my lucky Longhorns T-shirt that I wore when they won the Rose Bowl.

Bryn glanced at the faded orange and quirked an eyebrow.

"What?" I demanded. "This is a black-tie spell-casting?"

"Your new outfit's practical, but you can't expect me to view it as an improvement over the dress."

I blew a strand of hair out of my eyes and forced the frown from my face. "Sorry. I've still got the jitters."

"No need to apologize."

The driver slammed on the brakes, and the car screeched to a halt, causing us all to lurch forward.

Lennox grimaced and murmured, "He's fired."

"What happened?" Bryn asked.

"That leopard's in the road," the driver said.

"It's not a leopard," I said, opening the door. "Right?" I asked, looking pointedly at Bryn.

"No. Not a leopard."

"Of course not," I said, stepping out. "Mercutio," I called.

Merc sprang toward the car, startling me. He did look a lot like a leopard in the low light, but with prettier, rounder eyes than the leopards you see on *Animal Planet*.

"Will you stop creeping around like a cat?" I grumbled, but reached down to run a hand over his smooth fur. "Come on, we've got work to do."

Merc hissed at the backseat of the car.

"Yeah, I know. You smell dog—lots of them. You wouldn't believe what happened to us. I'm glad you didn't come," I said, climbing in. "Come on, Merc."

He hopped gingerly into the car and looked around before lying down on my feet. Occasionally during the drive to Bryn's house, Merc swiped the air in the car in a way that told me he could sense some things that I couldn't. Just one more reason I needed my cat.

When we got to the house, Bryn left Merc and me in the foyer while he walked Lennox to some downstairs guest bedroom. I was in a hurry to get on with things, but Lennox did look like he might just go on and collapse at any minute, so I couldn't blame Bryn for walking him.

When Bryn came back, I could tell by the way he moved that he was in pain. I folded my arms across my chest and gave him a stern look.

"Lennox needs to go to a hospital. And so do you." It was the third time I'd said so since we'd left the meeting.

"He won't go."

"You could make him go. We could've driven to a hospital like I suggested on the drive back. Not like he could've stopped us."

"You think they treat a lot of werewolf wounds?"

"I think they treat a lot of dog bites, and that's what he's got, basically."

"Sure, and a hurricane is just a breeze with a little extra wind," he said as he walked to the big staircase that looked like an extra set from *Titanic*.

"Well, kind of," I said mock cheerfully, just to be contrary. "And I still say they could help him."

"Come on," he said, waving to me.

I looked skeptically at the stairs. "Why?"

"You want help with your spell or not?" He continued to climb the stairs, not bothering to look back at me for an answer.

I glanced at Mercutio as I headed after Bryn. "Are you coming?"

Merc didn't budge.

I sighed. "Sometimes you're not the best sidekick," I hissed and jogged up the stairs.

Bryn waited for me next to a door.

"So my spell—" I said.

"We'll talk about it after I take a shower. Though I'm sure you're of the opinion that a dab of Neosporin and a Band-Aid would do—"

"I never said it wasn't a bad wound. Those werewolves are a real menace. What are you going to do about it?" I asked.

"What do you suggest? A strongly worded letter to the werewolf king informing him of their bad manners?"

"That's as good an idea as Cherry Coke, and I'll be ever so pleased to proofread the letter for you."

He grinned and leaned forward so his mouth was near mine. "You like to have the last word, don't you? That's going to be a problem in our relationship."

"We don't have a relationship. I don't go out with men who take me on dates where I nearly get eaten."

He raised an eyebrow. "Then you haven't had the right man nearly eat you."

I gasped, my jaw slack. He brushed his lips over mine, making them tingle.

"Yeah, somehow I figured I'd have the last word with that comment." He opened the door to the room and walked in, but I stood stuck to my place on the plush cream carpet.

Chapter 10

I hesitated outside Bryn's bedroom, but there was no way I could leave without his help, so I padded into it and looked around in awe. There was an enormous faceted skylight of leaded glass creating a prism effect of the night sky. The pearly white walls had some sort of gloss over them, so they shimmered and shined, reflecting the light. Large mirrors stood in each corner, making the huge room look huger. A sleek, black-silk duvet covered the king-size bed.

He nodded to a small sofa near the large bay window. I walked over and sat, looking down at the garden and pond that were lit up with landscaper's lights. It was like the pictures you see in *Architectural Digest*.

"Nice yard."

"Glad you approve." He pulled some clothes from a dresser, then went through a doorway that I guessed led to the master bath. When the door closed, I itched to get up and snoop around, but I sat still. I wasn't even supposed to talk to him. I should never have been in his house, but well, circumstances being what they were, there was no help for it.

I didn't move for the ten minutes it took for the door to open again. He walked out from the steam dressed only in jeans with a white gauze bandage taped to his wound. He was leaner than Zach, but still made of perfectly sculpted muscle, and I took a few extra moments to stare at his chest before looking away.

"All right, let me see it," he said.

"Are you going to finish getting dressed first?"

"Not yet. I want to see if this gauze stays dry." He held out his hand.

I pulled the paper with the spell from my pocket and handed it to him. He bent his head over the sheet for a minute and then looked up. "Not bad. Not the way I would have done it."

"Can you tell why it went wrong?"

He shook his head. "It's not the spell. I don't do much dirt magic, but this looks adequate for what you intended."

I pursed my lips. "Dirt magic?"

"Slang for Earth magic involving ground plants."

"Not a very nice way to describe it."

"No."

"And what kind of magic do you use?"

He looked back to the paper without answering. "The problem isn't the ingredients you put in, it's the magic."

"But I didn't put any magic in it. When Momma or Aunt Mel cast spells, they said they felt how much power they were using. But I never felt a thing."

He didn't respond.

"You can feel how much you use?"

"Yes."

"Since I didn't feel anything, do you think I actually used my own? Because I've never had any bona fide power. Maybe Momma and Aunt Mel's power is still in the house and yard, and I tapped in to it."

"No." Bryn went into his closet. I waited, drawing my brows together when he didn't come back. I stood and went over, peering inside. The closet, full of expensive designer suits, had a back door that led to a tiny workroom. Not exactly Narnia, but plenty intriguing.

Bryn leaned over an open book on a small antique desk.

"What are you looking at?" I asked, walking through the closet.

"A reference book."

"A spellbook? Can I see it?" I reached for the book, but he caught my hand, holding it and turning toward me.

"Didn't they teach you anything?"

I glared at him. "Of course they did."

He took a step forward so that our bodies were nearly touching. I took a step back.

"Then you know that you shouldn't touch another mage's book without permission."

"I wasn't going to cast a spell while touching it." I pulled my hand free of his.

"Give me a couple minutes. I'll be right out."

I walked back to the bedroom and sat on the bench at the end of his bed, feeling like a scolded child. I resented it and him and the whole darn mess.

I tapped my foot impatiently until he walked out with a couple pieces of paper. He sat on the edge of the bed, looking them over.

"Got it?" I asked, holding out a hand. I'd been gone for almost three hours, and I was anxious to get back to Glenfiddle.

He touched the bed next to him, and I moved to sit by him.

"Most of the fever-breaking spells were created to treat fevers that come from infection, not magic, but if the counterspell doesn't work, then you could try one. It might at least improve things temporarily."

I looked at the first sheet he handed me. It was marked "Fever Treatment Spell." It called for mixing henna with water and turmeric to make a paste that was supposed to be smeared above each eyebrow while reciting a healing blessing.

"What's the blessing?"

"You have to write it yourself. It's how you'll infuse your own power into the spell." I guess he could tell by the way I drew my brows together that I was skeptical about being able to put power in. He nodded encouragement, then added, "And here's a counterspell for you to cast." He handed me the second slip.

I looked over the list of herbs that were to be bundled together after being blessed by sacred verse. "I don't know if I have all of these."

"You can replace an herb if you have to, but just don't delete one. You'll also have to be sure the replacement herb has the same properties as the one you're removing."

I nodded. "You're not going to come with me?"

"No. I've got some of my own work to do, and it can't wait. But there is one other thing I can do to help prepare you."

"What?"

"Focusing energy is the most important part of casting any spell. You have to be able to ignore distractions."

"Not my best thing."

"Take off your shoes," he said, moving back on the bed and lying down.

"What have my shoes got to do with it?"

"Trust me. Take off your shoes and lie down." He stared up at the skylight.

This sure sounded like one of Zach's millions of ploys back in high school to separate me from my clothing and my virtue. But I imagined that Bryn's routines, by this point in his life, would somehow be a bit more sophisticated than trying to trick a girl into his enormous silk-covered bed.

"You forgot to put your shirt on. Maybe you want to do that before we start?"

He glanced over, looking me up and down. "Do you need me to?"

"Do *I* need . . . No, I'll be just fine. Right as rain." I lay down next to him on the bed.

"I want you to count the number of facets in the glass and then, with your eyes, trace the squares created by the lead between the panes. No matter what I do, keep your count."

I imagined him sliding his fingers over my skin and blushed. I hadn't even started counting, and it was already hard to concentrate, which was silly. It wasn't like he'd said "I want you to trace my muscles using your tongue." And, come to think of it, why the Sam Houston hadn't he? He'd been flirting nonstop, and now that he had me in his bedroom, he wasn't even going to try to trick me into having sex with him? In my book, we called that a tease.

I stared at the cut edges and began to count. I got to around five before he touched me, tapping my forearm with his thumb. I stopped and bit my lip. I started counting again.

He moved his hand to hook my jeans pocket closest to him. He tugged on the fabric.

"Darn it," I mumbled, starting to count again. I couldn't see his face, but felt sure he was laughing at me. I was only on number three when he laced his fingers through mine and pulled my hand to his body.

I turned my head to look at him. His perfect profile didn't move for several seconds as if he were studying the skylight, too.

The back of my hand lay against his side, growing warm.

"I can't do it. I can't concentrate."

He looked over. "No? Why not?" His fingers tightened his grasp on my hand.

"Because you're purposely trying to distract me, and it's distracting."

"You have to learn."

"Oh, really? And you could concentrate with a strange woman touching you?"

"Try me."

Uh-huh. "Recite something. Some poem out loud so I know you're not cheating and just telling me some number that you already have memorized."

"The sea is calm tonight. The tide is full, the moon lies fair upon the straits," he began.

I rolled onto my side, studying him.

"On the French coast, the light gleams and is gone."

I put my free hand on his stomach and slid it down to the waistband of his jeans and unbuttoned them.

His voice slowed, but continued. "The cliffs of England stand, glimmering and vast . . ."

I put my thumb just inside where I'd unbuttoned and rubbed it against his skin.

His voice trailed off, and he chuckled. "I know what you're thinking," he said as I pulled my hand back from his waist.

He rolled suddenly, knocking me onto my back and pinning me under him. I would have been shocked, if I'd been born yesterday. He'd reacted to being touched the way any guy would have. My body reacted to him lying on top of me in the usual way, too, but I didn't let it show.

"I was just proving a point. That wasn't a special invitation to make like a dog on a steak," I said.

"As a matter of fact, you didn't prove your point."

"You're counting ceiling glass with the eyes in the back of your head?" I asked.

He smiled. "I'm going to explain everything in a few minutes when I finish kissing you."

My heart sped up. "Don't you dare kiss me."

"Hold on to me," he whispered, then pressed his lips over mine. I felt hotter than a campfire, and it wasn't only from the velvety feel of his tongue parting my lips or his solid gorgeous male-smelling body pressing mine into the expensive feather bed.

He paused and mumbled something against my mouth, and white heat burned inside me, coiling like a spring. I writhed under him. The sensation was like moving toward orgasm, but it wasn't that kind of energy. I grabbed his back, digging my fingernails in, clawing against the unbearable tension. And then something flashed red before my eyes, and the spring snapped. It knocked him back, separating us. He knelt above me, head tossed back, and murmured something I didn't understand.

All the breath left my lungs and I was falling, breathless, suffocating and cold. I couldn't move, and a blue haze descended with a blistering wind gusting against me.

I stood on a playground. Georgia Sue, Zach, and I were out for recess from Ms. Smith's first-grade class. A pair of demons on purple horses galloped toward us with sickles drawn.

Chapter 11

* * * * *

I don't know how long I lay there hallucinating. I came back to myself, wrapped like a tamale in the silk-covered feather bed. My breath was frosty on the warm air. I coughed, shivering, and sat up, stiff as a plastic doll.

Bryn stood at the mirror. There were scratches on his back from my fingernails, but he peeled the gauze back, and the werewolf's gouges were gone. The skin looked smooth and perfect. He saw me staring at him in the mirror and turned.

"What did you do to me?" I asked, shaking like a newborn calf. I felt like I'd been doused with ice water and left in a freezer.

He walked back to the bed and crawled on it. "Cold?"

"Yes," I said as my teeth chattered.

He yanked the bedding from my fingers and pulled it loose. He pushed me back and curled up with me, covering us both. His body was like a furnace, and, as angry as I was, I couldn't resist the heat.

"We're a perfect match, magically speaking. I could have resisted your touching my body. Sexual excitement alone can't distract me when I focus. But your magic fits mine, tongue and groove, interlocking, like male and female body parts. Without any practice or training together, I can siphon energy from you," he said.

I slapped his shoulder. "I'm not a gas tank. You can't just steal my power."

He grinned. "Yes, I can, which is a good reason for you to apprentice yourself to me. I can teach you how to stop me."

"Oh, I know how to stop you." I kicked the covers off. His body heat and my anger had done the trick; I wasn't as cold anymore.

He reached for me, but I slapped his hands away, scooting off the bed.

"Tamara—"

"No," I snapped, collecting the two sheets of paper with the spells on them. They'd fallen off the bed in all the freaky sexlike magic.

"You can't cast spells tonight. They won't work."

I spun to face him. "Why not?"

"I've drawn too much power from you."

"Then get up off your butt and come with me. I've got people to save."

"I can't do that."

I flung my hand forward and pointed at him. "You bastard! No wonder you're on the list."

"I can give you some power to work with. Come back to me," he said, holding out a hand. He was heartbreakingly gorgeous as he tried to coax me, but I knew better than to trust him.

Those dark blue eyes glittered at me, sexy and dangerous. I

wanted him, and I knew he could tell. I closed my eyes and remembered the Glenfiddle workers. I thought about Stucky Clark's wedding, which was scheduled for next spring, and Lil Czarszak, six months pregnant. What would she do if Red died?

I clenched my fists and my jaw. My lids popped open, and I narrowed them at Bryn. "I don't have time to cuddle up with you right now. But I do have time to wait while you write me a spell of power that will give me enough juice to make these work," I said, shaking the pages at him.

He shook his head. "You would only hurt yourself. It's an upper-level skill to call power from nature. You're too inexperienced to make it work."

I pointed my finger at him again. "You healed your wound with a healing spell that was powered by the magic you stole from me. You owe me—"

"You're holding two spells that I gave you from one of my books. You can consider the power I took as payment for them. Reciprocity. And I'm offering to give you power back."

"You just want to experiment or something. I can tell by that look in your eyes that you want something. Zach gets the same look when he sees a Cobra Mustang." I marched over to the door. "And don't think I'll forget this. I *will* get even with you."

"That red hair suits you."

"Explain that!"

"Lots of passion, not much sense under its influence."

I spun to the rock bowl fountain and snatched a rock, which I whipped at him. He ducked, and it bounced off the mahogany headboard, leaving a big chip in the veneer. "That's for not helping me and for stealing from me and for being a total jerk!"

I flung the door open and marched out, stomping down the

hallway, then the stairs. I rushed out the front door, muttering curses. I realized when I got to the gate that I didn't have a key to get out or a car to drive home. I couldn't even buzz the security guy because the buzzer was on the outside of the gate. I stalked over a small hill to where I figured the security man might have a post.

A high-pitched whine froze me. I'd forgotten that I hadn't come alone to Bryn's.

"Mercutio!" I called. I ran toward the bushes, following the sound of panting. As I crawled to the hedge, Merc screeched at me.

"It's me!" I slid my hand in, heart hammering. I hoped he wouldn't bite me.

I felt his fur and pulled him to me. He lay limp and bloody, fur torn. "Oh no! Mercutio, what happened? What happened to you?" I sobbed.

I cuddled him to my chest, rushing back over the hill. I got just inside the door when I saw two black heads. My sneakers, which I'd forgotten, were in Bryn's left hand as he leaned over a large black Rottweiler that licked a bloody wound of his own.

"What have you been fighting, Angus?" Bryn asked, not seeing us.

Angus, spotting me and Mercutio, squared his broad shoulders and growled.

Bryn grabbed the dog's collar and held him back just as he lunged toward us. Mercutio hissed and twisted in my arms.

"I hate you and your dog!" I yelled.

Angus barked and gnashed his teeth at us. Bryn shouted at the dog in some language I couldn't even identify. He dragged Angus by the collar and locked him in a closet.

"Is he badly hurt?" Bryn asked grimly.

"I don't know," I said, tears running down my face.

"Here, give him to me. I'll take him to the vet."

"You're not putting him to sleep. No one is putting him to sleep. He's my cat!"

"I won't do anything without your permission. Give him to me. You don't have time to take him to the vet if you're going to try the counterspell."

"If you do anything to him, I swear I'll be the worst enemy you ever had."

"I very much doubt that, and you seem to forget that I'm the one who gave him to you."

I had forgotten that. Actually, I'd forgotten everything.

I handed Mercutio gingerly to Bryn. "You'll take him to the vet and make sure they help him?"

"I promise."

I rubbed the tears away from my eyes and pulled my shoes from Bryn's fingers.

"I can't get out the gate," I said as I shoved my feet into the sneakers.

"I'll let you out."

"You could have opened the gate for me earlier, couldn't you have? You could have done it from upstairs, right? You walked down here with my sneakers because you knew I'd be coming back in."

"My hair isn't red," he said with a shrug.

Arrogant freaking bastard. I tied my shoes, strangling my feet from yanking the laces so tight. I leaned over and kissed Mercutio's head. "I'm coming to get you right after I finish helping those people. Don't die. I'll buy you a lot of catnip this weekend, I promise. So don't die," I whispered.

Tears rolled down my cheeks again. If Bryn had been Zach, he wouldn't have let me go so upset, but Bryn just walked over to the phone. He held Mercutio with one arm and dialed with the other hand.

As I walked toward the door, I heard him talking.

"Mac, it's Bryn Lyons. No, Angus is fine, but I need to bring in a cat. Can you open the clinic? I'll meet you there."

I hurried out, trusting Bryn would take care of Mercutio because I had no choice. The limo was at the end of the drive, waiting for me. I opened the door and flung myself inside.

I didn't need to say anything to the driver. He passed the open gate and drove me to my house. I chewed my thumbnail, telling myself with each passing block that Mercutio was tough and would be okay.

At home, I quickly washed my face and set my mind to fixing things. I gathered the ingredients and focused all my energy on what I wanted to do, to heal the injured.

I felt a rustling of the wind and heard rain splatter against the roof as I finished the henna paste. *This is going to work,* I told myself over and over.

I remembered what Bryn had said about my not having enough power left to do the spells. I knew after tonight I wouldn't get another chance, so I had to draw magic to me or steal it from wherever I could.

I'd seen Aunt Mel work a power spell once in the backyard. I'd watched from the window but hadn't heard all the words. I did remember that she'd marked the corners and called to the earth. She'd been naked, but I couldn't see taking things that far.

I took off everything except my plum-colored bra and panties, then paused, wondering if I could really afford to hold back. I frowned.

But I don't want to. I really don't.

I stomped my foot at my hesitation. "Hey, lives are at stake. End of story." I took a deep breath, stripped naked as a june bug and marched out into the yard with a knife. I crouched on a small patch of grass and cut symbols in four corners. I hoped they were close enough to the ones I remembered seeing in the ground.

I cut the tip of my finger, yelping in pain. Good thing I wasn't going to do any spell-casting after the Glenfiddle problem was solved because I didn't like poking and cutting myself. My finger throbbed and blood dripped in a steady stream. Steadier than I'd planned. Could a person bleed to death from a pricked finger? I didn't think so, but felt a little woozy at the thought.

"Hear me, power of the earth, and feed me your strength as I give you mine. I call to the North, to the four corners, to the legacy of a family long faithful to the craft. Grant me your green energy." Green energy? Sounded like an eco-slogan. The earth must have been skeptical, too, because I didn't feel a thing. "Please, give me a little help. I need it and not for myself." I stretched my arms out and tossed my head back. "I call to you. I beseech you. I'm not a witch really. But I do respect the planet. I recycle. And if you help me, I'll start a program. Lord knows people throw away too much glass and plastic." Was I allowed to mention God in a quest for pagan power? "God, no offense here. If you want to grant me a miracle, that would be fine, too. Amen."

I shook my head. Probably that was the worst call for power that anyone ever performed. I was glad Mercutio wasn't here because it would have been embarrassing for him to hear me. I went back into the house and washed my finger, which was still pulsing blood. I pinched the tip.

"Ow, ow, ow!"

I'd just gotten it to stop bleeding and was putting on a Band-Aid when a loud knock at the door startled me. I scrambled into my clothes and rushed over to answer it, expecting it to be Bryn with Mercutio. I pulled the door open to find Zach, his expression as full of thunder as the impending storm.

"Girl, you better have a damn good explanation."

Chapter 12

"I do have a good explanation for running off, but I can't tell you what it is," I said.

The veins and muscles in Zach's neck popped up. I knew I was about to get an earful, but we didn't have time for that.

"I have special medicine. I was just on my way back to Glenfiddle."

"Sure you were."

"I don't lie." *About anything important . . . unless there's a real good reason.*

"What were you doing with Bryn Lyons?"

So he'd already heard? *Small-town folk are faster than DSL Internet. Darn them.*

"Can we talk about it on the way? And, hey, what are you doing here? Didn't the sheriff say we were all supposed to stay at the factory?"

"You ran off, and, like a damn fool, I came looking for you. Then I hear you're taking limo rides with Lyons," he spat. "You want to explain that to me? Not so's I'd care if he got struck down with whatever disease these people have got, but I do give a shit that you'd rather spend what could be your last hours with that arrogant SOB instead of me."

I looked at his handsome face, and something inside me started to hurt. Zach might be my difficult ex-husband, but he never would've taken power away from me that I planned to use to save people's lives in order to heal himself. He'd have stayed wounded and taken me to the people, and when we got home he'd have drunk a bottle of whiskey to kill the pain and told me to clean the wound for him and then to sit a spell and talk to take his mind off it.

I touched his face. "I only ever loved one man, and I'm looking at him."

"So what were you doing with him tonight? And what did he say to you to make you cry?"

I blinked and looked away. I guess washing my face hadn't made my eyes less red. I should have spilled some Visine in them, but heck, I'd had other things on my mind, and I wasn't expecting company.

"I was crying over Mercutio. He forgot he's a cat and got himself in a dogfight. So he's at the vet, and I don't know if he's going to be okay. I hope so. I really do hope so." I bit my lip and shook my head. I was pretty sure Mercutio wouldn't want me to get distracted at a time like this. "C'mon let's get to the factory and see if this medicine works. We'll talk about everything later."

"What kind of medicine is it, and where did you get it?"

"I got it from someone Bryn knows."

He didn't seem satisfied with that explanation, but before he could ask more, I said, "We're wasting time. Those people are dying!"

Zach walked out, and I followed him. I climbed into the front seat of his prowler, debating whether or not I should tell him everything. He didn't believe in magic. We'd had some whopper fights because I believed in Edie. If I told him about casting spells and werewolves, he would think I was crazy and have me committed, but how was I supposed to cast a counterspell with him watching? And how was I going to explain running around town in a trench coat with Bryn Lyons?

I avoided his questions during the drive by asking plenty of my own about how the Glenfiddle workers were doing. Zach told me that he and the sheriff had been busy, dousing the people with water, then turning the big fans on them to cool them off.

We got to the factory and found that the sheriff too had left the scene.

"Must've gone for help," Zach said. "We didn't want to risk infecting the rest of the town since we'd been exposed, and we kept expecting the radios to start working out here, but they never did. I don't know what's going on."

"Did you call for help once you got away from here?" I asked him.

"Yeah, should be on its way by now. They had to go over to Dyson to get some special protective suits that we don't have. Gear for coming into contact with hazardous materials. The question is why you didn't call for help right after you left. You let us sit here all night while you went to a party."

"I knew the sickness couldn't infect you." I walked to the doors, feeling decidedly uneasy about Zach watching me. And that wouldn't help my concentration, which, like Bryn Lyons said, I would need. I turned. "Can you do me a favor?"

"Like what?"

"I need to be alone to give them this medicine."

"Why? What is it?"

"Please." I walked over and grabbed his hands. "Can you just trust me? I need you to. I really need you to."

"I'm tired as hell, Tammy Jo."

"Please. This once, please just trust me." I don't know if he could hear the desperation or the tears in my voice, but he sighed.

"I'll take a walk to the end of the road and wait for the help to arrive."

I leaned forward and gave him a quick kiss and then spun toward the factory. I raced inside, closing the door behind me. The people were flushed and had dry, cracked lips from dehydration.

"Oh boy. Oh God, I need help. I sure do need it." I rushed from one to the next, rubbing the henna paste on their foreheads. By the time I got back to the first of the group, Tommy Kane, he already looked a little better. His skin was less hot at least.

"That's real good. This is all going to work." Then I heard the sound of sirens. "Shoot. They're here too fast," I muttered, scrambling to light the candle. I got it lit and then ran around the group five times, waving the herb bundle over their bodies. I set the herbs on fire and wafted the smoke over them.

"Smoky fire to warm the earth,
it receives their fever in her hearth.

A blessing here surrounds this girth,
dirt then water heralds calm rebirth."

I heard gravel crunch under the ambulance's tires. I clapped the fire out, preserving the hot ashes in my hands.

"Ow!" I whispered, blowing into my hands. I rushed out the back door, not wanting to get caught, and ran toward the stream. I was only about fifteen feet away when I slammed into something and fell down.

"Where the hell are you going?" Zach's voice said in the darkness.

Amazingly, I'd kept my hands cupped, but my butt wasn't happy about it.

"I need to wash this stuff off my hands," I said. "I need to hurry." I rolled onto my elbows and knees and pushed up, careful of my hands as I did. I got to the stream and realized I needed to be sure of which way the water was flowing, but it was too dark to tell. I put my foot in the water and felt it pushing my pant leg, then bent over and released the ashes, letting them flow away from me. I stepped out of the stream, my foot squelching in my shoe.

"Did you step in the water?" Zach asked.

"I guess so, by accident. Doesn't matter. We're already so drenched, you know?"

The sprinkling turned into another hard rain, and we hurried back toward the factory. My hands stung, but I didn't care. We suddenly heard noise and shouts and broke into a run, rushing to the door.

The Glenfiddle workers were sitting up and demanding water. *Thank you, Earth, and thank you, God, for the power and the miracle.* "Looks like the medicine worked," I said with a smile.

Zach slung an arm around my shoulder and planted a kiss on my cheek. "That's my girl."

* * *

Zach took me home, where I changed my clothes. I realized that I didn't have Bryn's cell phone number to call him at the vet, but I didn't have to wait long to find out what was happening. My phone rang just before I was ready to leave to drive there.

"He's okay. I'm bringing him home," Bryn said.

"Um, all right. Y'all be here soon?" I asked, glancing at Zach, who was standing in the living room waiting for me. He'd offered to drive me to the vet's, and although we hadn't really talked about all the details of the evening, because I'd said I was too tired and upset to talk, I knew Zach—he'd let things set only so long before he started an interrogation. And I'd be a captive suspect if he were driving me somewhere. On the other hand, I preferred riding in the car with him to having him getting in the middle of any talking between me and Bryn at this point.

"Yeah, I'm pulling up in your driveway," Bryn said.

Just peachy.

"All right then." I hung up the phone, trying hard not to grimace. I wished I'd had time to shoo Zach out before Bryn got there. The sound of a car door shutting drew Zach's gaze to the front of the house.

"That's Bryn Lyons. He's bringing Mercutio home. It was his dog that Mercutio got in a fight with."

"Is that so? And what were you and your cat doing at his house?" Zach asked, blocking my path to the front door.

The doorbell rang.

"I need to get that."

"I'm closer. I'll take care of it for you," he said with mock politeness, sweet as a honeybee right before it sticks its stinger in.

I frowned at him. "It's my house and my cat and my company."

Zach eyed me up and down and then turned and walked over to the door. I followed him, annoyed, but wanting to welcome Mercutio back.

Zach opened the door, and Bryn, with a sleeping Mercutio cradled in his arms, waited for Zach to open the screen door. Zach simply looked them over.

"Can you open the door?" I asked from over Zach's shoulder.

Zach's movements were slow, drawing the process out, making things tense in that way Zach does so well. Bryn stepped inside and passed Zach on his way into the house. I followed my cat, which Bryn laid carefully on the sofa. I immediately sat next to Mercutio, examining him.

"He's okay. He's got some stitches and a few punctured muscles, but Mac gave him a sedative and a painkiller. He should be back to normal in a week or two. Mac sent these," Bryn said, setting a couple bottles of medicine on the counter. "Antibiotics and pain medicine."

I leaned over and gently hugged Mercutio. I looked up at Bryn then. "Your dog's a menace. He needs to be tied up and neutered before he attacks any other innocent cats."

"He's a dog. It's his job to attack cats," Bryn said, but added more gently, "I suppose it's better in general if you don't bring Mercutio when you come over."

"Well, that won't be a problem in the future. Thank you again for helping me get the medicine for the Glenfiddle workers. They woke up and are doing fine."

"Are they? Well-done."

"Yeah, so it turns out the medicine was strong enough."

"Good."

Zach leaned against the wall, arms crossed against his broad chest, eyes boring into Bryn's back.

"There are a few things we need to talk about," Bryn said to me and paused.

"Go ahead," Zach said at the same time I said, "It's not a good time."

Bryn's eyes flicked to Zach for a moment and then focused on me again. "The unexpected visitors that came to the meeting are not satisfied with the results of their effort. There's reason to believe they plan to follow up on their objective."

I blanched at the reference to the vicious werewolves coming to town.

"I think you should consider staying at my house until the business is concluded. I can chain Angus outside; Mercutio can stay inside with you."

Zach cleared his throat, drawing my attention to him. "Is that something you're interested in doing? Staying at Lyons's house, Tammy Jo?"

Bryn didn't acknowledge the question. He just went on talking. "This isn't a matter you can rely on your ex-husband for help with. Don't let your anger cloud your judgment."

"Oh, I never do that. It's my red hair that interferes with my good sense. All that color so close to my brain, it plum disorients me most days. I'll stay at my own house, thank you."

"Tamara—"

Zach interrupted him, voice hard as granite. "She answered you. The answer was no. Now, it's been a long day. Why don't you take yourself back across town."

The edges of Bryn's mouth curved into a sardonic smile, and he walked over to the fridge. He lifted the erasable marker and wrote a phone number on the whiteboard I use for my grocery list.

"For when you change your mind," he said without bothering to look back at me for acknowledgment. He recapped the marker and let it drop to hang from its string, then walked down the hall and out of my house.

Zach walked over to the board, curling his hand into a fist.

"Don't," I said, but he ignored me and rubbed the number off the board. I sighed. I wasn't planning to call Bryn, but my life was so crazy these days, who knew?

"Who's coming to town, and why is that your problem?"

I sighed. Zach and I had broken up, but we were still all in each other's business. And it would really piss him off for some other guy, a guy he liked about as much as paying taxes, to know more about my life than he did.

"It's—" I put a hand to my head, shaking it slowly. I felt Zach close in on me.

"C'mon now. You got a problem, I'm your go-to guy, darlin'." He put his arms around me and hugged me against his warm, hard body. "Tell Big Zach about it."

When I'm worried or upset or even just under the influence of female hormones, any comfort makes me cry more than onions, and I was really close to tears at the moment. I looked up with swimming eyes. "It has to do with the ghost in my locket. I know you hate that subject."

Zach whistled slowly. "And Lyons is saying he believes in the girl in the locket, huh? C'mon, Tammy Jo, you know he's shining you on. His interest in helping you get your necklace back is to get close enough to get you into his bed."

"Could be."

"Not 'could be.' *Is*. And you don't need to worry. I'll get the locket back when this case gets solved."

"Are you close to solving it?"

He frowned. "Well, I been a little busy today, being quarantined without a radio."

"Right. Sorry."

"But everyone at the station is on this. We'll get it solved."

"I need it to happen soon."

"Why?"

I gently pulled away from him. "It has to do with the ghost."

He nodded silently. I was glad that he didn't yell and start us to fightin'. Edie had been a source of contention for a long time. I'd done things, bought things, and tried things that Zach didn't like because of her influence while we were married. Zach didn't believe in ghosts, so he felt like I'd created her because I didn't want to take responsibility for the stuff I did. And I probably shouldn't have listened to Edie, but it had been hard not to take her advice when I was fighting with Zach.

"Well, I ain't gonna say I believe in her when I don't. But I'm also not going to let Bryn Lyons move in on you without a fight. So you cozy up to him with that in mind."

I nodded. "Will you call me tomorrow?"

"Tomorrow? You kicking me out?"

"I need to pay attention to Mercutio and to shut my eyes for a while. I'm exhausted." Both things were true, but I also wanted a little time to myself to think about what was happening and what I would need to do about it. Edie and the locket were still missing, and I had to make a plan to rescue her. So I needed Zach gone, because I didn't want him scrutinizing my every facial expression and asking questions I couldn't answer.

"All right. I don't need to write my number on your fridge. You know how to get me when you want me."

I smiled at him, and he stepped forward.

"Gimme some sugar."

I leaned into him and kissed him. He held me tight for a few moments before he let me go. He didn't say anything else; he just winked at me, then turned and left.

Chapter 13

* * * * *

Sleep always makes trouble seem not as bad, so when I woke up on Tuesday, I was downright hopeful about things. After all, I'd returned Mrs. Barnaby to her grave and saved a bunch of people's lives, not to mention ensuring that the production of Glenfiddle whiskey would continue, thereby preventing a Duvall economic catastrophe.

"I'm a hero," I announced to myself in the mirror as I pulled my hair back. "Good for me. I deserve a super cake mixer and a nice pair of sandals."

I pinned my hair in a smooth knot at the nape of my neck. *And you can buy them, right after you rescue Edie and get a job.*

Unlike with witchcraft, when it comes to confection, I'm talented as all get-out. So despite Jenna's threats, I was sure that someone in town would hire me to bake. She might have pull, but I make Irish Cream chocolate truffles that melt in your mouth like

I stole the recipe from Lindt's. Unfortunately, things had to be: find Edie first, find a job second.

I'd been tossing and turning in bed, putting together a plan. I needed to do some old-fashioned detective work, I'd decided. Trouble was, I knew nothing whatsoever about detective work. Still, I didn't see how that should stop me. I didn't know too much about being a witch, and I'd done all right at that. Sort of.

My first order of business was to put on a Sunday church dress and pumps and go see Councilwoman Faber. Her Jag had been stolen, which might have just been a coincidence, but it was a flashy car, and it hadn't been recovered. I couldn't see thieves driving around in it for too long before getting caught, so they must have had a plan to hide it or sell it to a chop shop or something. Also, it was strange that they'd robbed the sheriff and a councilwoman. Robbing high-profile people would make it a high-priority case. Was that part of the point? Did they have something against the town government?

I would ask Mrs. Faber if she had any idea who they were. Then I was going to see the Deutches. Maybe someone had been admiring that big ring of Mrs. Deutch's. I also wanted to see Georgia Sue. Maybe someone at the party knew something about the thieves but was too embarrassed to tell the police. By now Georgia Sue would have called everyone on the guest list to talk about what had happened. She could be quite the source of information. Speaking of that, Johnny Nguyen might have some news. Yep, it was going to be a productive day, and I wouldn't even have to worry about casting any spells.

I buttoned up my periwinkle suit and slipped on my shoes. Then I hurried down the stairs. It was time for Mercutio's medicine, and I wanted to get it into him while he was still groggy. He hadn't much liked the taste of it the night before.

As I stepped off the bottom step, I spotted Merc. He stood at the door to the backyard with his head cocked.

"Good morning, Mercutio," I said.

He ignored me, but I attributed his rudeness to being wounded and medicated.

"You want to get a little fresh air?" I walked over to the door and opened it. "Hellfire and biscuits," I gasped.

The four spots where I had cut symbols into the ground were blackened and the usually lush tangle of green plants and bright flowers had turned brown and died overnight. The yard was barren, eerie, as dry and cracked as a southwest desert.

"Aunt Mel is going to kill me." I slapped a hand over my mouth and shook my head, heart racing.

Mercutio gave a speculative meow, and I could tell he was upset too, but this was no time for him to have palpitations. He was infirmed and needed his strength.

"It'll be all right," I told him. "I just need some topsoil and some seeds."

Mercutio cocked his head at me.

"A big heap of topsoil," I added. "We'll go on by the nursery right after we find the locket. Or after I do. You're going to stay home and eat some tuna with your medicine."

The doorbell rang, and I jumped. *What now?* "Oh, a visitor. Isn't that nice, Merc? Some company."

I went to the front door and pulled it open. Smitty—Calvin T. Smith to his momma—stood on my doorstep in his deputy's uniform. He was good Texas stock, built solid with a nice, slightly crooked smile and a clean shave. I'd been a bridesmaid at his wedding.

"Good morning, Smitty."

"Morning, Tammy Jo. How're you?"

"Oh, fine. Zach's not here. He's at his place."

"Actually, I came by to talk to you."

Uh-oh. "Oh, really? Well, come on in and have a cup of coffee."

"How come you're all dressed up? Job interview? We heard you quit Miss Cookie's." He walked in behind me and closed the door.

"Oh, you heard about that? Well, we had some creative differences over there." *'Cause I'm creative, and she's not.*

"Hmm. That never seemed to bother you much before."

"Oh, it's been on my mind on and off. I guess it just built up."

I took out a can of Maxwell House and pulled off the plastic lid.

"You don't need to make me coffee. I had some at work. Councilwoman Faber just put some fancy coffee machine in the town hall, and most of us been walking next door. You should come down and try some. It makes this white foam—"

"Smitty, what's goin' on?"

He stopped and looked as embarrassed as he had the time freshman year in high school when he'd had to give the oral report on human reproduction.

"Well, it's real awkward, Tammy Jo, you bein' a close family friend and all." He paused.

Don't you even . . .

"Turns out I'm here to arrest you."

Off the grill and into the gullet. The whole room spun around me. Turns out I was going to need more than a heap of topsoil to fix my day.

* * *

I sat down hard on the couch with Mercutio hissing at Smitty as he joined us in the living room.

"It's okay, Merc. Just a little misunderstanding. Smitty would never arrest me. After all, I broke down and wore a pea-soup-colored bridesmaid dress and a four-inch fake magnolia on my head for his wedding just to keep Heather happy."

Smitty cleared his throat and looked out in the yard. "Now, you know this wasn't my idea. But I am a deputy, and I've got to follow the law."

"So what are you charging me with? And does Zach know you're over here arresting me?"

"We all thought it best not to bother Zach with this until after lunch. He had a long day yesterday."

"*He* had a long day?" I sputtered. "What's the charge, Smitty?"

"Actually, there's a couple. They were working on the paperwork when I left to come get you."

"Working on the paperwork? This isn't some parking ticket! You'd better—"

"Now, get ahold of yourself. Yelling at the arresting officer isn't going to make the judge inclined toward leniency."

I'd had just about all I could take. I'd gone ahead and planned my day, and getting arrested was no part of it. I didn't have time for jail.

I lowered my voice to NutraSweet. "The charges?"

"Well, reckless endangerment. Lucy Reitgarten says you splashed them with some hazardous waste, and then they all got sick. Then you left the scene of the crime after the sheriff told you not to, putting the rest of the community at risk.

"The other charge is for indecent exposure. Hope Cuskin says you were prancing around naked last night in full view of her son's window. He's a minor, you know."

"What?" I gasped. "I was in my own yard last night. The only way Craig Cuskin saw me was with binoculars. And I'll just bet it wasn't Craig that Hope was worried about. You know, Judge Bob was always spying on Momma and Aunt Mel with his binoculars until Hope caught him at it. She told them she didn't want them sunbathing in the yard or even wearing shorts to water the lawn or wash the car. Now that is ridiculous. Just 'cause the Cuskins are rich and he's a judge doesn't mean they have say-so over what we wear or don't wear. It's our own private property."

"So you admit that you were outdoors naked last night?"

I pursed my lips and got up. "I'm going to give my cat his medicine. Then you can take me to the station. My first phone call will be to Zach, and we'll see what he has to say about the Cuskins spying on me. Judge or not, Zach's likely to knock Bob into next week."

"Now, the naked in the yard business is the least of it though. You got to understand that."

I ignored him. I'd forgotten that Lucy, Jenna's sister-in-law, worked at Glenfiddle. And how come the Glenfiddle workers remembered me splashing them with the passionflower potion? Weren't these potions supposed to cause at least a little bit of amnesia? I mean, how was a witch supposed to spell-cast without getting caught? I took a deep breath and blew it out. This was just one more reason why magic is not for me.

* * *

The cell at the station could have been cleaner, but it wasn't so bad, all things considered. Marvin, who supports the whiskey and ale businesses a little too vigorously, was asleep next to me on one of the benches in the cell. He'd gotten wet in the storm and had only partially dried into a horrible, musty, sweaty, drunken mess. He smelled extremely bad, and I would have paid a thousand dollars I didn't have for one spray of Lysol or a little pine-scented room freshener.

When Zach showed up, he was as angry as I'd seen him since the day the judge granted me a divorce despite his protests. Zach had contested the thing as though I'd asked for one of his kidneys in the settlement. The judge told him he should've poured that kind of energy into the marriage, and we might not have ended up in court. Yep, Zach had been really steamed that day.

Zach used a key to unlock the door. "They put you in with Marv?"

"Had to. Some frat boys home for the weekend were in the other one, and I didn't feel comfortable with them."

Zach clenched his teeth 'til I thought his jaw would snap. "Come on out of there," he said, taking my hand and pulling me right to him.

"It wasn't toxic waste. I swear it."

"You think I don't know that?" He paused. "And you don't know the guy that attacked them, right?"

"What guy?"

"Someone in costume. Same guy who left the corpse at the scene I expect."

Hmm. I didn't think that it would be helpful for me to mention that it was the corpse that did the attacking.

"Er—"

"Never mind. Don't answer that here. I don't want you saying a word until I've got you a lawyer. I'll have to go by the bank and work something with the mortgage."

"I don't want you to remortgage your place. That's not fair. I'll have to do it with my house."

"That house isn't yours, Tammy Jo. You can't go take out a mortgage on it."

"I can't let you risk your house. We're not even married."

"Where else are you going to get the money?"

"Maybe I can just talk to Judge Bob. He's got a soft spot for my family."

"What he's got for your family ain't soft. And you're not askin' him for a damn thing. We've got to get you a lawyer."

"She has a lawyer."

We both looked over to the doorway, where Bryn Lyons stood dressed in one of his designer suits. That man could put male models to shame with his good looks.

"No way," Zach ground out.

"For reasons I don't wish to discuss at this juncture, I'll be working gratis, which means free," Bryn said smoothly.

"You do family and corporate law. She doesn't need a divorce, and she isn't starting a business. You're not qualified to represent her in a criminal case. And besides which, no fucking way."

"Zach," I said gently. "He might be able to help get me out of here."

"Yeah, and so might I if I killed off the witnesses against you. Doesn't mean it'll work out for the best in the end. You let him represent you for free, he'll want something in return."

We both looked over to Bryn.

"The arrangements I work out with clients are always mutually acceptable. This is not a form of extortion. She needs legal counsel. I'm here to provide it."

I felt like a towel caught between a pair of dogs—I was very likely to be torn apart. But the bottom line was that I needed a lawyer, and free was all I could afford.

"You're hired," I said to Bryn.

The veins in Zach's neck threatened to burst, but he didn't say a word.

"Tell them I'll need a room to talk to my client in," Bryn said. "And tell them to bring me the warrant and every statement they've taken so far from witnesses. I want to see everything, right now."

"Lyons, I'm not your flunkie."

"If you want her out of here, you'll do what I ask."

They had a stare-down, all narrowed eyes and tight muscles, Zach looking ready to pummel Bryn, who never moved or took his eyes off his rival. Finally, Zach turned his head and looked at me.

"You remember what I told you the first night we went to New Braunfels?"

Sure, I remembered. Zach wasn't known for big romantic speeches, but he'd been young, in love, and more than a little drunk. I'd left camp, and he'd gone looking for me. "She's run off with the devil," Smitty had joked. "She doesn't run off," Zach told him. "If the devil's got her, it's 'cause he took her. And he's about to regret it when I get to Hell and kick his ass." Later, I'd asked him, "Would you really come after me in Hell?" To which, he'd answered, "If you're in trouble and I don't come, it's 'cause I'm dead and buried. As long as I'm alive, darlin', I'm comin'."

I stared at him now. He couldn't get me out of this trouble on his own, but he wouldn't leave me to face it alone either.

"I remember."

He nodded. "You go on and talk to the lawyer. I'm going to talk to a few people myself."

"Don't hit anyone."

He smiled, despite his grimness. "Oh, I doubt I'll have to, darlin'. Usually all I need to do is make a fist."

Chapter 14

* * * * *

Bryn and I sat across from each other at the conference table. He'd listened while I talked, all under the protection of attorney-client privilege. He took notes on a legal pad and looked so professional and detached that I felt like the whole night before had been just a dream.

"Fine," he said, closing the notebook when I finished. "Are you all right?"

"Oh sure. I've always wondered what it'd be like to be under arrest. It's not so bad really. I got a very nice cup of foamy cappuccino from City Hall, and I guess they'll be giving me a jumpsuit soon. Too bad it didn't happen before the Halloween party. Would have saved me some money on a costume."

"The reason I ask is that Bob Cuskin is conveniently out of town. My guess is that he wants to let things die down a bit before the bail hearing. I've made a couple calls for a substitute judge, but the soonest I can get someone here is tomorrow. You'll have to spend a night in jail."

I didn't have time to be in jail overnight. I was meant to be finding the locket. I put my head in my hands. "Know any good jailbreak spells?"

He chuckled. "You'll be fine. I'm certain Zach will make sure of that."

"If they let him."

"Think they could stop him?"

"Not unless they shoved him in a cell, too."

"Locked up with you, some men might not consider that such a hardship."

I looked up at him then. "You're not really gonna go there, are you?"

He grinned. "I suppose not. By the way, you made that henna paste pretty strong."

"So?"

He continued to smile, then laughed and shook his head.

"What?"

"All the Glenfiddle workers have dark brown smudges on their foreheads that won't wash off."

Jiminy Cricket. "Just great. They're disfigured. Next they'll be charging me with assault and battery."

"First of all, it's temporary. It'd be gone by the time they got you to court on that kind of charge. And second of all, no one saw you put that paste on anyone, and you're not going to testify that you did, so they've got no case."

"They might make one. Jenna and her sister-in-law would love to see me suffer, and they've got friends in high places. Like the Cuskins."

There was a rap on the door, and a young deputy who I didn't know looked in. "I'm sorry, ma'am. Time's up."

My heart did a tap dance in my chest. Back to that smelly, dingy cell where I'd never be able to sleep. "I'm ready," I said, despite the fact that my hands were trembling. The deputy closed the door to give us another moment.

"Listen, it's just as important to me to find my locket as it is for me to get out of jail. Have you made any progress on finding the thieves?"

"Not yet. One problem at a time."

I sighed as we both stood. Life wasn't going too good. If tomorrow's horoscope prediction was bad, I was liable to tear the whole newspaper to shreds.

I hesitated as we walked to the door. I looked Bryn full in the face. "I do appreciate this," I said. "After all the stuff I said and did last night, and you didn't even mention that. It's real gracious of you."

"We'll chalk what you said up to the red hair," he teased with a wry smile.

I turned to the door and pulled it open. "I'm not in a position to argue about it right at the moment." I glanced back and stared straight into his cobalt eyes, so clear and blue, like water in those pictures of the Caribbean. "But I'll think it over, and maybe if I ever get out of here, I'll dye it."

He leaned near me and said softly, "Don't you dare."

* * *

I spent the night in jail, but I had the cell to myself. Zach brought me a pillow and blanket from home and breadsticks and the lasagna I love from De Marco's. He left the cell door open all evening and played rummy with me until one in the morning. Then he kissed me good night and locked me inside. The guys on night duty came around every few hours to see if I needed anything and at nine in the morning, I got to take a shower and get ready for court. So my advice is, if you have to go to jail, make sure somebody you sleep with is holding the keys.

When I walked into court on Wednesday, there was a female judge with steely gray hair and an even steelier expression. My heart pounded, and I clasped my hands in front of me tightly, almost like my heart was in my grasp and if I squeezed hard enough I could make it go slower. Then I saw Bryn, and he nodded and waved to me in a confident way that reassured me. The bailiff led me over to him.

Smitty came in then with the prosecutor, and Smitty looked like he'd had skunk stew for breakfast. I cocked my head and then glanced at Bryn.

"What's going on?" I whispered.

"Give it a moment."

The prosecutor, who I'd never met, stood near his chair with Smitty sitting in the row behind him. Two rows back from them I spotted Jenna Reitgarten, giving me one of her usual holier-than-thou looks. I cringed. Could my humiliation get any worse? Did she have to be there to watch? I felt so nauseous I was frankly worried about Bryn's fancy briefcase sitting on the table in front of me.

I slid it to the side and forced myself not to put my head down. Bryn squeezed my arm in reassurance when I swayed. He leaned to me.

"Don't pass out."

But it seems like such a good time for it. I gripped the table until my hands were white.

After some announcement, the hearing was called to order, and the prosecutor stood.

"I've read Mr. Lyons's motion, Your Honor, and have had time to question the arresting officer. It seems that Mr. Lyons's statements are not incorrect. Ms. Trask was never advised of her Miranda rights at the time of the arrest. Officer Smith was also not able to inform her of the exact charges since he didn't have the warrant in his possession at the time that he arrested her."

The judge raised her eyebrows and then frowned at Smitty, who looked ashen.

"In light of these deviations, these serious deviations, and some other facts that have been brought to light, we are prepared to drop the charges against Ms. Trask."

The judge nodded. "Case dismissed."

People behind us gasped and mumbled, but I didn't look at them. I turned to Bryn, who smiled.

"Is that it?"

"That's it," he said.

"Oh my gosh," I stammered, too overwhelmed to speak.

Bryn slid his notepad into his black leather briefcase.

"I can't believe it." I put a hand to my forehead. I was still dizzy, but I was feeling better by the second. "Thank you," I said. "You're worth every penny of your fee."

He laughed. "You're welcome. There's always still a possibility of civil action, so don't talk about that night with anyone."

I gave him a hug, then started toward the back of the courtroom. I wanted the hell out of Dodge. That's when I saw Lucy

Reitgarten and a couple of women I didn't know, all of whom had large brown smudges on their foreheads, scowling at me from the back of the courtroom like the Furies.

I wanted to tell them the marks would wear off, but I remembered Bryn advising me not to talk about things, so I looked straight ahead and hurried past them.

When I got home, I gave Mercutio his medicine. He promptly went crazy, attacking the furniture and me. I had just cornered him with some throw pillows when the doorbell rang. As soon as my back was turned, he barreled by me.

My hair looked like I'd been in a NASA antigravity machine by the time I answered the door. I smoothed it down and gave Zach my most innocent face.

"Now what's going on?" he asked.

"Nothing. Just playing with Mercutio."

"Uh-huh, that's another thing we need to talk about. The vet says he's not a house cat."

"He does fine in the house," I said, trying to keep Zach from venturing into the living room where the disarray looked suspiciously like a tornado had come through.

"I ran into Mac. He says he's pretty sure it's an ocelot."

"A what?"

"A wild cat. Like a leopard, but smaller."

"Don't be silly. Mercutio's not a leopard. He'd have bitten me by now."

Mercutio did a flying leap into the foyer and onto Zach's leg, snagging his pants before landing and merrily pouncing on imaginary prey.

Zach looked at me.

"He's on medication."

Zach shook his head and walked around Mercutio, who seemed to have subdued whatever invisible foe he'd been battling.

"Texas has laws, Jo. No exotic animals as pets. You best say your good-byes and turn him over to a zoo before someone complains. And they will complain because the whole town's gonna be watching you."

"He's my cat. I'm not giving him up."

"You had such a good time in jail, you want to go back?"

I turned red, but put my fist on my hip and widened my stance to let him know just how serious I was about keeping Mercutio.

Zach walked into the kitchen, pulled open the cupboard and took down the coffee. I walked over and attempted to pull the can from his hand.

"It's my house. I'll make it."

He held fast to the can and eyed me as I tried to take it. "I can't make myself at home here anymore?" he asked.

I frowned. "That's not what I'm saying—"

"Then sit yourself in a chair, and let's talk about your locket. Who's seen it and asked about it? And who have you told that it's old and valuable?"

The locket! Yes, I did want to talk about that.

"Anybody who's known me and my family knows that we consider that locket our most important possession."

"Right, but someone just stole it recently. You been wearing it on the outside of your clothes lately? Mentioned it to anyone?"

I shrugged. "I don't know. Folks come into the bakery all day long. I can't remember what all's been said in the past few weeks. No one took an interest that I noticed."

"You told me once that you weren't the only person in town to see the ghost. Who else has claimed to see it?"

"Her. She's a her. And her name is Edie."

Zach gave me a pained look.

"And just why are you so interested all of a sudden?" I wondered if it might have been because Bryn had saved the day that morning, and Zach didn't intend for him to get all the glory in rescuing me.

The coffee percolated, and Zach got himself a cup. "I'm working on the case. Isn't that what you want me to do? Ilene Faber's Jag turned up in San Antonio. Who do you know with family or friends over there?"

"Nobody."

"Who claims to have seen the ghost?"

"Johnny Nguyen Ho."

"Of course," Zach mumbled. "He's probably also had visits from Elvis and James Dean."

"This was a very reliable Edie sighting. He described her perfectly, right down to the way she talks. I *know* he's seen her."

"Uh-huh. And did you open the locket to let her out for him to see?"

"No."

"So then how did he just happen to see her?"

"She doesn't need me to open the locket. She can get in and out whenever she wants to. And she went to his house. He was having a séance. Maybe she was the closest spirit to his place at the time."

I could see Zach's blood pressure rising, but he held his tongue like someone was likely to cut it off if he didn't.

"Has Johnny seen the locket?"

"Yes."

"Does he know that the ghost is attached to the locket?"

"Yes, but he wouldn't steal the locket. He doesn't need to. Edie likes him. She visits him."

"When she feels like it, huh?" Zach asked. "Maybe he wanted her to be the guest of honor at some séance, and she didn't show up like a trick pony. Maybe he thought if he had the locket, he could make her appear whenever he wanted her to."

"Oh, I don't think so."

"He's got out-of-town friends, more than most people around here. He could have asked them or paid them to get the locket."

"You're just too suspicious. Not everyone is out to break the law."

"Most times, people are out for what they can get away with. Now, who else knows how much you love that locket? Lyons?"

"He only found out it was important to me after the robbery."

"Did you tell him about the ghost?"

"As a matter of fact, no. I don't just go 'round telling everyone. You know I don't."

"Hey, you divorced me. How do I know what you do in your free time?"

"How do you know? That's a good question. 'Cause it sure seems like whatever I do gets right back to you. You've got more spies than the CIA."

"There you go exaggerating again. Now tell me about this ghost." He poured coffee into a mug and held it out to me. I took it, feeling strange about having this conversation with him. He'd never wanted to hear about Edie, and when he and I were breaking up, any mention of her had made him furious. Seeing my hesitation, he added, "C'mon, Tammy Jo, this is your big chance to tell me all about her."

Something in his tone rubbed me the wrong way. "Maybe I'm past wanting to tell you about her."

"You want me to find the locket for you or not?"

However uncomfortable I was about talking to him about Edie, I couldn't let it get in the way of his doing his job. I needed that locket found.

"There's not much to say that has anything to do with all this. She died a long time ago when she was twenty-four years old. The locket was her sister's. They were close and when Edie died, she attached herself to it. It might be that wherever she was supposed to go didn't want her or she didn't want it. But anyway, she's never left this world, or almost never left it. Except this one bad night of a Bryan Adams concert in 1984."

"What does that mean?"

"It's why I'm worried. I don't know what keeps her here, whether it's blood or memories or what. But something terrible will happen to her if she tries to appear and none of us has the locket. Back in the eighties, Momma and Aunt Mel shared the locket, and sometimes when they weren't wearing it, they left it lying around. Well, Aunt Mel's friend Lisa picked it up and put it on. They all went out, and Aunt Mel didn't remember to get the locket back, even though they knew it wasn't supposed to get taken anywhere without one of us.

"That night Momma and Mel had terrible nightmares and woke up hearing Edie screaming. She was being churned up and pulled into some hall of horrors. They ran out of the house, crying and hysterical. It was raining, and Momma crashed their car into a tree. Aunt Mel smashed her head against the windshield and was bleeding, but Momma couldn't even stay with her because she couldn't stand the shrieking. By the time she got to Lisa's house though, it all stopped.

"And when she got the locket, it was cold and dead, and Momma said she thought she'd die right along with Edie. She and Aunt Mel couldn't eat, couldn't sleep. They were so heartbroken.

"They called a ghost to make sure Edie made it to the other side, and it told them she wasn't totally gone. So they did something to call her back."

"Like what?" Zach asked. "A séance?"

I ignored the question because I still didn't like his tone. "So they pulled her back, but she wasn't the same. She used to talk and joke with them, tell stories, and give advice. But when she came back after that night, she would only stay in corners and sit curled up with her head down. She didn't talk or look at them for almost a year."

"Later, when she was a little better, she told them that it happened when she'd started to appear and couldn't tell where she was. She couldn't get her energy together. It was like being ripped apart by claws and sharp teeth she said. Well, Momma and Aunt Mel never took the locket off again. When one took a shower, the other wore it.

"When Momma and Aunt Mel left town, they gave it to me for safekeeping while they're gone. I promised I wouldn't take it off, and I didn't voluntarily." I shook my head angrily. "Those bandits, the bastards. I've got to get that locket back before she tries to come out. I just have to." I took a deep breath to compose myself as Zach watched me with a guarded expression. "I need it back before October twenty-fourth. It's an important anniversary." Edie's birthday as a witch. The day she'd successfully cast her first spell. "She always comes to visit on that day."

"C'mon," Zach said, getting up. "Let's go take a ride."

"Are you on duty?" I asked.

"Not officially, but you know I'm always on duty for you, darlin'."

Yeah, right.

Chapter 15

Johnny Nguyen was about as likely a crime boss as Mickey Mouse, but I didn't argue with Zach when he pulled up in front of Johnny's house. Johnny redecorated about once every six months, and I was looking forward to seeing what he'd done this time. My favorite had been the Bavarian lodge look. He'd had me make him a dish of pastries every week. I heard he had to crank up his air-conditioning to get all the heavy fabrics to work, so I guess it wasn't too practical.

Johnny's slate blue BMW was parked in front, so I rang the bell several times. Finally, he opened the door partway, but the chain was still firmly in place.

"Oh, hello, Tammy Jo," he said with a smile. He had a dark red smudge at the lower edge of his mouth. *Candy apple? No, lipstick. Yikes!*

"Hey."

"I sick with the flu. Come see me in salon next week."

Zach gently bumped me aside so that he could peer in through the crack at Johnny.

"We really need to talk to you today," Zach said.

"Oh, Deputy Sutton, it you. Such great hair, but it a little long. You should come and see me next week with Tammy Jo. I cut your hair free of charge."

"That's a generous offer, and I appreciate it, but I really just need to talk to you. Today."

"Just a minute then. I be right back." Johnny closed the door, and Zach scowled.

"I think maybe he's been trying on makeup. He's probably embarrassed," I said.

"Him, embarrassed? I don't think so." Zach grinned. "He got drunk one night and propositioned the sheriff in front of Miss Marlene."

"What'd the sheriff do? Arrest him?"

"Hell, no. And have to do the paperwork on that?" Still smiling, Zach shook his head. "The sheriff just went the other way like the bar was on fire."

I giggled. "Johnny's like five feet one and a hundred pounds. It's funny that you guys are so intimidated."

Zach rolled his eyes. "Intimidated? Yeah, right. Hell, if I clocked him one, I'd probably kill him."

"That's why you better never do it."

"Not plannin' to. He's a nice enough guy. Just can't hold his liquor, and he needs to remember he's in Duvall, Texas, not San Francisco. Howard Smith wanted to kick his ass when Johnny tried to flirt with Big Howard in front of Anita. Took Kenny and me both to hold him back."

"Johnny probably gets lonely here."

The front door opened, and Johnny stood before us in red silk pajamas and a matching kimono robe. I slapped a hand over my mouth to keep myself from laughing as I glanced over at Zach's face.

"Come in," he said.

The place was Moroccan-themed just like I'd heard from the rumors around town. Amethyst and garnet beads hung from the ceiling and plush jewel-tone pillows in ruby and sapphire surrounded a small carved table on the floor. I stood admiring the old metal lanterns and the gorgeous hand-beaded fabrics with elaborate patterns. It was all amazing.

Zach, who's about as exotic as apple pie, stood in the doorway, looking like he thought even setting foot inside might corrupt him in some terrible way.

"We just need to ask you a couple of questions. Do you know anyone in San Antonio?"

"Oh, San Antonio Riverwalk. Very nice. Yes, I have some friend there."

"Have any of them been to town to visit you recently?"

"No. Deputy, please, air-conditioning." Johnny waved Zach inside.

Zach closed the door behind him.

"Excuse please. Need Kleenex in kitchen," Johnny said, and when he turned I caught a glimpse of the chain around his neck. Old metal loops interlinked with white crystals. It was the chain that had held the Edie locket for the past five years.

I felt all the blood drain to my feet. First, Dr. Barnaby. Now Johnny Nguyen Ho. Was there anyone in town I could trust? Any friend that wouldn't completely betray me?

"Tammy Jo?" Zach said, moving close to me.

Johnny had already gone into the kitchen.

"He's wearing the necklace." I sat down hard on the pillows. It was a long way to fall.

"You're sure?"

I nodded.

"I'll get it." Zach squared his shoulders and marched down the short hall to the kitchen. I heard a startled shout from Johnny, followed by some rapid Vietnamese. Then Zach shouted, and a moment later I heard a muffled exchange and Zach stalked back out. He pulled me up by the arms.

"Did you get it?"

"He wasn't wearing any necklace."

"He was. He must have taken it off."

"He says he doesn't have it."

"Well, he put it somewhere. In a drawer or something," I said as Zach hauled me toward the front door.

"Stop. I'm not leaving without—"

"We're not staying." Zach yanked the door open and pulled me out with him.

"What are you doing?" I yelled.

"He has company. A guy dressed—There's no way we're playing 'find the locket' today."

"I don't care if he's got damned Osama Bin Laden in a daffodil print dress, I'm not leaving."

"What are you going to do? You can't search his place. And neither can I without a warrant."

"So we're just going to leave? We're just going to give him time to hide it somewhere good?"

"I'll talk to the sheriff. I'll tell him you saw the stolen property, but Johnny stashed it somewhere. They'll give me a warrant, and I'll come back."

"And what if he gives it to his boyfriend, and his boyfriend leaves town?"

"You want to stay and stake the place out?"

"I, at least, want to talk to him before I just go on home to wait for some stupid warrant."

Zach gave Johnny's front door an appraising look, then scowled and marched back over to it. I followed. He banged his fist against the door.

Johnny opened it warily.

"If you have something that belongs to my wife, I suggest you give it back."

"I never steal anything. Never."

"Johnny, I saw the necklace," I said.

"I no steal. You insult me very much."

"Where did you get it?" I asked.

"Not wearing—"

I leaned forward. "Listen to me," I whispered. "I don't care where you got it. Honestly, I don't. But I need it back. If you ever want us to see Edie again, you have to give it back to me. She needs for me to have the locket or her whole soul will get, like, ripped to pieces and evaporate."

"I not have your necklace."

"Okay. Okay, you don't have it. But if you did know who had it, you could just tell them to give it back. To put it in my mailbox or leave it in an envelope on my doorstep. I wouldn't ask any questions."

"I go now. Sick with flu, remember," he said, backing up and closing the door.

"He understands. He'll give it back. He has to," I mumbled to myself, ambling back over to the car.

Zach got in, shaking his head.

"What?"

"Never mind," he said and shuddered.

"The boyfriend was pretty?"

He shook his head. "There's a real good reason men don't put makeup on. Butt-ugly and freakish. I very nearly pulled my gun."

In spite of myself and the dire situation with the locket, I chuckled. He frowned. I giggled softly, then louder.

"Girl, don't start."

I clamped a hand over my mouth, but my shoulders shook as I laughed silently.

"We're going to Jammers. I need a beer."

* * *

Several of the patrons of Jammers had big brown splotches on their foreheads, and every one of them gave me an evil look. I slid into a booth and waved at Georgia Sue. She and Kenny owned Jammers, the favorite bar in town. As usual, the place was full.

"You want wings?" she called to us over the noise.

Zach nodded, holding up two fingers. He called the station on his cell phone and explained about needing a warrant for Johnny Nguyen's, but with the judge still out of town, it wasn't clear when that would happen.

A few minutes later, Georgia sashayed over with a tray and put down two baskets of spicy buffalo wings, a bottle of Armadillo Ale for Zach and a frozen margarita for me.

I took a gulp of my drink. "I think Johnny Nguyen Ho was behind the robbery at your party."

"What?" She dropped onto the bench next to me, and I told her about seeing the chain.

"You're sure it was the same one? I mean really sure? He's got that place all fixed up like India."

"Morocco."

"And I heard there are beads everywhere. So maybe it just looked like your necklace."

I took another big swallow of my drink and shook my head. "If it had been another necklace, he wouldn't have taken it off and hidden it in the kitchen. He knows he did wrong. I just hope he feels guilty enough to give it back. Otherwise . . ."

"Otherwise what?"

"Otherwise, I'm going to have to go get it."

"How? And can I come? I really want to see all those beads. Not to mention whatever kind of trouble you unload on him."

"Georgia Sue, don't encourage her," Zach said.

She fixed Zach with a look. "Well, he's got her necklace, Zach. You're her man. Just exactly what are you going to do about it?"

Zach raised his eyebrows and took a swig of his beer. "What would you like to see? Should I string him up by the nearest tree?"

"Now, I don't think we have to go that far," she said.

"Tar and feathers? A bullet—"

Georgia Sue clucked her tongue. "You're in an evil mood tonight."

"That's true enough. I just been to hell, and it looks a whole lot like Morocco these days. Get me another cold one, will you?"

Georgia Sue nodded and hopped up.

Zach leaned forward to say something but stopped when a tall man with greasy, shoulder-length brown hair passed the table slowly, staring at me the whole time.

"You know him?" Zach asked.

I shook my head.

"Well then, that just wasn't polite, now was it?" Zach said, voice low and menacing.

I could see where this was headed. He was still wound up from Johnny's, and a confrontation would suit him just fine as a way to blow off steam.

"You know it's getting late. I should be getting home to check on Mercutio."

"That wildcat? Like he needs you babysitting. He'll be taking down livestock in a couple weeks."

I opened my mouth to explain that Mercutio was just a baby, but I never got a chance to speak because Bryn Lyons walked up.

"I need to speak to you," Bryn said.

"She's busy. Having dinner with me," Zach said through clenched teeth.

"Dinner?" Bryn asked, glancing at the wings dismissively.

"That's right. Sometimes us poor folk have bar food for dinner. Now, why don't you take your rich ass back to Dallas and pick up another deb with a price tag hangin' from her nose, and leave the real women in town to the real men in town?"

"If she prefers your company to mine, that's her unimaginable choice. But I do need to speak to her, if, that is, you're not too insecure to let her do that for five minutes."

Zach laughed. "Still sore that the prettiest girl in town never gave you the time of day? Can't say as I blame you." Zach paused. "You can talk to her if she wants to talk to you. It's a free country, after all. Plenty of my family died to make sure of that."

Bryn rolled his eyes and leaned toward me, sliding a hand

under the booth's table. He pressed his hand to mine, and I felt several small cool objects fall into my hand.

"They're here," he whispered, making my spine tremble. Then he turned and walked away.

I glanced down into my upturned palm where several silver bullets lay. From the look of them, they were .38 caliber.

A memory of the bloody muzzles of those wolves from the witches' meeting flashed in my head, making me as scared as a turkey on Thanksgiving morning.

"Zach, what kind of gun do you carry?"

"Thirty-eight, darlin', why?"

"No reason," I said with forced cheer, "except that I'll maybe need to borrow it."

He cast a speculative look to where Bryn Lyons had sat back down. "Someone you need me to shoot for you?"

"Oh, I don't think so. I just want it for show. Maybe I'll have to wave it around and act fierce. That'll do the trick." *I hope.*

I craned my neck to look around. If the wolves were around, where exactly? I spotted the guy who'd made such a point of checking me out when he walked by. He was sitting at the bar, and when he caught me watching him, he gave me a hard look. Definitely not looking at me because he thought I looked cute in my ponytail. Plus, he had a suspiciously long face. The kind that could turn into a muzzle faster than you can say canines.

Zach got up, drawing my attention to him as he strode around the bar, right up to the guy.

Uh-oh.

"Got a problem, friend?" Zach asked, shoulders square, stance wide and solid.

The man shook his head.

"Want one? Seems like you do, since you keep staring at my girl."

"Just leaving," the guy said, standing up.

Zach's eyes never left the guy as he moved around him and walked to the door. I watched him leave, feeling better. I glanced over to Bryn to see if that put him at ease, but he's always got a poker face, and, as usual, I couldn't read him.

Zach grabbed another beer and slid back into the booth. "You comin' home with me?"

I shook my head. "I have to give my cat his medicine."

"Then I'll come home with you."

I considered his offer. Burglars and werewolves running around town, Mercutio too drugged to keep watch, and the only gun I was likely to get ahold of came with the good-looking man sitting across from me. The choice was easy, so I nodded.

"I'll finish this one, and we'll go. I want to talk to you about what Lyons said that has got you so worried."

Great. Couldn't wait.

I glanced at Bryn again and noticed he'd gotten up and was leaning over saying something to Georgia Sue. Then he walked to the back of the bar and through the doorway that led to the kitchen.

"Now why does he need to go out the back way?" Zach asked.

I wondered the same thing but quickly turned my eyes back to stare straight across the table.

"You want to talk to the man? Go ahead," Zach said, but I knew him saying that was just like me saying "You want to watch football all day instead of coming over? Go ahead."

I shook my head. "Finish up, and let's go home."

Chapter 16

You'd think that all that rain would've cooled things off, but it was hot and muggy when we walked out of Jammers. I wasn't happy that it had gotten dark, and my gaze darted to the sky. I could see about half the moon.

I followed Zach around the building to the lot behind it. I paused, feeling something strange, a thickness in the air, like it was about to storm, but different. My heart thudded in my chest.

Zach slowed his pace too and looked around. I squinted, scanning the cars, and stopped walking. Anything could be scrunched up behind a parked car, waiting. The air caught in my throat, and I had to take a deep breath, but it didn't help. It was like I couldn't take a big enough gulp.

Faint ringing in my ears made me start to run. "Zach, honey," I gasped. He turned just in time to catch me as I slammed into him.

"What?" He slung one arm around my waist, holding me to him as he looked around.

I dug through my purse, only coming up with a couple of the silver bullets. "I want you to put these in your gun," I whispered.

"My gun's loaded, darlin'. And you can stop shaking. There's nothing out here for you to be afraid of. But it does stink to high heaven. Smells like something foul overflowed with all the rain."

I licked my dry lips as I turned my head from side to side. It didn't smell like a sewer to me, but there was something rank. I heard a scratching sound and felt Zach's muscles tense. He reached lazily to his gun holster and unsnapped it. "You go on and hop in the truck," he said, handing me his keys.

I took them with trembling fingers, but didn't move. I didn't want to leave him all alone with a werewolf if there was one. I had the silver bullets.

"Go on now," he said, giving me a gentle shove away from him as he started toward the trees at the edge of the lot.

"Come with me, Zach. There's nothing out there. Probably just a mangy dog or raccoon."

Zach ignored me, walking with purpose. And then I saw yellow eyes peering out of the darkness and screamed. Zach half turned toward me, and the wolf-man sprung from the brush.

It came for me, but Zach moved into its path, and it slammed him to the concrete. I shrieked, knowing it was too late to do anything to help. The bared teeth ripped into him. Then a blast of frigid air from behind me knocked me to my knees.

The wolf howled and rolled backward. I gagged on the smell of seared flesh as the wolf dashed back into the woods. I looked over my shoulder and saw Bryn Lyons standing on the roof of Jammers, his arm stretched out toward us.

I stumbled to my feet and ran to Zach.

"Oh, God. Zach, honey, can you hear me?" Blood soaked his

shirt. I pulled it down and saw four punctures, two on the right side of Zach's neck and two slightly torn wounds just under the left collarbone. The wolf had been about to rip Zach's throat open. But Zach was still breathing, his pulse a steady throb under his skin.

I shoved his shoulder. "Zach!" I shook him gently, but his eyes stayed stubbornly closed.

He stirred but didn't wake. I glanced up when I heard Bryn walk to us.

"Concussion," Bryn said, not bothering to bend down to check on Zach. He murmured something in Latin and walked to the edge of the trees.

"Show yourself, or you'll regret it," Bryn said.

The tall man from the bar rose and stepped forward, blood and saliva smeared on his chin, his eyes an evil yellow. So he could obviously change forms as much as he wanted. In partial wolf form, he'd been bigger than a real wolf with clawed hands rather than paws.

"I'm just the tracker," he said in a gravelly, inhuman voice. "The pack will be here soon, wizard. Kill me and my blood will mark you. Just as Jeff's blood marks that little bitch," he said, nodding to me. My heart slammed against my ribs.

"She cut him while defending herself."

The man smiled, showing viciously long teeth. "She was already an enemy of the pack. She should've let him kill her because Samuel won't stop there. He'll make her suffer." His laughter was crazed. "You stay out of their way, or they'll kill you, too."

The man-animal turned and leapt into the wood. The rustling of the brush lasted only a few seconds and then there was only silence again.

I bit my lip, looking at Zach, whose head was cradled on my lap. I could feel the knot on the back of his scalp where his skull had hit the ground. I pulled my purse to me and yanked my cell phone out to call the town paramedics, but there was no signal.

"I need your phone," I stammered.

Bryn shook his head. "Mine won't work either. Magic shorts them out until it dissipates."

"Well, run into the bar and get help."

He shook his head and held out a hand to me. "We'll send help when we get away from here."

"I'm not leaving him!" I gasped.

Bryn scowled. "He's safer without you. They want you, and they'll kill him to get to you. That tracker is one of the weaker members of the pack. Clearly Sutton can't be effective against them. Leave him. Save both your lives," he said, curling the fingers of his outstretched hand to beckon me to him.

Tears blurred my eyes. "I can't just leave him lying in a parking lot."

Bryn shook his head and sighed.

Zach stirred again, and I looked down at him.

"What's up?" Zach mumbled, his speech slightly slurred. He twisted suddenly, and his head slid from my lap and banged on the concrete.

"Honey, be still. You want your brains scrambled?" I said, grabbing his head.

He opened his eyes. "Hey, darlin'." He winced as he moved his left arm. He reached over with his right hand and touched the opposite side of his upper chest. "I'm not drunk enough to be on the ground," he said and twisted from my hands, sitting up. He swayed for a moment, but then looked steady. He held his fingers up to his face to examine his blood. "Someone shot me?"

I didn't answer. Bryn had receded into the shadows. Zach's gaze went to the trees. "I was going to the woods, and you screamed. I turned my head, and that's all I remember." His hand went back to his chest. "Am I shot?"

"No, it was a dog. A wolf, I think. It knocked you unconscious and bit you, but something scared it off."

"A wolf knocked me on my ass?" he asked incredulously as he rolled onto his knees, then stood up.

"Maybe you should stay lying down."

"The hell I will," he grumbled. "I need a flashlight. Run on up to the bar and get me one." He pulled his gun out.

"You have a concussion. I don't think you should try to shoot right now."

He laughed softly. "I'm all right, darlin'. You know I've got the thickest skull in three counties. You used to say as much all the time."

I smiled. "Let's go home."

"You really think I'm gonna leave an animal hunting this close to town that could knock *me* on *my* ass? Folks have kids, Tammy Jo. Go on now, and when you get me that flashlight, tell Kenny to call the station. Tell the boys to come with some shotguns and the dogs."

I walked to the bar shaking my head, but if Zach was on his own I guessed he wasn't likely to get attacked again since it was me the wolves wanted to kill. And why was that? Bryn had defended himself too. Why did they hate me in particular? And why did the wolf-man say I was *already* an enemy of the pack? I'd never hurt any wolves before that meeting. I don't hunt, and I always loved *White Fang.*

* * *

It took about twenty minutes for the phones inside Jammers to start working again, then we called for reinforcements. With Zach and the other deputies crashing around the woods with dogs and guns, I was on my own, and it was hard to decide what to do first. Highest on my list was getting the locket back. I went home, hoping to find the locket in the mailbox, but it wasn't there. Shame on Johnny Nguyen.

The other thing that I needed was protection. Silver bullets, a gun, and a protection spell to cast over myself, the house, and Mercutio. I looked forlornly in the direction of the dead herb garden. It was unlikely that I'd be able to find all the right herbs in my cupboards. Also, where was I going to come up with a very powerful protection spell? I couldn't count on an Internet spell to be strong enough to hold back a pack of werewolves. To have any kind of a chance, I needed a real spellbook.

I could try to buy or rent one from Bryn. If money changed hands, I wouldn't have to owe him any more favors, and I was sure he'd have some books around that he wasn't using. On the other hand, he didn't need my money. Plus, did I even want to take a chance using a book that might be tainted with his magic?

Odds were good that I'd have to make a run to Austin for my own book. I stood in the kitchen, encouraging Mercutio to eat his tuna fish while I chewed on my lip. I had to have money.

"They'll kill me," I mumbled, going to the stairs. I stood looking up the steps, contemplating. I chewed on my thumbnail some and then looked back over at Mercutio, who was circling his bowl of tuna like I'd put in some arsenic instead of antibiotics.

"Just eat it!"

He blinked and meowed, swiping a paw at the air in my general direction.

"Sorry," I said and marched up the stairs. I went to Momma's room and opened the middle drawer with the false bottom. I popped it open and looked down. Momma's ruby heart pendant, Aunt Mel's emerald drop earrings, and my wedding ring. I scooped them up, closing my fist around them. "It's just stuff," I said, trying to convince myself.

I jogged back downstairs. "Mercutio, I need to go see Earl Stanton, and then I'm going to pay a call to Bryn Lyons. His horrible dog might be loose, so you're staying here. I'll be back in a couple hours."

Mercutio stood and walked over.

"No, you stay inside and rest while I'm gone. There are wolves out there. They'll probably get me, and I can't see any reason they should get to eat our whole family in one night."

Mercutio bounded to the door as I tried to leave. "You cannot come. You're a cat. You do what I say." We struggled at the door. I didn't want to be too rough, him being hurt and all. He wasn't as ethical about it. I had scratches and snags in my clothes.

I sighed. "In the car. That's as far as you're going with me." I flung the door open, and he sauntered out. Typical male, stubborn and bullying his way into things he ought to leave alone.

I bit my lip, hoping I wasn't going to get us both killed. I probably should have hid out until morning, but I couldn't just wait around for the wolves to show up at my house. It felt less scary to be trying to do something to protect myself.

I drove ten blocks to Earl's and knocked on his door. Mercutio danced around the front porch, climbing and pouncing, oblivious to the fact that he was supposed to be injured.

I laughed, watching him. "When we get home, you mind if I try some of your medicine? It seems to work real good."

He meowed generously just as Earl opened the door. Earl used to have a nice six-pack of muscle in high school, but in five years he'd managed to bury it pretty effectively with hundreds of six-packs of Armadillo Ale.

"Hey there."

"Hey there, Tammy Jo." He looked around behind me. "Zach with you?"

"Nope. Just me and my cat. Mercutio, Earl. Earl, Mercutio."

"Hey," Earl said amiably to Merc. "So what are you doing at my door in the middle of the night all by your lonesome?"

"I need to pawn some stuff, Earl."

"Do you? How come?"

"Well, like most people that pawn stuff, I'm in need of money."

"Uh-huh. How come?"

Earl and I had been friends in high school. I was just starting to ask myself why that was. "As it happens I'm between jobs."

"Yeah, I *heard* that. Why don't you ask Zach for money?"

"Zach and I are divorced."

"Uh-huh. He know that?"

"What exactly are you getting at, Earl? 'Cause I'm in kind of a hurry."

"I figured since these aren't exactly business hours." He looked me up and down. "Well, come on in." Earl rubbed a hand through his greasy hair. When had he decided that shampoo was optional? I followed him into the living room.

"Here's what I have," I said.

Earl looked the jewelry over and then walked to a desk with a hutch and pulled out a little thingy that you use to look closely at gemstones. He examined them and nodded.

He walked over to the couch and sat down next to me. I got a whiff of whiskey when he exhaled, so I leaned back. "And whose wedding ring is this?"

"Mine."

"You going to part with something that's got so much sentimental value?"

Like I had a choice. I clenched my jaw. "Apparently I am."

"You know I was thinking of asking you out when you and Zach split up, and he let it be known that he wasn't in favor of it. Put this notch in my nose."

So that's why Earl and Zach weren't friends anymore. I'd wondered about that. They used to fish together twice a month.

"So how much can you give me for all this beautiful jewelry?"

"I guess that depends on you. See if you and I were dating, I'd be inclined—"

You have got to be kidding me. "Oh, Earl, that sure is sweet, but . . ."

Mercutio seemed to sense my uneasiness, and he hissed.

"I don't think so," I said.

"Doesn't hurt to ask." Earl reached over and stroked a strand of my hair. I leaned back.

"So, how much?"

"Two hundred."

I gaped. The pendant alone was worth five hundred. "I'm pretty sure you can do better, Earl."

Earl grinned, showing his perpetually crooked bottom teeth.

His momma had wanted to get them fixed, but he wouldn't go to the orthodontist appointments. So he'd basically been a pain in the behind his whole life.

"You know, I probably could do better. Let's have us a little drink and talk it over."

"I don't really have time tonight," I said, starting to stand up. He grabbed my arm and squeezed.

"Now, don't be like that. Sit yourself down." He yanked on me so that I fell onto the couch and him.

"Earl James Stanton, you take your hands off me this minute, or I will tell your momma about this."

He laughed, leaning to give me a kiss while he held me down.

"Stop it!" I yelled.

Mercutio landed right on Earl's neck and did his signature swipe. Earl hollered and flung me to the floor. He reached for Mercutio, who darted away. Earl's face was purple with rage. "I'm gonna kill that cat."

Earl stumbled to the gun case.

"Run, Mercutio!" I screamed as Earl yanked the glass door open. Mercutio leapt over the couch as Earl swung the shotgun around.

Boom. I blinked. Earl had blown a huge hole in his living room wall, missing Mercutio by at least five feet. Merc raced through the room, and Earl swiveled the gun after him. I hopped up and grabbed the brass lion lamp from the sideboard table.

The second shot rang out just as loud as the first. Me clocking Earl with the lamp was real quiet in comparison. Earl staggered and fell to his knees and then passed out face down on the rug. I bent over and checked his pulse.

Mercutio poked his head around the corner.

"Bad news, Merc. He's alive."

Mercutio sneezed and then I swear he smiled at me. I laughed nervously and then put a hand to my forehead and sighed.

"I need money. He offered us two hundred dollars." I dug into Earl's pocket and pulled out his wallet. I took out four hundred. "But two hundred wasn't really a fair price. I'm sure he'll see that when he sobers up in the morning. Now, you know what else we need to borrow?"

Mercutio purred.

"Darn straight," I said, opening the gun case and pulling out a .38 special that was lying on the bottom. "This sure is convenient. Almost like it's a sign. Pretty sure it is a sign," I said, popping the revolver open and dumping out the regular bullets. "I'm definitely going to church this Sunday to tell God how much I appreciate His help this week," I said, loading the chambers with the silver bullets that were rolling around the bottom of my purse. "You remind me Saturday night, Merc. The way things are going, I might be distracted and forget." I slapped the revolver shut and tucked it in my purse.

I grabbed the throw blanket off the couch and laid it over Earl.

To Mercutio, I said, "All set."

Chapter 17

Mercutio and I trotted back out to the car and drove over to Bryn Lyons's house. I wanted to try to get him to sell me a spell-book or the spells I needed. If he did, it would save me a trip to Austin and all that time spent driving that I didn't have. Also, I needed some answers from him.

I buzzed the security man. "It's Tammy Jo Trask. I'd like to see Mr. Bryn Lyons, please."

"Just a minute, Ms. Trask," came the deep voice through the speaker. A few moments later the gate swung open. I pressed the buzzer again.

"Ma'am?"

"It doesn't seem too polite that I don't even know your name."

There was a pause. "Steve."

"Good evening, Steve. Where do you sit, by the way? Last time I was here, I was wondering that."

"I have an office in the house, ma'am. On the first floor."

"Oh, right. Well, I'll probably see you in there then. If I don't, have a good night, Steve."

I heard him chuckle softly, and then he said, "You, too."

"Oh, Steve?"

"Yes?"

"My cat's with me, so could you tell your boss to put his serial killer dog outside?"

"Already taken care of, ma'am."

"Steve, you can call me Tammy Jo. Everyone does."

"Yes, ma'am."

I swung the car up the drive and parked it right in front. You never know when you're going to have to make a quick getaway. And I could hopefully trust Steve to help me out with the gate now that we were on a first-name basis.

The front door opened, and Bryn leaned against the frame with a coffee cup in his hand.

Merc and I got out and walked up, and I realized that he was as dressed down as I'd ever seen him. Faded jeans and a black T-shirt that had white lettering that read, "Sarcasm is just one more service we offer free."

I nodded to the shirt. "That your firm's new marketing slogan?"

"You got it."

"I'm surprised you own that shirt. I've never seen you wearing anything like that around town."

"There are one or two things about me that you don't know."

"Such as?"

He closed the front door behind us.

"How's Zach?"

"Out hunting werewolves."

"I wish him well."

"So what do you know about them?"

"That's a very broad question," he said, waving for me to follow him.

"I'd like a very broad answer, as quick as you can give it."

We went down a wide hallway with lots of big impressive paintings and ended up in a kitchen that most chefs only dream about. I walked directly to the double oven and ran my hand over it longingly. I took another minute to admire his stainless steel appliances.

Bryn moved past me and opened the fridge. He pulled out a Tupperware dish and opened it. There was a perfectly arranged meal. Roast beef in gravy, green beans with slivered almonds, broccoli in butter. My mouth watered.

"Sit," he said, nodding toward the round granite-topped table.

"Who cooks here?" I asked, looking around reverently.

"A chef-for-hire during the workweek. On the weekends, it's generally empty."

"That sure is a shame."

He popped the food in the microwave and hit the start button.

"You're free to come over and use it anytime you like."

I bit my lip at the temptation and shook my head. *He's on the damn list. Get ahold of yourself!* "So you were going to talk about these werewolves."

"There's not much I can tell you."

"Why are they after me?"

"You stabbed one of them."

"But the wolf-man tonight said I was their enemy before that. Why?"

He leaned against the counter, as sexy as the stainless steel. "You tell me."

"How should I know? I'm a pastry chef."

"You never cast any spells before you got fired?"

"Never. Never ever!"

Bryn shrugged. "I don't know."

"That's it? You're supposed to be a brilliant lawyer."

He grinned. "And when they sue you, I'll have an answer for every question and a plan for every courtroom eventuality."

"I don't need courtroom help. I need to know how to stop them from coming after me. Have you got a plan for that?"

The microwave beeped.

"It happens that I might," he said, and I heard that faint Irish lilt again.

He took the food out and set it in front of me with a beautifully polished silver knife and fork and a navy blue linen napkin. He got me a glass of water and a glass of red wine.

"So, are you going to tell me?" I asked impatiently as I placed the napkin on my lap.

He sat down at the table across from me. "We'll need to strike a bargain. I don't offer preternatural services gratis."

I chewed the delicious roast beef silently. "I'm broke. I have four hundred dollars left to my name." *Which is kind of stolen, and which I'll need to return eventually to get the family jewels back.* "But if you'll sell me a protection spell, that'd be a good use of what I have."

"I can't do that. It's illegal for me to sell spells."

"How come there are stores that can sell spellbooks then?"

"The books' former owners are dead. The spells are sort of public domain, waiting for a new witch or wizard to claim the compilation and make it his or her own."

"But you gave me spells."

He smiled. "I did. It was supposed to be a one-time occurrence . . . because there were special circumstances."

"Well, right, but some more special circumstances have come up."

"They always do," he said, laughing softly. "No one with power ever stops with one spell."

"Hey, I'm gonna stop. Just as soon as I get a chance to." I ate my vegetables and took a gulp of wine. "So. What do you want in exchange for help with the werewolves?"

"I want you to apprentice yourself to me."

"Not going to happen."

"You do realize that your life is at stake?"

"Of course, I do. I wouldn't be here if I didn't know that."

Suddenly a disembodied voice boomed overhead, startling me. "Mr. Lyons, pick up. We have a situation."

Bryn stood and walked over to a wall phone. He picked it up and asked, "What's going on, Steve?" Bryn listened and frowned. "Detain them at the front."

There was suddenly a pounding on the back door to the kitchen. I jumped up and yanked the gun from my purse, pointing it.

Bryn raised his eyebrows. "It's not the werewolves. You can put that away."

I ignored him. "Aren't you going to answer it?"

"Why don't you wait in the foyer?"

"No way."

"This doesn't concern you. Wait in the foyer."

Whoever was outside pounded again.

"And I won't need a gun?"

"Not unless you're planning to shoot the flower arrangement in the foyer. Go, now."

I grabbed my purse and spun on my heel. I left the kitchen and walked about five feet down the hall. *One one thousand. Two one thousand. Three one thousand.* I stopped counting when a young guy in a security uniform started coming down the hall toward me.

"Steve?" I asked.

"Ms. Trask, can I show you the front hall?"

"Sure," I said with a smile, then I turned and darted back to the kitchen.

As a chef, I've seen plenty of disasters in the kitchen, but in all my days, I've never seen anything that shocked me so much as the scene in Bryn's.

Georgia Sue lay unconscious on the table where I'd just had dinner. She looked like she'd been carved from ivory; she was that white. Bryn and Lennox Lyons leaned over her.

"What? What?" I yelled, rushing to her. There were a few drops of blood on the collar of her white Jammers work shirt. Then I saw the two tiny bite marks.

"You're vampires!" I screamed, yanking my gun back out.

"No," Bryn said holding his arms out.

Suddenly, Lennox Lyons looking so pale and ill made sense. He was a vampire, and he hadn't been letting himself feed.

"You get away from her, right now." They backed up.

"She has been bitten, but I didn't bite her," Lennox said. "She was in Magnolia Park."

"Liar! She wouldn't have been in the park alone. She's married, and she got married so she'd never have to go anywhere alone, unless it was the hairdresser or the spa, which the park at night sure isn't. Now pick up that phone and call nine-one-one."

"She'll be dead before they get here. She needs blood right now," Lennox said. He still had his arms in the air.

"We have blood here. We can save her, if you put down your gun," Bryn said.

"I don't need to put down my gun for you to save her. Go ahead."

Lennox walked over to a small stand-alone cupboard and took out a stash of medical supplies. "Steve, go to the small fridge and get two packets of blood."

Steve looked unhappy, but he turned and hurried down the hall.

I stared incredulously as Lennox pushed up Georgia's sleeve and expertly started an IV. A minute later, Steve was back with a packet of blood that was labeled like it had been stolen from a blood bank or hospital.

"Can you just give her that? Doesn't it have to be, what do you call it, checked to be sure it matches her blood?"

"This blood is type O negative. It can safely be given to anyone," Lennox said.

The gun in my hand shook as Lennox connected the blood to the IV and it started to drip into Georgia's arm. Bryn lunged forward as the gun dropped to the floor and caught me just before I hit the ground.

The room spun around me for a few moments, and I felt distinctly sick as sweat popped out on my forehead.

"You're all right," Bryn said soothingly. "Steve, a wet cloth."

A moment later, a cool rag was lying across my eyes, and I did feel better.

"How does he know how to start an IV?"

"He's been sick. He's had to take transfusions himself. He doesn't like hospitals."

"What's wrong with him?"

"A blood disease."

Like vampirism? I'd heard that some vampires who were too weak to drink blood had it poured right into their veins by others in their covens.

"He found her vein pretty darn easy," I mumbled.

Lennox cleared his throat. "I had a small drug habit in the early eighties. Fortunately for your friend, I can always find a vein."

I pushed the washrag up from my right eye and looked at him. "A small drug habit?"

He inclined his head. "Heroin."

A real-live heroin addict in Duvall? And everyone said we couldn't get any of the big drugs so far from the big cities. "You're still using?"

"Not that it's any of your business, but no. And why exactly are you here?" Lennox asked. "Aren't you banned from fraternizing with us?" His tone was like he was talking down to a half-wit.

I glared at him. "What do you know about it?" I asked, noticing that Bryn was watching him intently.

Lennox shrugged. "What could I know about it? When the second bag goes in, she may regain consciousness, Bryn. We'll need to get her out of here."

I sat up slowly. "We'll call an ambulance."

Lennox ignored me. "I'll take her back to the park and call an ambulance from the pay phone a block away. She'll survive long enough for them to arrive."

"You could have called the ambulance when you found her," Bryn said.

"The ambulances don't carry blood, and the house was closer." Neither Bryn nor I said anything, and Lennox added softly, "And I owed her husband a favor. Debt settled."

I noticed then that Lennox looked a little pale and sweaty himself. Did he need the blood he'd given Georgia Sue? What would happen to him without it?

"Bryn, put Georgia back in the car," Lennox said.

"I'll take her to the park," Bryn said.

"No, my contact may still be in the vicinity. I'll have a look around."

"I'll take care of it—"

"I want to keep you out of it."

"That gets less and less possible," Bryn observed, shifting so that I was sitting on my own. He stood and walked to Georgia Sue as Lennox hung the second bag of blood. It ran into her quickly, and she looked pinker.

"I'm going to the park. I'll wait with her until the ambulance comes," I said.

"No," Lennox said.

I stood up, took Earl's gun from the table where Bryn had put it, and dropped it into my purse. "She's my best friend. I'm going."

The phone rang, and Bryn walked over and picked it up. "Hello?" He paused. "Astrid, it's not a good time."

I chewed on my lip, glancing anxiously at Georgia Sue.

"I understand that, but you can't come to the house tonight. In the morning if you like, but not tonight." He paused again. "Cast a Garner-Stills. That should put them off." He paused again. "No, he's not here. He's out. I'll speak to you in the morning." Bryn hung up the phone.

"She asked to speak to me?" Lennox asked.

Bryn nodded. "I don't want her here tonight."

"So you'll leave her to the wolves?" Lennox said.

Bryn's eyes were hard as sapphires as he stared at Lennox. Bryn said something in a weird language, and Lennox looked away. I held Georgia's limp hand. What had happened to my happy little town? Once upon a time, there were only four people with magic in town, my momma and aunt, and Bryn and Lennox. And they were all real quiet about the other world. No normal people in town ever had reason to suspect it existed. Now we had corpses rising from graves, werewolves in our bars, and vampires in our parks. Crime sprees and the occult in Duvall. This wasn't going to look good in the visitor's brochure.

Chapter 18

* * * * *

Bryn put Georgia Sue in the back of the Mercedes, and I climbed in next to her. It was the second time that night I'd had to cuddle someone I loved and hope they didn't die. A person could go on and get an ulcer from so much stress, and I know from the one or two hangovers I've had in my life that I can't even swallow Alka Seltzer.

Bryn leaned into the open window. "If she comes around, don't let her sit up. She'll be better off lying down so the blood doesn't have to travel against gravity."

"Nearly bled to death before?"

"No, but I've been dehydrated a few times."

Lennox cleared his throat as he slid into the driver's seat. "Shall we continue to have social hour? Or are you interested in saving your friend's life?" he asked, looking at me in the rearview mirror.

"We were waiting for you," I said, making a face at him like I'd just started sucking on a lemon drop.

"Bring Tamara back with you when you've gotten help for her friend," Bryn said to Lennox as he stood and took a step back from the car.

"It's not up to him," I called over the sound of the motor starting.

If Bryn heard me, he didn't let on. He walked back to the house as Lennox swung the car around and headed down the drive. I smoothed back Georgia Sue's damp hair. She was still pale and sweaty.

"So, Bryn said that you had an amulet stolen during the robbery at Georgia Sue's house."

"Not an amulet. A locket."

"Valuable?"

"To me it is."

He nodded, eyeing me in the mirror. "Was it yours or a family piece?"

"Why are you interested?"

"I'm good at location spells. If the locket has any magical properties, I might be able to help you locate it."

"Why would you do that?" I didn't like to sound suspicious, but Lennox hadn't exactly been a goodwill ambassador to me and my family in the past.

Lennox coughed, and I could hear a slight wheeze. He took a couple of deep breaths and turned left on Sandstone Street toward the park.

"Bryn mentioned that you helped him work a healing spell."

"Uh-huh? And you were thinking maybe I could let him steal some more energy from me to heal you?"

"Would it really be considered theft if you gave him permission?" he asked, tone light as a soufflé.

I didn't answer. I was still kind of sore about that stolen power incident.

"But if the locket isn't important enough for you to engage in that sort of bargain, it's understandable."

I pursed my lips, annoyed. Lennox was a Lyons, so also on the list, and spoiled milk's got a sweeter disposition than he does, so I wasn't at all tempted to make a deal with this particular devil.

"I have a good idea who was behind the robbery, and I'm going to handle it myself."

"Solved the crime, have you? Let's hear it."

It was none of his beeswax. Lennox hadn't had anything stolen since he hadn't been at the party, so he didn't have a stake in seeing the case solved. And I might still be negotiating with Johnny. I didn't want to blab it around town that he was guilty.

"Here's the park," I said.

"So it is. If your theory proves wrong, my offer stands."

Sure, I'll take you up on that when the devil invests in long underwear. "Well, I'll sure keep that in mind, if things don't work out."

Lennox and I got out of the car and worked together to get Georgia out without jostling her too much. We laid her down on the top of a picnic table.

"You wait with her while I call emergency services and look around. We'll leave when we hear the sirens."

"Leave? I'm not going anywhere except on an ambulance ride with Georgia Sue. Now hurry up, and go call."

"We'll discuss this in a moment," he said, walking briskly across the street. I sat in the dark, listening to Georgia Sue breathe quick, shallow breaths. I looked around at the trees. Boy, they looked sinister with only one streetlight casting shadows off them.

I fished Earl's gun out of my purse and let it rest in my right hand. With my left hand, I stroked Georgia's hair, which was stiff with gel and pointing at crazy angles.

"We're going to be all right. With all the hairspray you wear, you wouldn't taste good to any dumb werewolves. Nope, you're going to be just fine sitting here with me." I untangled her curls to give myself something to do besides shaking. "What they ought to be doing is shopping for some breath mints. Ugh. You would not believe how those muzzles stank."

A few minutes later, Lennox strolled back up.

"You called?"

He nodded.

"And did you find your friend?"

He sighed and shook his head. "Not a friend. A blood-and-bones witch's apprentice."

"What's a blood-and-bones witch?"

"One who specializes in magic of the flesh, life-and-death magic, usually healing spells. It's an exceptionally rare talent. I spent a fortune in money and promised power to get one here, but it looks like the ongoing wolf attacks have scared him off."

"I'm sorry," I said.

"So am I. Now, why don't you come and sit with me in the car while we wait for the ambulance to pick Georgia up?"

"Not going to happen. I go where she goes."

"Are you aware that ninety-eight percent of werewolves drive trucks and SUVs? It wouldn't take many of them to surround and stop one ambulance."

My heart kicked up a fuss in my chest, but I stuck my chin out stubbornly. "There's something you might have heard about," I said with false sweetness. "It's called loyalty. My friend is not going to die, but if she was going to die, she wouldn't be doing it alone on a beat-up picnic table. Wherever she's going, I'm going with her. So you can just run along because my ride will be here in a minute."

"Remember the Alamo," he murmured.

"Got that right."

"Good night then. I sincerely hope you don't get ripped to pieces, because I look forward to seeing how my son plans to handle you in the future."

I frowned. "Your son's not going to be handling anything."

"I'll pass that along to him. Good night." He walked away, and I was left sitting in the dark, hoping I could live up to all my tough talk.

* * *

The ambulance siren was still so faint I could barely hear it when Kenny's black Trans Am screeched to a halt at the edge of the park.

Kenny's door jerked open, and he scrambled out and ran across the park, stumbling once and getting a huge grass stain on his jeans.

"What happened?" he stammered, dropping to his knees on the bench of the picnic table and gathering Georgia in his arms.

"I don't know. I found her," I mumbled.

Kenny's face was so full of anguish that the bubble of shock and disbelief I'd been in popped like it'd been made of soap. My eyes welled up, and tears spilled down my face again.

He rocked her in his arms. "Wake up now, Georgia. C'mon."

I put my head in my hands and sobbed.

"What happened? She said she was going to see about your necklace. What the hell happened, Tammy Jo? What were you girls up to?"

I gulped back another sob and garbled out, "My necklace?"

He nodded, looking at me and then back down at her.

"She didn't call me. I don't know what she was doing," I said, rubbing the heel of my hand over my cheek.

The ambulance pulled up, and the guys hopped out with an orange rolling stretcher. They rushed over to us and knelt down with their special equipment to check her vital signs.

"Her heart's racing, but she's got a good pulse," Marty, one of the EMTs, said. "Let's package her up and take her to Dallas."

"Dallas?" I croaked.

"Sure, you think Doc Padovny can handle this at the urgent care center?" Marty asked as they put Georgia on the stretcher.

I shrugged. I hadn't thought. She probably would be better off in a big city hospital, but would she survive the drive? Well, they were going in an ambulance, so it would be as fast as possible. Yeah, she would definitely make it, I told myself.

"Okay," I said, following them.

"There's no room for you in the ambulance, Tammy Jo, if Kenny comes."

"I'm coming," Kenny said.

"I'll follow you," I said.

"No," Kenny said, turning to me. "I need you to go back to the bar. I didn't lock anything up. I just ran out of there." He pressed his keys into my hand.

"I'll take care of it. Will you call me as soon as she wakes up?"

He nodded, gave me a fierce hug, then climbed into the ambulance.

* * *

I didn't hesitate. I hopped into Kenny's Trans Am and peeled away from the curb and drove to Jammers. I was on a mission, and God help anyone who tried to so much as steal a bowl of wings while Kenny and Georgia Sue were on their way to Dallas. I was loaded for werewolf, but that didn't have to stop me from firing a couple of warning shots if people got rowdy.

When I hurried into Jammers, I found that there was no mayhem at all. Zach had rolled up his shirtsleeves and was behind the bar. I was sure glad to see him looking okay, given the werewolf bite.

"What happened?" he asked as soon as I got close enough. "Kenny said Georgia Sue had an accident, but the station didn't get the call. I talked to dispatch and heard it was a medical emergency, not a wreck."

"I'll tell you about it later," I said, the adrenaline wearing off and leaving me shaky yet again.

"She'll be all right?"

I nodded, hoping that was true. "What happened with the wolf?"

"Dogs lost the scent. I came to return the flashlights when Kenny got the call about Georgia Sue."

"So you took over the bar?"

"Seemed like the best way for me to help. He left here at a dead run without leaving anyone in charge. Didn't even answer me when I asked if he wanted me to drive him."

Georgia Sue and Kenny were my friends, not really Zach's. Zach and Kenny had even had a couple shouting matches when Zach acted like a jerk during the divorce. Zach wasn't too fond of people passing judgment on him, so it was more comfortable plucking my eyebrows than hanging around together as a foursome anymore. Yet here Zach was, keeping things orderly for my friends who were in trouble.

I flipped up the flap and walked behind the bar, straight to him. I flung my arms around his neck, kissing him full on the lips. "Some days I do love you, Zachary Taylor Sutton."

He grinned at me. "Likewise."

"How are you though? How's that bite?"

"Fine."

"Really?" I asked.

"Smarts a little. Ain't no big thing," he said.

I studied Zach for a minute, trying to figure out if he was telling the truth. Right after he'd ruined his knee playing football, I met him in the locker room and asked him how bad it was. He'd just gotten through throwing up from the pain and had gotten a shot of morphine from the trainer, but Zach said his knee wasn't too bad and he'd be ready to play in the next week's game against A&M. Turned out the MRI showed he'd ripped most of the ligaments off the bone, and the joint was full of blood. Turned out there would never be any more college football games for him, and, two surgeries later, I could tell it still hurt him by the way he wrapped it and ate a couple aspirins some mornings, but Zach never complained.

"You sure you're okay?" I asked.

He nodded, and I decided to believe him since he didn't look pale or sick.

"Can you close this place up for them? Here's Kenny's keys," I said, pulling the bar keys off the ring.

"Why? Where are you going?"

"I need to go by Georgia's momma's house to tell her what's going on. You know how she gets the wheezes. I don't want her to hear the news alone." That was true enough, but not my first stop. Georgia's momma sleeps like the dead and would never wake up at the phone ringing after midnight. I'd be able to take care of one or two things before going to hammer on her back door.

I marched out and flung myself back behind the wheel of Kenny's car. I liked the leather bucket seats, the roar of the engine, and the squeal of the tires. The only thing it needed was a kitty cat companion in the passenger seat, and it would have been perfect.

I thought about swinging by Bryn's to pick up Mercutio, but the way my night was going, some other big catastrophe would happen and put me off from getting to the locket. Time was running short; everything else could wait until I got Edie back.

I got to Johnny's house in record time, thinking I really did have to get me a Trans Am. I shook my head at the hour. I don't normally drop in on people so late, but I think anyone would agree that these were special circumstances.

I knocked very loudly on the door and contemplated whether I wanted to waste one of my silver bullets shooting his door lock.

Finally, the door swung open, and what I saw next would have knocked me right out of my pantyhose if I'd been wearing any. A lanky, black-haired, six-and-a-half-feet-tall man in four-inch stilettos, a black kimono, and three-alarm-fire-red lipstick stood with his hands on his hips.

"Settle down, Miss Thing, or I may have to drink a couple pints of that rudeness right out of you." With that he flashed a smile that showed off pearly white fangs.

Chapter 19

* * * * *

I squeaked in alarm and took a step back, fumbling through my purse for Earl's .38. The vampire's gaze swept over me, and he rolled his eyes, looked bored, and turned and walked into the Moroccan oasis.

I got the gun in my hand, gripped it firmly and walked in behind him. "Where's Johnny?"

He kept walking, not bothering to answer me. I followed him to the bedroom where Johnny was leaning heavily on a dresser, barely standing.

"It's just Pippi Longstocking here for a visit. Now, let's get you back to bed." The vampire picked up the diminutive hairdresser and tucked him under the covers.

"Rollie, be pleasant. Tammy Jo my good friend."

"Rollie?" I echoed.

"Roland Spears. No relation." He walked to a stack of clothes that were piled on the edge of the bed and flung a swirled green-beaded cape around his shoulders. "This is fabulous," he said as he walked over to the full-length mirror in the corner to admire himself. "Hard to pull off with jeans unless you're totally fierce, but fortunately for me, I am." He puckered his lips and blew himself a kiss and then turned and blew one to Johnny.

"Did you bite Georgia Sue?" I demanded, pointing the gun at him.

"Was that her name?"

"Rollie!" Johnny snapped. "You say you only going to get cough medicine for me."

"I was, but I got hungry."

"You only supposed to bite me when you in town."

"I can't bite you. You're too weak. Drink some more of that echinacea tea."

"Such a disobedient vampire. You not welcome in my house anymore. Get out."

Rollie thrust his lip out in a pout.

"Tammy Jo, how is Miss Georgia?"

"Real sick. She lost so much blood she's in a coma, and she might die." My voice cracked, and I blinked back tears.

"She's not going to die," Rollie said, snapping his fingers impatiently. "I'd never kill anyone with hair that fabulous. All those Shirley Temple curls. Amazing." He dropped on the bed with a dramatic sigh.

"She's in a coma!" I screamed at him.

"Easy, cheetah. She's only sleepy-time because I stuck her with a little dart."

"What?"

"A wonderful little sedative dart. It slows the bodily functions until the victim can be found and also keeps them from remembering what happened. I was going to make an anonymous call for help for her, but then that gorgeous man showed up. He's a little thin; someone should tell him heroin chic is out. He carried her off. She'll get a couple of pints at the hospital and be good as new. Better. That sedative dart is fabulous. It'll be the best sleep she's ever had."

"There is no hospital in town. There's no blood bank," I said.

"What?" He looked at Johnny with wide eyes.

Johnny nodded.

"No hospital? Where are we, the third world? Oh right, Podunk. So ridiculous. Every town should have a blood bank. Vampire tourism is on the rise, especially in places like this, though I can't imagine why. I'm a city girl myself. Normally, if you don't have Versace in a twenty-five-mile radius, there's just no reason for me to visit."

I lowered the gun and continued to stare at him, dumbfounded. "Do silver bullets kill vampires?"

"No, but they do make us very testy. And if you put a hole in this cape, I will kill you, fabulous hair or not."

I turned to Johnny. "If Georgia Sue dies or has brain damage, or even nightmares, I'm going to hold you and your friend responsible."

"I very sorry about Georgia Sue, but if Rollie say she be okay, she will."

"You should never have invited him here! Vampires don't belong in Duvall."

"Oh, don't we?" Rollie said, stealing glances at himself in the mirror. "Johnny didn't invite me. My coven sent me to see what's going on in this town."

"What's going on? What do you mean?"

"Oh don't play innocent, Miss Sabrina Teenage Witch. You've been spell-casting. I can smell it from here. And, in fact, the town reeks of it." He wrinkled his thin nose. "Plus, we heard that a pack of wild dogs was headed this way. And I'm here to see what that's about and to report back. We couldn't care less about your little hamlet, but we don't want the *Call of the Wild* bunch to go on a rampage that includes Dallas. That town and its Galleria Mall are ours."

I thought about Bryn saying that he could feel me casting spells and that others outside Duvall would feel it, too. But what did that have to do with the werewolves?

"Why would werewolves come to Duvall? Are they drawn to witch's magic?"

He shook his head.

"So then why?"

"How should I know? Do I look like some mangy mutt to you?" he asked, running his knuckles over his cheek. "Have you seen them? All that hair." He shuddered. "One would need a fifty-gallon drum of wax every full moon." He ran his finger over a perfectly arched eyebrow.

"What makes them mad? What would someone have to do to become their enemy?"

"Breathe?" He shrugged dramatically, causing the beads to sparkle and reflect the light. "They pretend they're only Rage in a Cage on the full moon, but the truth is they're all about the anger every day. Too much testosterone. They could so stand to get in touch with their feminine sides. A little spandex and a rosewater bath would go a long way."

"How does someone turn into a werewolf?" I said.

"A bite and the predisposition."

"Predisposition? What's that?"

"Somewhere in the genes you've got to have the switch waiting to be flipped."

"And if you don't, you're okay," I said, hoping Zach didn't have any doggy DNA buried inside him.

"Oh, no. Humans die if they don't turn. So does any other part-human creature with a serious bite. Werewolf bites don't heal. They bleed on and off until the body's defenses give out and the person collapses."

"No."

"Yes, and most humans don't turn."

The room spun slowly, and my legs folded under me.

"That is it," I mumbled, staring up at Johnny's bedroom ceiling. "I have had enough now. I'm done, Lord." I closed my eyes. I'm not sure if I fainted or not. When I opened my eyes I was still on the floor of Johnny's room. Johnny had crawled to the foot of the bed and was peering down at me while Rollie stood over me looking like a goth tower.

"There must be a magical way to stop the werewolf transformation or the bleeding," I said.

"If there were, witches and warlocks would be making a fortune. Imagine how much people would pay for that cure. No, doesn't exist." He flipped his hair. "Why? Who got bit?"

"My ex, Zach."

"Oh, the uber-butch muscleman cop. Yeah, invest in some heavy-duty barber shears. He's just the type to go furry."

I slapped a hand over my eyes. "Okay, I'm going to have a nervous breakdown. I really am. But before I do, I'd like to do one thing right." I moved my hand and looked at Johnny with pleading eyes. "Give me the locket. I'm begging you."

"I not have it," Johnny said sadly. "Rollie, go to kitchen please and get my necklace. It in the silverware drawer. I show her."

Rollie left and came back. The chain was an exact replica of the chain I wore the locket on, but the locket was a little different.

"Where did you get this?"

"I always like yours, and I love Edie. So I make a sketch and have a jeweler in Dallas make for me. And I get a spellbook from the store Edie talk about in Austin, but I not able to put the magic to the locket. Edie not come when I ask her to." He sighed. "And when she does visit next time, she tease me. Say it not very original. She say she disappointed to see Johnny go for knock-off. So I not want you to see it. I embarrassed about copying. And then you accuse me of stealing. You make me angry, so I wanted you to go."

I closed my eyes. I wished I could be in a coma with Georgia Sue. I was not one step closer to finding the locket. Plus, there was a pack of werewolves in town to kill me for some unknown reason, and they'd already taken a poisonous bite out of Zach. I wanted to run away from my life, but the best I could do was escape for a few minutes by fainting, and I was fixing to do that when I heard Rollie's voice echoing down.

"She looks pale, and I haven't even bitten her yet."

The hell you say! My eyes popped open, and I glared at him.

"Rollie, that not a funny joke. Things very serious."

Rollie clucked his tongue in annoyance. "Well, for someone with red hair, she's not much fun. She should watch *Will and Grace* reruns." He cocked his head thoughtfully. "You know, if I were on that show, I'd want to be Karen."

* * *

I rolled onto my side and pushed myself up. I walked stiffly to the bathroom, still feeling woozy and sick about Zach and Edie and everything. I ran cold water on a washcloth and put it on the back of my neck while I leaned over the sink.

"You better get a grip, Tammy Jo. There's no time to fall apart. Maybe in a couple of days, but not right now. And what would Mercutio say if he could see you now? He fights off burglars five times his size when he's only seven months old." I took a deep breath and straightened up. I grimaced at the state of my eyes. Time to invest in some waterproof mascara. I pulled the cloth clear of my neck and ran it under some warm water.

"Rollie?" I called.

"Present," he said dryly, and I could hear beads hitting the floor. Was he still trying on Johnny Nguyen ensembles?

"Johnny said he got a spellbook from a place in Austin that Edie recommended. I need to see that book."

Rollie's long maudlin face appeared in the doorway, startling me, and I glimpsed lavender fabric around his neck but couldn't get a good look at what he was wearing.

"Why? Are we doing some magic? Can we conjure up a blond-haired boy with Raphaelite curls?"

"Oh, you don't want me trying to conjure up your dreamboy. We'd probably end up with a roomful of cherubs with wooden stakes for arrows. I'm really barely a witch at all."

"So then why would I get the book for you?"

"It's an emergency. The family ghost will have her soul shredded to confetti if I don't find my locket, and I'm just not fixin' to have that happen. Now, I'd really be grateful if you could help me by getting me that book. And I promise to do something nice for you when things settle down."

"She a very excellent chef. Makes cakes and pies."

"So a nice bread pudding with blood sauce at my next soiree then?"

"Oh," I said, going pale again. "I'll see what I can do. Does it have to be human blood?"

He laughed. "I guess she's kind of cute," he said over his shoulder to Johnny. "Some of my coven mates have human teenage girls for pets. They send them shopping during the daylight hours. I never really wanted one myself, but maybe I could find something for her to do for me." He looked me over. "I guess you're as pretty as a lovebird or a Siamese cat. And you don't shed or have paper to change."

"What happened to my gun?" I asked, trying to peek around him.

He laughed at my tone. "Spellbook coming up."

"I'm not a teenager," I grumbled. I walked out and sat on the edge of the bed. "How in the world did you meet him?" I asked Johnny.

"Oh, I not remember," Johnny said, blushing.

"Just as well."

"Well," Rollie said, sweeping back into the room. He was wearing a lavender chiffon gown that was several inches too short for him, but the train made a lovely swish behind him nonetheless. "This book could stand to be redone. With all the computerized scrapbook-making software, there's just no excuse for this type of shoddy presentation."

He held up a worn book with a tattered leather cover. My pulse kicked into high gear. I knew an authentic spellbook when I saw one.

"Gimme," I said, snatching it and flipping it open. The pages were yellow and stiff with ink that seemed to have come from a fountain pen. There were symbols, etchings, and even dried herbs and flowers tethered with thread to some pages. "Jackpot, Batman."

"It a good book?"

"I don't have enough money for this. It was more than five hundred dollars, I'm sure."

Johnny nodded. "Very expensive."

"I don't have that much, but I can give you four hundred, and I'll bring you goodies three times a week for the rest of the year, if you give me this book."

Johnny smiled. "No need, Tammy Jo. It a present. Find locket. Save Edie."

Tears sprung to my eyes. I'm an all-occasion crier, and I was more relieved than I could say. If I didn't have to buy a spellbook, I wouldn't have to drive to Austin. Plus, I could get back my family's jewels from Earl right away. It was like the answer to a prayer.

I set the book aside and gave Johnny a fierce you're-my-hero hug. "Thank you so much. You're such a great friend."

Rollie sniffled above my head. "That settles it. I'm adopting her. My very own redhead!"

I laughed in spite of myself. "I don't think the lavender suits you. The cloak was real nice though."

"I knew it!" Rollie said, stalking over to the mirror. "Yes, it's much too pale with my skin. Makes me look chalky and severe."

Nobody ever told me how vain vampires are. If I'd had time to sit around and smile, I would have, but I had to get back to my coming-apart-at-the-seams life.

"I'll see you boys later," I said, hefting the book into my arms.

Chapter 20

* * * * *

When I got home, there were three messages. One from Kenny saying that Georgia Sue had woken up halfway to Dallas and was doing okay. They were going to Parkland Hospital anyway to have her checked out.

There were also messages from Zach, saying he'd be stopping by, and from Bryn, telling me that the werewolf count in Duvall was up to thirty and asking me to come back to his house for my own protection.

I chewed on my lip as I set the book down on the kitchen table and went through it. There were no spells in it for curing lycanthropy, which made me stand up and pace for a few minutes. I couldn't help but feel sick about Zach. It was my fault that he'd gotten attacked. But maybe Rollie was wrong about what would happen with that wound.

I poured a glass of milk, ate a handful of Hershey's miniatures, and sat back down, flipping through the book. I found a complex protection spell, but I didn't have the right ingredients for it. Where was I supposed to get the blood of a medieval knight and a square inch of scrap metal from a suit of armor? It occurred to me that my new spellbook might be a tad out of date.

I pressed on, still determined to use it. Unfortunately, all the scrying spells had a component of concentration that I wasn't sure I was up to, but I needed a way to find that locket. I came to an astral-projection spell and paused over it. It didn't seem to require concentration. There was a recitation portion and then a part where the mind had to wander. I was kind of afraid where my mind might wander to, but if I did some recitation at first about going to Edie, it might just work out. I looked at the list of ingredients, and I had most of them. I'd just have to find some substitutes in the dried herbs in the cupboards.

I lit a vanilla candle and set it next to the counter, then started to scavenge through the cupboards. I was on my knees behind the counter when I heard a loud scratching sound.

I froze for a second, startled, then stood up. There were two men with long narrow faces at the back sliding-glass door. Hellfires! How had they gotten in the yard?

I ran around the counter and got to my purse just as one of them yanked, and the door lock popped with a horrible cracking sound. They slid the door open. Both of them had shoulder-length hair and beards and creepy yellow eyes. I pointed Earl's gun at them and shook my head.

"Y'all can just go back out the way you came in."

The darker-haired one sniffed the air. "It can be painless or it can be agony. Put down the gun." They took a step forward, and I knew if they got too close I wouldn't have time, so I took a deep breath and pulled the trigger.

The sound was so loud it made me jump as the dark-haired one howled and went down.

"Silver," he growled, grabbing his wounded thigh.

The other held out his arms for a moment and then bent and grabbed his friend. He turned and sprung out into the yard so fast that they disappeared into the darkness almost instantly.

My heart pounded, and I stood like I was glued to the linoleum.

Can't stay here.

Finally, I rushed to the counter, blew out the candle, and grabbed a plastic grocery bag, throwing in a bunch of herbs and extracts. I put the book in a tote bag and rushed to the front door. Just as I got there, I heard squealing tires. *Now what?*

I looked out the front door and saw Astrid's sports car sideways in my driveway and another car barreling down the street toward the house.

Astrid flung her door open and ran to my front door as I yanked it open for her.

"Oh my God!" I screamed, seeing a whole carload of wolf-men.

"I can't stop them!" she screamed, shoving the door closed.

"The back is open. We're not safe here!" I yelled. I only had a few silver bullets left. Not enough when the whole crew came through the door.

"Steel knives and mirrors!" she yelled, running to the counter. She pulled a butcher's knife free and spun around. "A big mirror and a strong lamp!"

"Upstairs," I said, rushing toward the steps. She ran after me.

We heard the door splinter.

"Oh, God! They're going to kill us!" I said, hyperventilating. We rushed to Aunt Mel's room, and I pointed at the mirror. Astrid dragged it to the doorway, facing it outward. She grabbed a lamp and laid it on its side to light up the mirror.

"What are you doing?"

"Seeing their reflection repels weak-willed werewolves. I'll add an enchantment. If we're lucky, this will turn them back." She panted with the exertion, then cast a quick spell and stood with her knife at the ready.

They growled as they came up the stairs. It was still the worst sound I'd ever heard in my life. My legs were locked stiff as two-by-fours. I widened my stance and pointed the gun at the doorway.

"You don't have a lot of bullets," I told myself in a whisper. "Focus. Aim. Just like shooting cans with Zach for fun. You can do this. You can do this."

They rushed the doorway, but three turned back at the mirror.

I pointed and pulled the trigger. I got one in the chest and another in the shoulder. They fell, scrambling toward us, knocking the mirror onto its side. Astrid stepped forward and slit their throats, making me wince. She stood the mirror back up.

"Good!" she said with a quick glance at me. "The same way when they come again." She said some words that I guessed were for another spell, but I didn't even process what she was saying. My whole mind was focused on the doorway. I wanted to live.

There were sirens, shrill and getting louder. And then I heard a car door slam and a motor start.

"Do not move," Astrid said, walking to the window behind me. "Ha! They go. *Pendejos!*"

My arms burned from holding the gun outstretched, but I couldn't seem to move. I wasn't sure they were all gone. I couldn't let my guard down.

I saw flashes of light from the squad cars reflected off the wall.

"The police. *Bien.*"

I waited with the gun still gripped tight in my hand.

"Tammy Jo!"

I didn't answer. I just stood where I was until Zach bounded up the stairs and appeared in the doorway. I lowered the gun.

"What the hell?" he said, looking at the pair of dead men on the pale gray carpet. Those stains were never coming out.

"They broke in and tried to kill us," Astrid said.

Zach looked at the pedestal mirror.

"To block the door and slow them down," she added.

"Hey," Zach said softly, stepping over the bodies. "C'mon to me, darlin'. C'mon."

The other deputies shouted to each other downstairs. They were sweeping through, I guessed. I dropped the gun into the tote bag that was next to my leg.

Zach put his arms around me, and I put my forehead against his chest. "Easy there, baby girl. You did right."

I didn't cry. The well had run dry, I guess. I just trembled, and my teeth chattered a little.

"That's all right. You just lean on me," Zach said, and I did.

"What the hell! They broke through the front and the back?" someone downstairs shouted to someone else.

"How many were there, Jo?"

"Too many," I whispered. "They're crazy psychos, and regular ammunition won't stop them. You and the other guys need to load your weapons with silver bullets."

"Easy now. Don't get yourself more worked up."

"I'm not kidding," I said, pulling away. "And you will darn well listen to me." I poked him in the chest. "I'm not letting any of you get killed."

He cocked his head to one side.

"Something bad is happening in this town," I whispered. "Was I right about the special medicine to get those people at Glenfiddle out of their comas?"

He nodded.

"Trust me again. You need *silver* bullets."

"Well, not having many visits from the Lone Ranger, we don't keep a supply of them at the station."

"Bryn Lyons gave me some. He must know a supplier."

Zach clenched his teeth. "Lyons again."

"That's a very good idea. Let's go to Bryn's house. He can help us," Astrid said.

I rubbed my tired eyes. I knew Zach wouldn't go for that. "How's that bite doing? Has it been bleeding a lot?"

"Nah, it's just a scratch. Here, sit down," he said, maneuvering me to the bed. I sat, trying to figure out what to do. If the wolves were tracking my magic, I didn't want to cast the astral-projection spell from anyone else's house. But I couldn't exactly stay in my house with its busted-in doors either.

"I need help," I murmured.

"I'm here," Zach said.

I nodded. I wondered if the wolves would be brazen enough to attack the jail. If the cops had silver ammunition, they wouldn't get far.

I took a deep breath. "All right, I have a plan."

"A plan to do what exactly?" Zach asked.

"I have to go to Bryn Lyons's house. After that I want to stay at the police station. If I meet you there, will you put me in a cell for protective custody?"

"In a cell?" he echoed. "You can stay at my house."

I shook my head. "They're killers, Zach. You couldn't shoot them all fast enough."

"Who are they, and what do they want with you?"

"Revenge. They tried to kill me, but I didn't let them, and they're mad about it. I guess it makes them look bad if a girl like me can get away." I didn't even know what I was saying. I was just talking to get us where we needed to be, armed to the teeth and barricaded in the jailhouse.

"Who are they?"

"I'm not really sure."

"How many are there?"

"I don't exactly know."

"Well, we'll call in backup from the surrounding towns. This ain't the old West, you know. And if you're going to Lyons's house, I'm going with you. I'd like to have a talk with him. Seems like it's been since you started spending time with him that all this trouble started."

I didn't know what to say.

"Good, I'll join you," Astrid said. "Let's go now. You may ride over with me," she said to me.

I understood her ploy. Bryn had turned her away, and she thought if I was with her she'd have a better chance of getting in. I could've been annoyed at being used, but I didn't blame her for being scared. I was scared, too. And I wasn't sure why he didn't want her in his house, but it seemed pretty low to leave her running around town without a place to go.

"We'll caravan over there," I said. "But I'm going to ride with Zach." I stood and reached for my tote bag, but Zach grabbed it and shouldered it.

"Remember when I used to go out shooting with you all the time?" I asked. "I just did it to keep you company because I wanted to be near you."

"I know."

"And you used to say it was a good skill for a girl to have, just in case."

He nodded as we stepped over the bodies in the doorway.

"You can go on and say 'I told you so' if you feel like it."

"I don't." He grabbed my hand and held it as we walked down the stairs.

"Sutton, you taking her to the station?" Sheriff Hobbs asked as we passed him in the living room.

"Yes, sir."

"You go on and let someone else drive her. She's your ex-wife, and we don't want it to look irregular in the reports."

Zach nodded. "We'll be outside." I didn't need to ask. I felt the purpose in Zach's step.

"You're going to get yourself fired," I said as we crossed the lawn.

He opened the passenger door of his prowler, and I slid inside.

We drove across town to Bryn's house, where security let us in after a short delay. Astrid and Zach parked, blocking my car in, which was still there from earlier.

Bryn stood in the doorway when we got to it. "Astrid, you'll stay in the guest house with Lennox."

"It's under your protection?" she asked.

He nodded.

"Is Lennox armed?"

Bryn nodded again as Security Steve pulled up in a golf cart.

"All right," she said. Astrid climbed in and was whisked down a dark path.

"Bryn, my house was attacked," I said.

"I heard. Are you all right?" he asked, waving us into the foyer.

I nodded. "I shot three of them using the silver bullets you gave me."

He shook his head and smiled. "You're full of surprises."

"What can we do to make them go—"

"Who are they?" Zach cut in.

Bryn looked at Zach. "A gang."

"Yeah, I got that," Zach said. "Biker gang? Street gang? And where from?" As he waited for Bryn to answer, sweat popped out on Zach's forehead and upper lip. My head tilted, and I opened my mouth to ask him if he was okay as crimson blossomed on his upper shirt.

"Lie down on the bench, Sutton," Bryn said, motioning to an expensive-looking settee in a small alcove near the door.

"I'm fine," Zach said, wiping the sweat from his forehead. "Git to talking. I don't have all night."

"You're right about that," Bryn said grimly.

"Zach, honey, let's sit down. I'm dead on my feet."

Zach let me maneuver him to the bench. I took the keys and tote from his grip and set them down on the floor.

"Don't fuss. I'm all right."

"I know." I pressed my hand over the fabric, pushing down on the wound. As the cloth touched his skin lower down, blood seeped into it. The blood was running down his chest.

Chapter 21

"Lay him down," Bryn said.

I looked at him sharply. "What can we do? You healed yourself with that energy we created. If we were to—"

"No. Scratches are one thing. A bite's another."

Zach leaned back, putting his head against the wall and closing his eyes.

"We can give him a blood transfusion," I said. "Like Lennox did for—"

"It won't last."

"I'll be all right in a minute," Zach said, but he looked pale.

I got up and pulled on Zach. He was heavy and hard to move. I panted with the exertion of positioning him flat and turned to Bryn, feeling helpless and overwhelmed.

"If you know anything, please . . ." I clenched my fists at my sides and blinked back my tears. "Please."

He sighed. "Keep him flat. There's something that can be done to slow the bleeding, but I'm telling you it won't solve the problem."

"But it'll keep him alive while we think of something else?"

"It'll keep him alive awhile, but there's nothing I can do to save him."

He walked to a wall phone and picked it up. He spoke softly and quickly, then hung up.

"What language was that?"

"Gaelic."

Gay-lick? What in the world? Sounded like something Johnny Nguyen would be interested in.

"Keep his heart lower than his legs. There are some cushions on the couch," he said, nodding to the room down the hall. "Lennox only has two packets of blood left. He'll be up to give the transfusion. I'll be back in a few minutes." He walked past me to the front door.

"Bryn, thank you."

He didn't answer as he walked out. I hurried down the hall and stopped in the incredibly opulent living room, which was decorated in shades of purple from dark blue-violet to periwinkle with silver accents.

I loaded my arms up with pillows and went back to Zach. He was too tall for the antique bench, but I got the pillows under his thighs while his calves dangled off the end of it.

"Better flip those burgers 'fore they burn," he mumbled.

I bit my lip and unbuttoned his shirt. I grimaced and pressed the heel of my hand over the wound where his blood was draining from it.

"Oh, Zach, I'm so sorry," I whispered.

A few minutes later, Lennox arrived. He put an IV in each of

Zach's arms and let the blood run in. It was just finishing when Bryn came back.

"All right, Tamara, hold the door open for me."

I rushed to the door as Bryn and Lennox pulled Zach up, and Bryn lifted him in a fireman's carry.

I started to follow them out, but Lennox caught my arm. "No. You'll stay here until we're done."

"But—"

"Don't argue! You owe us more than you can repay already," Lennox snapped.

I went as still as if he'd clocked me with his fist. I kept my mouth firmly shut and my feet planted as I watched them load Zach into the golf cart. After they left, I closed the front door and paced back and forth, still shaking from having been yelled at. When I stopped to think about it, I knew it was just plain silly to be worried about that with so many worse things going on, but I couldn't stop. Lennox made me feel like I was pushy and ungrateful, and that just wasn't the way girls in Duvall were raised to be. Lennox could be a terrible jerk, but he had helped me. I'd try to remember to use my best manners even when I didn't feel like he deserved them.

Finally, I sat down with the spellbook and started searching for strong healing spells.

* * *

A half hour later, Bryn came into the house. He was soaking wet and smelled like a shrimp salad gone bad.

"How did things go?" I asked.

"The bleeding stopped better than I expected, and he's awake."

"Thank goodness for that."

Bryn walked past me to the laundry room, and I trailed after him.

"He's in bed in the guest house. It was closer. And he walked in there under his own power. He's tough. I'll give him that."

"Thank you so much for your help, Bryn. So what are we going to try next? I've got this old spellbook. It's powerful, and I found a couple of healing spells that might do the trick. Nothing that mentions werewolves, but—"

Bryn yanked his shirt off, and something that sounded like hail on a tin roof fell to the floor. I bent, but he picked up the pearly white bits and tossed them in the garbage.

"Crushed seashells," he said, unbuttoning his pants.

I turned to face the door but didn't leave. "So, what do you think? Use the book I've got or one of yours?"

"We can't spell-cast. I've done everything I can to cloak this property. There are still twenty-eight angry werewolves looking for us. The minute we cast a spell, they will track us here. I can't risk it. Not for Sutton or anyone." He reached past my shoulder and grabbed a bathrobe from the hook. "I'm going to take a shower, then I have to drive somewhere far enough away to draw power without compromising this house. The highest priority now is survival for the maximum number of people, which includes the townspeople. Werewolves aren't especially patient. Sooner or later, if they get frustrated enough that they can't find us, they'll start attacking innocent people."

"Zach is innocent," I said.

He turned me to face him. "I've done what I can for him. Now, I need you to share power with me to help me do what has to be done. Are you with me or not?"

I needed to find the locket and to heal Zach. Edie was always a wealth of advice. She'd been around more than a hundred years now. She might know some rare cure for a werewolf bite that we didn't. I couldn't take a chance that Bryn would steal too much energy from me and leave me without enough juice to power the spells I was determined to cast.

I looked at Bryn, who was waiting for my answer. "I'm sorry. I can't."

"Saving it for Sutton, huh? He doesn't deserve it."

"Maybe not," I said softly. "But I got him into this."

Bryn walked out of the laundry room.

"Hey, I'm real sorry. I'll make it up to you," I called.

He didn't slow his stride. "I hope you get the chance."

* * *

Just as I was leaving the laundry room, Mercutio ran up and darted past me.

"Hey, where have you been?" I demanded as he careened into the hamper and knocked it over.

He rooted around in its spilled contents.

"No crab legs in there. Just stinky clothes. And I don't know why swimming in seafood bisque would help a wolf wound, but I don't have time to think about it. I've got to cast a spell and find a locket. I can't go home. I can't do it here. I can't go to any of my friends' houses. What do you think?"

Mercutio ignored me. He was intent on licking the fabric of Bryn's damp clothes.

"Easy!" I said as he began chewing, putting puncture holes into the jeans. I sighed. "Great. You don't think he's mad enough at me?" I paced back and forth, and Merc cocked his head, looking at me. Then he walked over and rubbed his furry body against my legs. And just like that, I had to forgive him.

"Uh-huh. So where are we going to go?"

Mercutio hopped on top of the washing machine and surveyed the room. The way he was perched gave me an idea.

"We can go to the tor. I'll park on top to cast my spell. If they show up too soon, we'll just hightail it out of there. What do you say? Wanna be my lookout?"

Mercutio gave a rough purr that I took for his agreement.

"Okay, let's go," I said, turning and marching out. Mercutio padded along with me. I picked up my tote bag and the keys to Zach's squad car.

"Our ride's a police car. Too bad you weren't with me earlier. You'd have liked that Trans Am—real fast and pretty. Maybe when I get another job, I'll buy a used one. You know, I don't think they make them anymore though. How do you feel about vintage? I like antique stuff. You?"

We walked out the front door, and I spotted the golf cart, which made me think of Zach. If I was going out to possibly become a sandwitch for a pack of wolves, I should at least say good-bye. Plus Bryn had said Lennox was armed in the guesthouse, so maybe he had a few silver bullets to spare. There was a better than average chance I was going to need them.

"You like the wind in your hair?" I asked Mercutio as I got in the cart. He hopped in too, and I drove in the direction I'd seen them go.

The "guesthouse" was bigger than I expected. I'd pictured a cottage, but this looked like it could sleep half a dozen people. There was a flower border of pretty impatiens lining the walk, but I didn't stop to admire them.

I knocked on the door and opened it when no one answered. I walked through the family room, which was decorated Southwestern-style with big leather couches, American Indian throw blankets in deep orange and brown, and a big stone fireplace.

I found Zach in one of the bedrooms down the hall, and my jaw dropped when I poked my head inside. Zach sat up in bed, his naked chest partially wrapped with a tight Ace bandage. On a chair next to the bed was Astrid, her long legs propped up and resting on part of the mattress.

"Are you kidding me?" I asked, stepping into the room.

"Hey there, darlin'. Lyons said you were at the big house, sleeping." His hair was disheveled, but he looked as handsome as ever. And the way Astrid studied him, I was sure she'd noticed.

"Do you think I'd just tuck myself in for a nap while you were—" I paused, catching myself before I said the word *dying*. "While you were so sick?"

"You were exhausted."

"Sure I am, but I thought I'd check on you. Glad to see you're all recovered." My gaze slid to Astrid, who had a rather smug expression on her stunning face.

"Oh c'mon, Tammy Jo, we're just shooting the shit."

I glanced at him. He had an earnest expression and looked as innocent as someone with that many muscles can.

It didn't matter. I was still ridiculously jealous. "I'll see you later."

"Hang on," he said. "Where do you think you're going?"

"Out," I announced as I turned and left the room.

He caught me a few steps later, proof that he was feeling pretty strong again. He turned me by the shoulders, and I couldn't help but glance down. He had a towel tied around his hips. So he'd been sitting naked in a strange bed with a strange woman for company, as easy as you please.

"You don't need to go off half-cocked," he said. "I talked to the sheriff. Told him I fell sick from this bite before we could get to the station. He says they've been patrolling the town, and there are no signs of any gangs, but we've got five cars from the surrounding counties coming. They'll get everything squared away, and we can talk about the details of what happened at your house so that your story's straight when they question you. I'm sure Miss Astrid can find something better to do than jaw with me. Why don't you come cuddle up in bed?"

I shrugged his warm hands off my shoulders. I'd only ever seen Zach sick a couple times, and both times when he'd recovered, he'd had one thing on his mind, proving just how strong and alive he was. As tempting as he was, there was no time for that now.

"I can't." A blur of spotted fur caught my eye, and I turned my head. Mercutio, who had been perched on top of a tall bureau, had jumped down and walked the hall to the front door. "Mercutio's ready to go. We're heading to Georgia Sue's to wait for her to come home," I lied. I couldn't take Zach with me to Macon Hill. "I'll talk to you tomorrow."

"You're leaving me here?"

"I figured you'd want to question Bryn some more."

"And you'll be at Kenny and Georgia Sue's? When I'm done here, I can meet up with you there?"

I nodded. He gave me a quick kiss, and I left him there.

I walked through the quiet house, listening. When I heard the rustle of papers from a hallway to the right, I followed it to a door that was partially ajar.

I tapped lightly.

"Come," Lennox said.

I pushed the door open slowly. He looked up at me from a pile of papers and charts.

"Yes?" he asked, his tone neutral enough.

"Just wanted to say thank you. And if you tell me where you get those bags of blood from, I'll get you some more to replace the ones you used."

The corners of his mouth quirked into a wry smile. "The blood is obtained by means that your ex-husband, the local law enforcement, wouldn't approve of. But it was good of you to offer."

"I'm going out to do some . . . well, to do some things. And afterward, when the main stuff is taken care of, I'd be pleased to help Bryn try to cast a spell to fix your blood disease."

"Thank you."

"Welcome," I said and turned to leave. "Mr. Lyons?" I said, remembering the other reason I'd come. "Do you happen to have any spare thirty-eight caliber silver bullets? In case I run into trouble out there?"

He opened the bottom drawer of his desk and dug through the contents. He held out a four-by-six-inch wood box with a lone star carved in the top. I took off the lid and looked down at the shiny ammunition.

"Thank you."

He nodded and turned back to the stack of papers on his desk.

Chapter 22

* * * * *

When I was eight years old, I wrote a report for science class on Macon Hill, aka the Duvall tor. All the information I used in the report came straight from Edie. I'd snuck the locket out on a chain that had it hanging to my belly button and rode my My Little Pony bike to the hill where I spent the whole day. I sat on the grass with my loose-leaf notebook, scrawling down the stuff Edie said as she floated around, scaring wasps.

I caught hell for being gone all day, for taking the locket without permission, and most of all, for writing a report all about magic. Momma finally gave me a kiss on the head just before she burned all my notes and the painstakingly written report.

Edie and I were both furious. From then on, I kept the things Edie told me a secret, locked away in my diary under a small brass lock.

Since the days of my pink bike, the town had built a nice paved road to the hilltop, and First Methodist of Duvall had built a very pretty stone chapel at the peak. From the west-facing bay window, you could see most of our gorgeous green town.

I drove up the hill, listening to the police radio. No signs of trouble to hear the sheriff and his merry men tell it. Mercutio's window was open, and he seemed to be tasting the wind, his rough pink tongue darting out between pointed front teeth. He sure took up a lot of the passenger seat, and I had to own the fact that he most likely wasn't a house cat.

"Merc, what's an ocelot anyway? Jungle cat?"

Mercutio's gravel-voiced purr was rhythmic and unperturbed.

"Well, there isn't any decent jungle around here. So frankly I think it's best if you just keep on living with me."

He didn't disagree, and I thought that even Zach would have to admit that Merc's downright friendly for a wild animal.

"Here we are," I said, stopping on the drive several feet from the landscaped lawn of the chapel. I walked around to the west side to where Beverly Stucky's fourth grade class had created a rock garden.

"Like Bryn, Edie says this tor is a ley center, Merc. That's a place of magical power. Perfect place for us to cast spells." I walked to the largest stone that was hammered on top to form a seat where three adults could fit comfortably. I sat down with my tote. Mercutio hopped up and sat next to me.

"I miss Edie. Isn't that funny? She really doesn't visit much, but just when someone leaves town is when you really feel like talking to them, you know. Why is that? I guess people hate to lose anything, even the stuff they take for granted and never appreciate while they have it."

I lit the vanilla candle. Mercutio jumped down and tugged on my right shoe.

"What?"

He meowed unhelpfully, but then pulled again and bit my big toe. Not hard, but enough for me to catch the drift.

"It's been raining cats and dogs, Merc, and it's muddy as all get-out."

Mercutio looked at me with his big eyes. I sighed and stripped my feet bare. He got back on the rock with me while I burned herbs. I took a breath and closed my eyes to relax.

"Feel anything?" I whispered, then yawned. "Besides sleepy?" I twisted around so I could recline in a fetal position, curling around the lit candle. I sprinkled more herbs into the flame. It smelled nice, like spicy perfume.

I put my cheek on the cool stone and thought about the power of the earth and how I hoped it would bring Edie to me. Mercutio's soft fur rubbed my arm as he lay next to me.

"Edie, I miss you," I whispered. "Sure would be nice to walk the earth, to feel the grass between our toes, the peace and power, the energy, and to be together."

As I breathed in the warm, relaxing fragrances, I concentrated on getting my mind to separate from my body. If the spell worked and transported my consciousness to Edie and the locket, I would see where they were. Once I knew that, my mind could come home and tell my body, so I could go retrieve them. Real easy . . . in theory. I felt myself drifting.

I woke up when Merc's paw batted my nose. My back was arched over the rock like I was a human horseshoe, my fingers touching the dirt on one side of the rock and my toes poking into the mud on the other. I had the worst kink in my back.

"Arg, I'm in no shape for this," I grumbled, twisting onto my side. "I'll need to take yoga if I do any more spells like this. Ow!"

I straightened up and heard a car door shut. My heart thumped quicker.

"Who's that?" I whispered.

Mercutio hissed. *Uh-oh.* I picked up my gun. Mercutio hopped down and sprung forth, fearless as ever despite the stitches that should have reminded him not to tangle with big dogs.

I slid from the rock, and my feet squished in the soft warm mud. I curled my toes, thinking how energized I felt after my nap. *Somebody should build a spa up here.* I stretched my arms over my head. I licked my tingling lips. Boy, I was buzzed. *Adrenaline sure is fun.* It was like I'd had three margaritas on an empty stomach.

The night's silence was punctuated with the sounds of a fight. Mercutio's high-pitched meows and men's shouts, then howling.

"I do love that cat. He's going to be a force to be reckoned with when he grows up, which could be any minute now." I needed higher ground, all the better to ambush a pack of wild dogs. I climbed onto the stone and stood up.

I leaned over and gripped the rose trellis, pulling myself onto it. Thorns scratched my legs, but I didn't give them the satisfaction of yelping in pain. I just climbed and pressed myself onto the chapel shingles. I strolled to the edge, wishing my feet were ankle deep in the wet soil. Hmm, maybe the nice buzzed feeling wasn't adrenaline after all.

I could feel Edie's pull, her cool aura rubbing my skin and her memories dancing at the edge of my mind. I tried to focus, reaching for her world, but I couldn't quite get into it.

The especially bright moonlight lit the roof. I admired the way Mercutio darted between the big wolves with their snapping teeth. He reminded me of a running back slipping between lumbering defensive linemen.

"You darn wolf-men, stand still," I muttered as I cocked the hammer back on Earl's gun, pointed it, and pulled the trigger. The wolves howled and scattered.

"Mercutio, stop foolin' with them. I've got to hurry up and shoot them so we can round up my family."

I heard the sound of claws and turned. A wolf-man was almost on me when I shot him, but it all happened in slow motion, so I had plenty of time. He collapsed at my feet. The bulky pelt shimmered and then faded as he shrunk back to a man.

"I'm reloading," I announced. "If you don't want to be shot full of holes, y'all can leave. Otherwise, it's Swiss cheese time."

I heard Mercutio screech and then a loud *pop* clapped the night and bits of roof went flying.

"Oh, now you're shooting?" I dropped to my belly and peered over the edge of the roof, thinking that someone really needed to clean the chapel's gutters.

"Big nasty teeth aren't enough, huh? You've got to resort to guns to kill one girl? You'll be a laughingstock, but you know, do what you have to."

I followed the sound of Mercutio's pissed-off meows and spotted dog fur moving. I squeezed off three more rounds, hearing yelping. Then I felt something cold and hard pressed to the back of my neck.

"Drop it," said a guttural voice dripping with malice.

I should have peed my pants, but I just plain didn't feel like it. My hand clenched my gun tighter than ever, my blood as cold as Edie's iced martinis.

"They got me, Merc. Run on home now," I called.

The metal banged on my head in a sharp rap. It stung like hell. "I said drop your gun," he growled.

Kiss my ass! I took a deep breath. *Now, remember about minding your manners, Tammy Jo.* "I don't believe I will. Go on and shoot me."

Suddenly, I was ripped up off the roof to a standing position, and he spun me to face him. The greasy black hair hung down around his pockmarked face. The eyes were flat and human, but he had a muzzle instead of a mouth, and it was dripping saliva and twisted like he was in need of some serious plastic surgery.

With better speed than The Flash, he knocked the gun from my hand, but I just stared into his hateful yellow eyes. All I could think was that if I were dead, I'd have a really good shot at finding Edie, and I could lead her to the other side with me. I'd miss Earth, but Heaven's rumored to be real nice.

"I'm going to rip your throat out."

"I know, but you probably can't help it. You *were* raised by wolves."

He growled menacingly and shook me by the arms until my teeth rattled. "Fear me!" he raged.

I blinked in surprise. "I do," I said, but he was right, I wasn't really feeling it like I should have.

Over his shoulder, there were a bunch of other creepy wolves gathered on the edge of the roof.

"Kill. Kill. Kill," they chanted.

"Who helped you kill Diego?" he growled.

"Who's Diego?"

He howled loud enough to be heard three counties over. He shoved me, knocking me down.

The slope of the roof took me, and I rolled right off, landing butt-first in a hydrangea bush before thumping to the ground. The earth shook when I landed, and I heard wolves yelp in surprise. There were several loud thumps as some must have fallen off the roof on the other side.

I scrambled to my feet and, as my toes nestled in the mud, the power of the crossing ley lines bubbled through me like a mimosa.

Mercutio darted out from the shadows, and we ran. I heard the wolves growling behind us. I reached the prowler and yanked the door open. Mercutio jumped in. The lead wolf, muzzle snapping the air, raced toward me. I dropped into the driver's seat and slammed the door hard, hitting the power lock. He crashed into the side. I grimaced. "That's going to leave a dent. Don't know how Zach's going to explain it to the sheriff."

I gunned the engine and swung the car around. I drove over a couple of wolves as fast as I could. The rest scattered out of my way as I rammed into one who didn't make way. I backed the car up and spun the wheel to get me back on the driving path.

I spotted a bunch of wolves chasing the car as I gunned the engine. The car jerked over some rocks at the edge of the path as I struggled to keep the wheel straight. We barreled down the hill at a hundred miles per hour.

The wolves broke pursuit and ran back up the hill to where their trucks were parked. I kept my foot pressed all the way down on the accelerator, fighting against the urge to stop the car so I could walk around with my toes in the grass and dirt of that fantastic hill.

"You know what, Mercutio? I think that went pretty well, all things considered." I lay a hand on Mercutio's fur. Wet?

I pulled my hand up and saw blood.

"Is that your blood?" I sighed. "The vet's going to think I'm not a very good pet owner. Lie down, okay? And try not to bleed too much. Right after I get my locket, I'm going to get you some medical attention."

I turned on the radio. "Robert Earl!" I yelled, slapping my thigh happily. "Don't that just beat all? My favorite singer on the radio when I'm feeling so good." I crooned along, "They got a motel by the water, a quart of Bombay Gin. The road goes on forever and the party never ends."

Mercutio cocked his head at me.

"Well, I know that he sings it better than me, but I love this song. And we escaped instead of getting eaten. Doesn't that make you feel like singing?"

It didn't seem to, but I went right on, hoping he'd join in.

Chapter 23

*

I don't know why I don't wear more black eyeliner. Smoky eyes are sexy. I smeared some red lip gloss on my lips as I swung the wheel and pulled into Johnny Nguyen's driveway.

"Come on, Mercutio," I said, opening the passenger door. The cat hesitated before getting out, but he finally did.

I knocked on Johnny's door, and Rollie answered.

"Nice lip gloss, but *what* in the world is happening with your feet?"

I came to the right place. "Exactly. I need a makeover, real quick like." I pushed past him into the house.

Mercutio hissed slightly before following me in.

"Your cat, I take it. Does he bite people?"

"Not so far as I know, but he does sometimes do stuff that surprises me. Johnny?" I called, walking back to the bedroom.

Johnny looked up groggily from a pile of fuchsia pillows.

"Hey there. I'm going to rescue Edie, and I want to look good doing it. Can you help me?"

"Huh?"

"She's always better dressed than me, and she's dead for cryin' out loud. For once I want to show up and impress her."

"Oh. Can wait to the morning?"

"No."

"Oh," he said, rubbing his eyes.

"Hey," I said, spotting a pack of Kool cigarettes on the nightstand. "Can I have one of those? It's been so long since I smoked."

"When you smoke, Tammy Jo?"

"Well, actually never. So you see my point? I've been good for twenty-three years. I'm entitled to one cigarette without a federal case being made." I picked up the pack and tapped one out. I popped it between my lips and fired it up with a match.

"Now, I need a dress. I'd like something short with fringe. Black would be good. Can I use your shower?"

"I didn't know Duvall had any good drugs in town," Rollie said. "Who on earth is your supplier?"

I took a long drag and only coughed a couple of times. Not bad for my first time. "This has to be like really quick. Can you get him up please?" I said to Rollie, nodding at Johnny.

"You are a pushy little thing." He looked at Johnny. "The girls in Dallas will go crazy over her."

"I'm not pushy. I said 'please.'" I marched into the bathroom, puffing away on my cigarette. I twisted my hair up into a towel to keep it dry. Definitely not enough time to shampoo it. I set my cigarette on the corner of the sink and stripped out of my clothes. I took a fast, hot shower and went back to smoking while I dried off. Cigarettes really do taste good. No wonder people are willing to get cancer to smoke them.

I marched out of the bathroom wrapped in a towel. If Zach could walk around in front of strangers in a towel, so could I.

Rollie and Johnny went to work on me and fifteen minutes later I was dressed to kill. Too bad I'd lost my gun.

"You gorgeous," Johnny said, fluffing my hair as Rollie put a third coat of mascara on me.

"Forget this town. Let's take her to New York and make her a supermodel."

"She not tall enough."

"She's what, five-seven? Kate Moss is five-seven. And Kate's a crazy drug addict, too. Our little redhead will fit right in."

"Can I have another cigarette?"

"No, you not smoke," Johnny scolded.

"Hmm. Can anybody say gateway?" Rollie said.

I looked myself over in the big mirror. Fringed green beaded minidress, gemstone encrusted gold shoes by some Italian shoe designer whose name I couldn't pronounce, and five pounds of the sexiest makeup ever worn by anyone in Duvall, except maybe Rollie himself.

"This dress is the berries," I said with a smile.

Rollie gasped. "I haven't heard that expression since Cool Cal was president."

"Huh?" I asked, cocking my head.

"Calvin Coolidge. He ran the place about eighty years ago."

"Hmm. Well, wish me luck. I'm going to get our ghost back. And anyone who tries to stop me is going to get a mascara wand jabbed in his eye."

"Good luck, Tammy Jo," Rollie and Johnny said.

* * *

Mercutio and I zoomed across town, not having to run over any werewolves on the way. I could feel the pull of Edie's spirit. My tor spell was working like gangbusters.

Then I drove straight up to Bryn Lyons's gate.

"Well, butter my butt and call me a biscuit. Will you just look where we are?" I said to Mercutio while checking out my lip gloss in the rearview mirror. "So Mr. Tall, Dark, and Gorgeous was in on it all along. No wonder he was at Georgia Sue's instead of at the mayor's party. Well, don't you worry. He's not going to outsmart me again." I pressed the security buzzer.

"Yes?" the security box said.

"Steve, is that you?"

"Yes, ma'am."

"Tammy Jo here. Is he home?"

"He is."

"Can I come on in? Pretty please?"

"Are you alone?"

"Just me and my kitten, Mercutio." Mercutio looked at me. I took my finger off the buzzer. "What? You're seven months old. That makes you a kitten," I whispered. "And we're trying to seem nonthreatening."

The gate slid open.

I grinned. "Say what you want about the guy, Merc, but I like that Steve. He's always been on our side." I drove up to the house and shimmied out of the driver's seat, liking the swish of my fringe.

I opened the door, catching a faint smell of bleach in the air. Who the heck had been cleaning at this time of night? Bryn was coming down the stairs but stopped when he saw me.

"Hello."

"Hello yourself," I said.

He looked as gorgeous as ever, but better. His blue eyes were super vibrant, like a bolt of electricity had lit them up.

"How'd your night go? Were you struck by lightning or anything?" I asked.

"No, you?"

"Nope, but I think I did cause an earthquake. Did you feel it?"

"Actually, yes." He came down the rest of the stairs and walked over, stopping when he was only a few inches away from me. "Did you go to a party afterward?"

"No, just got cleaned up. My feet were kind of muddy. You know how I like that dirty magic."

His mouth quirked into a smile that made my heart pound. The lying, thieving bastard from the forbidden families list. Why did he have to be like a movie star, except better looking?

"Do you smoke?" I asked.

"No."

"I'd like a cigarette."

"Can't help you with that. What else can I do for you?"

I leaned forward. He smelled like sandalwood soap and magic. I licked my lips. "Have you had any luck recovering your watch? Your this-doesn't-go-with-my-Zorro-costume Rolex?"

"I knew which watch you meant, and no, I haven't gotten it back."

"Maybe I should cast a spell to try to find it. I'm really getting the hang of my powers." *Sort of.*

Bryn raised his eyebrows. "Is that so?"

"Yeah. I defeated a bunch of werewolves single-handedly." I

glanced over toward the door. "Well, Zach's car and Mercutio helped a little."

"You shouldn't be casting spells you don't understand. It's reckless."

It wasn't as much fun when Bryn wasn't flirting and looking at me like I was dinner, so I decided to get down to business. "Where's my locket?"

"I don't know."

He was lying. It was around somewhere, but his power was interfering with my Edie-reception. I needed to put his power out, or to steal it. I smiled at the thought. Wouldn't that just fix his little red wagon? And then I'd be strong enough to find my locket, heal Zach from the werewolf bite, and probably cure cancer.

I took a couple of steps forward and put my hands on his chest. Power sizzled between us like a Fourth of July sparkler.

"I think we should work together on a spell to banish the werewolves. Want to make some magic with me?" I whispered.

Bryn stared into my eyes, his lids drifting to half-mast. "What I want . . ." His voice trailed off, and he pressed his lips against mine. He tasted like peppermint schnapps and dark chocolate.

I slipped my arms around his neck, my fingers into his hair, and pulled his power right up to mine, wind and earth, mingling just like they're meant to.

He kissed me like the last bit of oxygen in Texas was left in my lungs, and he wanted it. He pressed me up against him, and I let my body melt on his, sharing that heat.

He broke the kiss, drawing in a long breath and licking his lips. "You're not yourself," he said in a husky voice, curled with passion and power.

"Whoever I am, do you want me?"

"Be careful what you offer."

The corners of my mouth turned up, not afraid of the game. "Been careful most of my life. Not my turn anymore. Maybe *you* should be careful," I challenged.

He let me go slowly, rubbing the excess gloss from his lips with his thumb. "Caution is not what interests me." He looked me over, making my whole body tingle. "But I'll give you a chance to think. I'll go upstairs alone. You can hide in the guesthouse until whatever you've done is undone. Or you can come to my room, and see how that turns out," he said and went up.

I started to follow, but Mercutio hurried over to the stairs and lay across the bottom one like a big feline doorstop blocking my path.

"Hey now, you heard him dare me."

I stepped, and Merc stood when I had one foot over him. I had to grab the rail, but still managed to crash-land on my butt on the second step. I glared at him, and pulled myself up.

"Don't be a flat tire. I'm just interested in some button shining," I said, but I bet he knew I had more than close slow-dancing in mind.

He pressed my legs, trying to get me to turn back, but I wouldn't. I was motivated like it was a hundred-and-five-degree day and the only snow cone in the state was upstairs.

When I got around him, he darted down the step and sauntered toward the kitchen. I smiled, satisfied with my victory.

I walked up, having a flash of memory. I saw the fringe of my dress swish and my feet in patent-leather shoes kicking up and outward. It sure wasn't a two-step.

I held the banister until I could see again. My locket waited for me, and I wanted it. But I couldn't tell whether it was upstairs or down, inside the house or somewhere on the grounds. I decided it didn't matter. After I shorted out Bryn's power, I'd find it easy and dance the Charleston to celebrate.

At the top, I slipped my shoes off and let them dangle from my hand, enjoying the feel of the soft carpet almost as much as the feel of the mud earlier in the night.

I leaned against the doorway and tapped my knuckles on the door. He opened it and smiled at me, all glossy black hair and blindingly beautiful face. He leaned toward me, but I stopped his lips with a fingertip.

"I'll have a drink."

"Of?"

I looked him over. "What have you got?"

He pulled me into the room, and I kept moving until the length of my body was pressed to his. He laughed softly then kissed me. My toes curled in the carpet, and the shoes dropped from my fingertips.

I could feel the room, particles buzzing by, atoms dancing, electrons orbiting, and every bit of energy seemed focused on where our bodies touched.

He tasted so good, more delicious than food, more necessary than water. I licked his tongue, and his hands pressed my back, fusing us together.

I leaned back finally, dragging my mouth free of his. "About that drink?"

"Are you toying with me, Tamara?"

I watched his blue eyes glitter, fascinated as ever by them. "Yeah, like it?"

"Very much," he whispered. He went to a piece of furniture

with a cabinet top and opened it. There were decanters of golden brown liquor the color of sun-kissed skin. He filled a pair of crystal glasses and walked back to me. He handed me mine and then tipped back his, draining it in an instant.

I sipped, the liquid all fiery smooth, like him. He set his glass on the bench at the end of the bed, then dropped to his knees in front of me. I looked down at him as I sipped some more.

He put his hands on my bare thighs just where the fringe stopped. The touch was warm and intimate, but his hands were still. "Where did you get this flapper dress?"

"From Johnny."

"Of course," he murmured, bending his head. He ran his tongue between two columns of hanging beads, setting my skin ablaze. He kissed me, sucking on the skin lazily before leaning back. "I'm going to buy you a lot of dresses from him." He didn't look up and make eye contact. It was like he was having a conversation with my legs.

"When?" I asked, trying to draw his attention up.

He shrugged, still focused on my legs. "Whenever I feel like it." He ran his lips over my knee then upward as his hands slid under the dress. "You have the most amazing skin." His fingertips caught the edge of my panties and slid them off my hips, down, down, down to my ankles. I stepped out of them and walked away from him, dipping my tongue into the mostly empty glass. I stood at the edge of the bed, staring up at the skylight. The black sky was dusted with glittering stars, seemingly ready to rain down on us.

I felt the power first, then felt his body touching mine. He leaned and his mouth was near my ear. "Did you walk away from me to see if I'd chase you? I can end the suspense. I always will," he whispered. My body hummed, making my head swim.

I heard the fabric slide off his skin and closed my eyes, feeling him take the glass from my hand. He turned me toward him and drew us onto the bed.

"How do you feel about roller coasters?"

I opened my eyes, seeing his face just above mine. "Never been on one."

He smiled softly as he slid the edge of my dress up. "Hang on."

He didn't move fast, but time seemed to be lost. One minute I was one person, aware of the world around me. The next, he was inside me, part of me, and the world closed in and slammed through me.

Our hearts beat like a drum in my ears, pounding under my skin, then I was like a peach he'd bitten into, dripping juice, bursting with flavor. I tried not to be torn apart. Something tried to turn me inside out, and I wrapped my arms and legs around the only bit of the solid world still left.

I tried to hold the power. I wanted him to share it with me.

Energy exploded in the room, fire and water, searing, quenching, and I fell and fell and fell.

* * *

Bryn roared. Glossy with sweat and blazing with energy, his aura glowed white-hot, and I had to close my eyes or go blind.

"Stop," I whispered hoarsely, but I doubt he heard me.

My body was slack, burned up and drowned at once. I heard him fling open a door and turned to see him on the terrace. He stretched his arms out and shouted a spell, cursing into the night.

The house shook with a countershock, and the lights flickered and went out.

I lay limp and exhausted, but in the distance I heard him laugh. He sounded so happy it was near impossible to be sorry I'd lost the power struggle.

Chapter 24

I woke later to the sound of shouting. Sunlight streamed in from all the glass windows, and I rolled onto my side and saw Zach slam Bryn into the wall. Bryn ducked as Zach's fist smashed into the plaster.

"You son of a bitch!" Zach stalked over to the bench and grabbed a crystal tumbler. "You had to get her drunk?" He whipped the glass across the room, and it shattered against the wall.

I wanted to say something, but didn't know what. It didn't matter since Zach didn't look like he wanted to talk anyway.

"You want to stay here?" he demanded, looking down at me.

"Yes, she wants to stay," Bryn said. He was dressed in jeans and a white shirt. He looked ready for the day.

I felt like a Ford F-250 had run me over. I put an arm over my eyes.

"I don't feel good," I mumbled.

"I hope the fuck not," Zach said, scooping me up. The sheet slid off my bare legs. The world lurched, and I squeezed my eyes shut as I pushed my dress down to cover as much as possible.

"Get out of my way," Zach ground out. I opened my eyes to see Bryn standing in the doorway.

"Tamara, do you want to stay or go?"

I felt like a prizefighter the day after the big fight. I rested my head against Zach's shoulder.

"Go."

"There are only ten left. The others were cast out. We did that," Bryn said.

Ten what? Werewolves? How? Had he used our combined power to cast a killing spell? That seemed, well, kind of wrong. Sure I'd been all fired up to shoot them, but killing them from a distance seemed unfair, like we should have gotten a penalty for unsportsmanlike conduct.

The room was slightly blurry, but I focused on Bryn's face. "I'm tired."

He reached a hand out toward me, but stopped short.

"You touch her, and I'll set her down long enough to knock your head off your shoulders."

Bryn smiled. "I'll let him take you because he doesn't have much time left with you. When you feel better, pack a bag, because the next time you find yourself in my house, you'll be staying longer than the night." Bryn stepped aside.

I felt myself shifting. Zach was going to put me down to fight with him.

I clutched Zach's shoulder. "No, take me home."

I closed my eyes and didn't open them again until I told Zach to pull the car over so I could be sick. When I was finished, he put me back in, silently. He stalked back around to the driver's side, and I could feel the accusation in his stiff movements.

I'd betrayed him. I knew he wanted to shout and smash things, but I was in no shape for it. The silence was so thick it was hard to breathe.

And worst of all, it was already afternoon on Thursday, October twenty-third. I had less than twenty-four hours left, and I didn't have the energy to lift my head, let alone to cast a spell. Not that I could be trusted to spell-cast. Astral projection was supposed to have taken me to the locket, not made me channel Edie, causing my body to house my soul and part of hers. I couldn't deny that it had felt great to be as bold and fearless as Edie, her twenties slang dripping from my tongue. I'd been drunk with power and confidence, overconfidence actually.

Bryn was right. I should never have cast spells without training. Now I'd had my fun, and I would pay for it with Edie's soul and a guilty conscience that wouldn't give me peace for the rest of my life.

* * *

Zach's little brick house feels a lot like home sometimes, but not when we're fighting. I dropped down on the lumpy blue couch and tipped my head back, resting my neck on the cushion.

Zach went into the kitchen, and five minutes later, bacon and eggs were sizzling in the frying pan. He came out and handed me a glass of sugar water. We'd figured out in high school that eating a packet of sugar is a good way to recover from a hangover for some reason. I swallowed the sweet liquid, not sure at all that it would work for a magical hangover, but, twenty minutes later, I felt better and sat down at the old Formica-topped kitchen table.

Zach set down two plates of food, one in front of me and one for himself.

"You're bleeding again," I said, seeing a small red spot that had soaked through the shirt's maroon bloodstain from the night before.

He didn't say anything, just got to shoveling food into his mouth.

"Zach, I'm sorry." I paused. "I feel better, so if you want to yell at me, go ahead."

He ignored me, going back to the skillet for more bacon.

"I didn't do it to hurt you."

He looked over and fixed me with a hard look. "That just makes it worse, doesn't it?"

I opened my mouth, but couldn't think of what to say. He'd have rather I'd done it to make him jealous or something than because I'd wanted to do it. "I just meant—"

"I don't want to talk about it."

Me either. I hated seeing him in pain.

"I think you need to go to a hospital in Dallas. If that wound keeps bleeding, you need to be in a place where they can give you another blood transfusion."

"There's trouble in Duvall. I ain't goin' anywhere until that's settled."

"The sheriff and the others can handle it. You said they have backup."

"You need to wash all that shit off your face. If you're done eating, get to taking a shower. I need one too before I go to work."

"Zach, you could bleed to death."

"Then bury me next to Momma at Lakeside," he said flippantly. He finished his food and tossed his dish in the sink.

"There's no talking to you!"

He walked over and picked up the newspaper from the counter before proceeding to the living room with it. I followed him.

"Why did you even bring me here if you don't want to talk about things?" This was so typical of Zach. No problem at home was too big to be ignored. When he didn't answer, I walked over to where he'd sat down and snatched the paper from his grasp, crumpling it.

"Girl, I'm at my limit today. Don't push me."

"I can take a shower at my own house. Just drive me home."

"I'm not dropping you off looking like some tramp who's been turning tricks for tequila shots. Now, go on in and take a shower."

"What do you care what my neighbors think? I'm not your responsibility. We're divorced!"

"I said for better or worse, and I meant it. Gettin' divorced was your idea."

"When we were married you barely knew I was there!"

"First off, that's a hell of an exaggeration. Second, today's maybe not the best day for you to get on a high horse about anything." His tone was hard and flat, and it cut me deeper than a steak knife could have.

I clenched my fists. "We're not married, you and me. I can do whatever I want."

"You best hope I *do* bleed to death then, 'cause otherwise you're going to have a big problem with me from here on out."

"It's none of your business."

"I married you, darlin'. You'll be my business 'til we're both dead."

"There's no talking to you."

"Then stop tryin' to," he said, yanking the paper from me and nodding toward the hallway where the bathroom was.

I marched down the hall and slammed the door closed. I nearly shouted in surprise at the sight of my black-smudged reflection in the vanity mirror. The aftermath of three coats of mascara is a good reason to stick to one.

I showered, scrubbing myself with soap and water, then went to his room and threw on one of his Cowboys jerseys. It hung to my thighs and was just about the length of my dress from the night before. I found an old pair of my jeans in the bottom of the closet and slid into them.

After Zach took a shower, he walked into the room naked except for the towel he had pressed to his chest.

I walked over immediately. "Sit down, and let me see it."

"Gonna kiss it and make it better?"

"No."

"Then I'm not interested."

He walked to the dresser and yanked open a drawer. He tossed the bloody towel on the bed long enough to pull on a pair of boxers and jeans. Blood dripped from the wound, and he mopped it up just before it reached the waistband at his hips.

I dug through a box on the closet floor and pulled out an Ace bandage we'd used on his knee a couple of times after football injuries.

I tossed the bandage on the bed and went to get some gauze pads. When I returned he was sitting on the edge of the bed, waiting.

I didn't say a thing. I taped the gauze in place and then wrapped the bandage tight, pressing on it, relieved when the blood didn't seep through.

"Does it hurt a lot?"

"Been hurt worse."

I looked into the denim-colored eyes that were studying me.

"I'm sorry," I whispered.

He slid a hand up and into my hair, pulling my head down. A moment later, I was flat on my back with him on top of me. We kissed for a few minutes, and I could feel that not all of him was mad at me.

When he finally rolled off me, we were both breathless.

"Glad we understand each other," he said.

He got up slowly, holding out a hand to me. I let him pull me up, and we stood toe to toe.

"Where you want to stay while I'm at work? TJ's? I don't want you at Kenny and Georgia's until Kenny's home." The look on his face told me that he wasn't going to drop me off anyplace where I would be alone, and his brother TJ, like all the Sutton boys, had a house full of guns that he wouldn't be shy about using if trouble came knocking.

"TJ's is fine."

* * *

The Sutton boys, as they were known growing up, were all named after U.S. presidents, GW the oldest, for George Washington, of course. TJ for Thomas Jefferson and Zach for "Old Rough and Ready" Zachary Taylor.

They'd all married young, but continued to raise hell despite that. Owing to a very bad example set by their hard-drinking father, they liked to stay out all night in bars, drinking and swapping stories, and sometimes getting reckless. To this day, I couldn't even talk to Zach about the time TJ had wrecked a new car while they were drag racing. Zach just shrugged things like that off. When I said I worried that one of them might end up really hurt or dead if they didn't knock that stuff off, he just grinned and kissed me and said they'd be all right. There was no talking to the man.

It was too bad they'd all been cursed with good looks and easy charm, or they might have stood a chance at staying single, but, as things were, the women they couldn't resist couldn't resist them either. Me included.

I'd been warned. My future sisters-in-law, Sherry and Nadine, had taken me aside right before my wedding shower, and Nadine had asked, "Do you love him?" I'd been startled, but replied quickly enough, "Of course." Sherry had shaken her head and said, "We're sure sorry to hear that, but welcome to the family."

Zach and I pulled into TJ's driveway. I smiled at Nadine, who waved as she collected a bunch of plastic toys from the front lawn.

"Hey there," Nadine said, leaning in Zach's window to give him a kiss on the cheek.

"Hot enough for you?" he asked.

"Hotter than a barbeque in hell," Nadine said with a grin. "I'm so glad you talked TJ into coming home to keep an eye on things. I've got that upstairs bathroom sink that's leaking. It's just been waiting for him to have a chance to fix it."

"Always glad to be of help. Y'all stay out of trouble," Zach said.

I stood in the drive and watched Zach pull away.

"Well, it's good to see you, honey." Nadine said, her dark blond hair swinging stubbornly despite the humidity's fight to weigh it down. "Come on, let's go drink a gallon of iced tea."

"Got anything stronger?"

"Oh it's like that, is it?" She laughed and then said thoughtfully, "I poured TJ's last bottle of Jim Beam down the drain after he drove that riding lawnmower of his through my sunflowers."

She shook her head. "He had the nerve to say he thought they were weeds! And that it was my own damn fault for nagging him about the lawn and spurring him on to cut the grass at one in the a.m. when he couldn't see straight. Nagging my ass. He's lucky I don't just—"

Three children burst out the front door, making as much racket as a fifty-member marching band.

"Crockett, where's your sister?"

"Tied up in the backyard," the boy said, running by without missing a step.

"Well, you better go untie her before your daddy gets home. You know he'll whip your butt if he sees you torturing his baby."

Crockett considered this and seemed to weigh his options. Clearly seeing the wisdom of avoiding a confrontation with his father, who had a hundred and fifty pounds of muscle on him, he asked, "When will he be home?"

"Any minute so far as I know," she said.

Crockett turned and ran back into the house.

"He looks so much like Zach," I said with a smile.

"Yeah, they don't come any cuter, God help us." She gave me a sideways look. "You know, you could get your man to help you make one of your own."

"Zach's not really my man anymore," I said, but didn't even sound convincing to myself.

"That right?" she asked mildly. "Zach was over here one night telling us some story about you with that smile he always gets when he talks about you. And TJ said, 'Son, what are you doin' still in love with that woman?' Zach just grinned and said, 'Hell, that's the only good habit I've got. Not planning to give it up anytime soon.' "

I smiled and shook my head.

"So when *are* you gonna get married again? Zach thought by summer, but here it is fall, and you're still divorced."

Zach had thought we'd be remarried by summer? He'd never mentioned it to me. "Well, there have been a few hitches. Like me sleeping with Bryn Lyons." I clapped a hand over my mouth, not believing I'd let that pop out.

"Oh my God. When?"

"Kind of . . . yesterday."

"And Zach knows?"

I nodded grimly.

"Hmm. It's sure a good thing Zach's a deputy because I wouldn't want TJ going to jail for helping Zach bury the body."

"That's not funny."

Nadine grinned again. Then she laughed, making me laugh with her. "I'm so sorry, but between TJ and the kids, I guess I've gone crazy. Now," she said, fixing me with a pointed look. "What's your excuse?"

Chapter 25

I had half a glass of iced tea and then, when Nadine was busy untangling a walloping fight down the block between her kids and four kids from neighboring houses, I wrote her a nice note and stole her Dodge Ram. I don't know why people pay for rental cars when so many friends and family members just leave their keys lying around unattended.

I had no business going to see Bryn Lyons, and, if Zach didn't die or turn into a werewolf, he was likely to kill me or Bryn, or both of us, if he found out. On the other hand, Bryn was in possession of my cat, my car, my spellbook from Johnny, and very possibly my Edie locket. Wild mustangs with demon riders couldn't keep me away.

I pressed the security buzzer determinedly.

"Can I help you?"

I didn't recognize the voice. "Where's Steve?"

"Sleeping. He pulled a double yesterday."

"Who are you?"

"Security for Mr. Lyons. Who are you?"

The new guy wasn't nearly as nice as Steve. "Tammy Jo Trask. I'd like to see Mr. Lyons and to retrieve my house cat, Mercutio. You might have seen him around. He's got spots like a leopard, but he's a lot sweeter."

"Trask. You're on the list, but Mr. Lyons is out."

"Can I come in and get my cat?"

"Sure. Report to Mr. Jenson."

"Okey dokey." The gate slid open. Easy as shooting fish in a bathtub.

I drove up to the house, and Mr. Jenson met me in the foyer.

"Hey there," I said. "I left this morning in kind of a hurry."

"Your undergarments are in the dryer. They will be ready shortly."

I just know my face turned red as a candy apple. "Oh . . . I was actually talking . . ."

"Mercutio has been fed. He is in the solarium pursuing the birds."

"What's a solarium?"

"Shall I show you?"

"Not right now. Did you happen to come across an old book in or near a cabbage-rose-print tote bag?"

"No."

"It might have been in Mr. Lyons's room with . . . the other things I left."

"I didn't see it."

"You know what else I lost? An antique locket. I asked Bryn to hold it for me a few days ago and forgot to get it back from him. Have you seen that?"

It was long shot, but you never make a fourth-down touchdown from your own twenty-yard line if you don't throw a Hail Mary pass now and then.

"A woman's locket? No."

"Well, I'll just have a quick look in Mr. Lyons's room for my book." I thought about Bryn's office nook in the closet. If he hadn't put my spellbook there, I could just borrow one of his. And maybe find my locket, too.

"I think Mr. Lyons would prefer for you to wait in the living room for him until he returns. May I get you something to drink? Something cold and carbonated, perhaps?"

"Mr. Jenson, if you and Mr. Lyons ever have a falling-out, I want you to know that I'll find room for you to live with me. I couldn't pay much, but I'd make you a torte every week."

Jenson smiled. "I will bear that in mind. And may I say that I understand why Mr. Lyons finds you so charming?"

"Thank you. I wish I could say it was mutual, but, between you and me, I have reason to think that Mr. Lyons has done something pretty low."

"To whom? You?"

I nodded.

"I shouldn't think so, Miss Tamara. Between the two of us, as you say, I have it on good authority that Mr. Lyons hopes to see a great deal of you. I don't believe he would jeopardize his friendship with you."

He hopes to see a great deal of me out of my underwear while siphoning power off me like some people steal cable. "You could be right. I'll have a seat," I said, going to the living room.

My "Cowboy, Take Me Away" ring tone went off, and I started searching for my cell. Turns out my tote bag was behind the couch, but there was no spellbook in it.

I pulled the phone out. Zach's picture was displayed on the little screen and I grimaced, glancing out the window at Nadine's Ram in the circular drive. I thought about ignoring it, then I thought about him bleeding and maybe needing me to drive him to Dallas.

"Hello," I said.

"Where are you?"

"Me? Oh, I'm just fine. How's your chest?"

"Where the hell are you?"

"I'm picking up my cat."

"You stole my brother's wife's car to go back to Lyons's place?" he asked, sounding like he'd asked, "You stole a car to drive to a nursery and murder babies?"

"There's a dog named Angus who lives here. I have to rescue Mercutio."

"Yeah, the safety of your cat was your top priority last night." He paused.

I didn't answer, because what was there to say to that?

"Nadine won't press charges if you return the car by the time she has to drop the kids at her momma's."

"Nadine won't press charges whether I return the car or not. No wife of a Sutton is ever going to send another one to jail. We've got a right to go crazy once a week. Just ask Nadine."

"TJ is my brother, Jo. I tell him you're messing around with Bryn Lyons, and I promise you he'll let me put you in jail for your own good."

I paced up and down on the plush carpet. "You can't arrest me for having an affair."

"I can't arrest you if I say that's the reason," he agreed. "Now, I've got a warrant to search Johnny Nguyen Ho's house. If you want to be there when I search, you should meet me."

"Oh, I went to Johnny's. He doesn't have the locket."

"Tammy Jo!"

"I thought he did. I swear it! And it sure was sweet of you to get a warrant."

There was a long pause, and I was grateful that he didn't say out loud all the curses he was thinking. Finally he said, "So you're staying at Bryn Lyons's?"

"No, of course I'm not. I'm getting my cat." *And my underwear.*

"And then where will you be?"

"Well, I'm not exactly sure. I'm having to fly by the seat of my Levi's just now."

"Girl, you're makin' me crazy. Why don't you come on home and behave yourself."

"I'm gonna. Real soon."

"Let me talk to Lyons for a minute."

"He's not here."

"That right? Guess God's not as pissed off at me as He has been. All right, get your cat and get out of there."

"I'll talk to you later."

"Count on it."

I flipped my phone shut.

"Your ex-husband?"

I spun around to find Astrid standing right next to me.

I nodded.

"You make a nice couple. *Es muy* . . . he's very handsome."

"Thank you." Too bad I didn't have Mercutio's paws to claw her eyes out with.

"I have an idea, a way that we can get these wolves off our backs as you say."

"Just why are they on your back?" I asked, thinking maybe I could figure out why they were after me, too.

"I killed one of them at the meeting. My magic marks his blood, and the wolves in his pack will track me with it until I'm dead or until they can be thrown from the scent."

"We were just defending ourselves."

"Yes, I was. Will you help me in casting a spell?"

I gave her a once-over, trying to figure out her game. "Why do you need me?"

"I don't have power enough to do it myself, and Bryn prefers not to share power. But you've got some very nice raw energy. I'll tell you the words, and we can work the magic together and get these wolves to leave your town."

Astrid cared about Duvall about as much as she cared about the state of Barbara Bush's pedicure, but she wanted to save her own skin and that could work out for both of us.

"I would love for them to hightail it out of Duvall. I really would, but I've got to get a couple of things. You think you could distract Bryn's butler for a few minutes?"

"Certainly. A few minutes is not difficult."

Fish in a bathtub. I hurried out of the room and up the stairs. I opened the door to Bryn's room and stopped at the delicious smell. Sandalwood and sex magic clung to the air, making my knees quake.

I felt like rolling around on the feather duvet and maybe licking some strawberry sauce off Bryn's naked body. But I vetoed this idea since, one, I had important things to do, and two, he wasn't around.

I searched the obvious hiding places for my stuff, under the bed, in the drawers, under the bathroom sink, but didn't find anything. I zipped to the back of the closet. I wished there were some fur coats I could just magically walk through, but no such luck. It was all silk ties, Italian shoes, and a lock that was determined to keep me out.

Pushing against the door though, I realized it wasn't that thick. I walked to the beginning of the closet, dug the heels of my boots in and ran.

I slammed my shoulder into the door, and it snapped open. I landed on the floor, glad and not-so-glad at once. I rubbed my arm, where I was sure to have a Texas-size bruise in the morning, then got up. At the desk, I lifted a framed antique photograph of the Gulf coast and Galveston Bay and, right under it, I found my spellbook sitting on the desk.

"Thief." I shook my head. I looked on the shelves and quickly rifled through the desk drawers. I got my hopes up at a small padded velvet pouch. Inside, I found seven amazingly shiny gold coins, older than Edie, and nearly as pretty. Not my locket at all, but valuable and tucked away like they meant something important to Bryn. And I needed leverage. I got to thinking maybe I could trade them back to him for my locket. I didn't want to play dirty pool, but October twenty-third was nearly a memory.

I grabbed a piece of paper and scrawled a note. I left it under a pewter paperweight of the planet Saturn. I got to the hall and dumped my book in my tote bag and ran down the stairs. "Astrid!" I stage whispered.

"Here," she said, walking out of the living room.

"Let's go," I said, rushing to the front door and flinging it open. I looked around then ran to the Dodge.

"We can take my car. It's fast," she called.

"No, we'll drive separate," I said.

"Fine. We'll meet at the tor."

I stopped. "Oh, no. Not that place!"

"We need its power. No time to argue," she said, getting in her car.

I chewed my lip, but didn't really have any choice. I hopped into the Dodge and gunned it to the gate. How could I make a quick getaway if the gate didn't open? Then I noticed a security intercom I hadn't seen before because it was hidden by a hedge. "Now how was I supposed to see that?" What were they trying to do? Make things look nice? Ridiculous. I stabbed the button with my finger. "Hi, I'm leaving now."

"I don't think so," the security guy said.

"What? Why not?"

"I saw you on the upstairs hallway camera. You stole something from Mr. Lyons."

True. "No, I didn't. It was my book that I was putting in my bag. I left it here last night."

"Mr. Lyons will be home soon. He can confirm that."

"I don't have time to wait for him. Besides he knows where I live. He'll track me down soon enough if he sees fit to. Now open the gate."

"I don't think so."

"The Duvall sheriff's office is on my cell phone's speed dial. If you don't let me out right now, I guarantee you'll have a heap of questions to answer."

I waited, holding my breath. I had a sack of stolen coins and a witch's spellbook. If I called the sheriff they'd be bound to search through my tote bag, and just what was I going to say about the contents? Nope, definitely bluffing about that call. Lucky for me, the guy's not a poker player.

The gate slid open.

"Yippee!" I shouted in a whisper.

I zoomed past the gate and onto the street. Then I paused to let Astrid zip out in front of me. From the Ram, it looked like she was driving a matchbook car.

I hoped Mercutio was having fun with the Solarium birds because he was going to miss one hell of an adventure with me and Astrid banishing all the wolves with a spell. Probably after today, I'd be retired from adventures. But that would be all right. I was pretty sure Merc would enjoy the quiet cake-baking life as much as me. After all, he'd get to eat his share of heavy cream while I whipped up desserts.

Yep, all I needed was to drive the werewolves off, find Edie, cure Zach, and get a new job. Piece of cake. Well, a five-layer, two-days-in-the-making, and every-pan-in-the-kitchen-dirty Death by Chocolate Cake maybe.

* * *

We got to the tor, and I broke out in a sweat at the thought of going back up there and drawing on that power. I wanted it and dreaded it, too. It was the same way I felt about being with Zach or Bryn for that matter. And I didn't see why things couldn't just be nice and simple for once. Didn't I deserve a break for working really hard and having good intentions?

But maybe things were going to be okay. I only had a few big problems, and I was about to solve one. I just needed to stay focused and think positive thoughts. I parked the Ram behind Astrid's little car and followed her to the chapel.

"We're going to do it inside?" I asked. I'd never known Momma or Aunt Mel to cast spells in Holy places.

I'd gotten half a step in when someone grabbed me. My mouth opened to scream, but nothing came out. I was face-to-face with the werewolf who had ambushed me on the chapel roof. The one who'd been mad that I hadn't been afraid of him. He wouldn't have to get mad today.

Chapter 26

*   *
  *   *
   *

I looked around the chapel. There were three of the wolf-men inside. One that I didn't recognize was at the window, keeping watch. The third one was the lanky man, the tracker from Jammers. He stepped forward, and his straight, greasy hair and patchy beard made me very much want to direct him to Johnny's hair salon, but it wasn't the time. He stood in front of me and patted me down for weapons while the guy from the roof held my wrists in a tight grip behind my back.

I looked at Astrid, but she wouldn't make eye contact with me.

"You have her now," she said.

Next time a strange witch asks me to cast a spell with her, I'm going to be busy making pancakes or waffles. If the town has to get eaten by werewolves or walloped by plagues, that's just not going to be my problem.

My mouth was dry and my hands trembled as I tried to think of a way to get out. The tracker pushed Astrid away from me until she was pressed to the wall, then bent his head to the crook of her neck. She squirmed.

"Enough of this," she said. "I've kept my part of the agreement. I expect you to keep yours. As you see, I was not a party to whatever she did before the meeting."

"I didn't do anything," I protested.

The lanky man took a deep breath and then stepped back from Astrid. "She's clean."

"Go," the one holding me said to Astrid.

"I'm clean, too. I used plenty of Dial soap in my shower today." I tried to keep things light and casual, which is hard to do when you're a hostage. My heart hammered, but I tried not to pass out.

Astrid left without so much as a good-bye. The lanky guy stepped up to me, leaning to put his nose right into the vee of the jersey. I tried to back up, but ran into the canine wall behind me.

"It's like I told you, Samuel. She wounded Jeff at the witches' meeting, but she didn't kill Diego. I can't even pick up Diego's scent on her anymore."

"But her house had it," he growled from behind me.

"Yeah, Diego's scent mixed with blood and magic. Someone else's blood, not hers."

Samuel spun me around to face him, squeezing hard on my upper arms. He growled, showing long, jagged teeth. "Who killed Diego?"

My heart raced as fast as my mind. "I sure don't know. I never met anyone called Diego. And there weren't any murders in Duvall before you showed up."

He grabbed my throat with one hand and squeezed. Lights danced before my eyes, and my knees went watery. "The only ones dying around here have been wolves, but that's going to change. I promise you."

He was strong enough to crush my windpipe and kill me with one hand, but he didn't. He let go of my throat, but kept a hold on my arm.

"I'm telling you. Diego bit whoever attacked him," the tracker said.

Samuel glanced at him. "We've been over this," he growled. "I don't care how powerful a witch or wizard it was; Diego's bite would have killed whoever it was by now. We're still tracking Diego's scent, so the killer is alive. And if this bitch didn't do it, she's at least had him into her house." He yanked on my arm, making me stumble.

Nobody had come to my house and bled on the furniture. Could I have picked up the scent somewhere and tracked it in on my shoes?

"Tell me what you know."

"I don't know anything. I'm not even really a witch—"

The blow caught me across the cheek and knocked me down.

"You lie to me again, and I'll break all the bones in your left arm."

"Samuel!" the man at the window growled as Samuel caught me by the arm and pulled me back to my feet.

"What?"

"Police cars."

I rubbed my cheek as the door swung in. Zach stood in the doorway with a shotgun leveled into the room. Samuel yanked me in front of him.

"Y'all wanna live, you might want to think about lettin' her go,"

Zach drawled, voice smooth and easy like he was asking them to pass him a bag of Cheetos.

Samuel glanced at the window and made a tiny motion with his head. In a flash of speed, the other two crashed through it and were gone. I heard the popping of gunfire from outside, but Zach didn't look to the window. He watched us.

Samuel dragged me toward the window, whispering in my ear. "I want you to know I'm going to kill you. Before that though, you're going to suffer the Ritual of the Nine. Nine hours of having your bones broken from smallest to largest. Pain beyond imagining."

My heart seized up in a sharp contraction, and I bit down on my lip as I started to shake. Zach walked into the chapel with us, calm as sunshine, waiting for his moment.

Suddenly I was flying forward. Zach got the gun barrel up just in time. I crashed into him and fell to the floor.

Zach swung the gun and fired it. The thundering blast echoed in my ears, and my wrist ached where I'd landed on it, but I didn't care. They were gone, and I was still alive.

Zach ran to the window and looked out. "Winged him, but he kept going." He walked over to me with a grim expression.

"The other two?" I asked.

"Gone, I guess. You all right?" he said, putting a hand out to lift me up.

I moved my wrist gingerly. It was mighty sore, but not broken. "I'm okay."

He tipped up my chin so he could look at my cheek.

"When I catch that son of a bitch, he's going to fall down a couple flights of stairs before I throw his ass in a cell."

I sat down on a wood bench so I could shake without falling down. "How did you find me?"

"I got to Lyons's house just as you were coming out. Followed you." Not all jealous ex-husbands come in handy, but mine definitely does. "Now, are you going to tell me what this is all about?"

"I don't know."

"You must know something. What did they say?"

I shuddered, thinking about the torture ritual. "One of their gang members was killed, and they thought I might have done it."

Zach's eyebrows shot up in surprise. "You?"

"They don't know me."

Zach looked me over. "But where would they even get an idea like that? I'm looking at you, and I can't see how anyone with half a brain would jump to that conclusion."

I thought about my quick-draw routine on the chapel roof. "Um, I don't know. They got some bad information."

"From who? Astrid?"

"For one," I said, my lips curling into an angry frown.

"She brought you up here to them? And left you?"

I nodded. "She traded me to save her own skin."

"She's Lyons's friend." He paused. "How does he fit into this?"

I shrugged.

"You better not protect the guy, Tammy Jo. He got you mixed up in this, and it could've got you killed. Now where did you go with him the other night?"

My phone rang, and I pulled it out of my pocket. Speak of the devil.

"Hang on a minute," I said to Zach and flipped it open.

"Where are you?" Bryn asked.

"None of your business."

"Security said you and Astrid left together. Are you still following her?"

"Mmm hmm."

"Stop your car, so we can talk."

"We can talk. Go ahead."

"Don't go any farther. She can't be trusted."

"How do you know she can't be trusted?"

He hesitated, but I waited in silence, trying to ignore the hole Zach's eyes were trying to bore into me.

"I saw it," Bryn said finally.

"Saw what?"

"You're familiar with Tarot cards?"

"Yes."

"I practice something along those lines. Astrid came up with the symbol for betrayal more than once."

"But she's a friend of yours."

"She's an acquaintance, not a friend."

I remembered Astrid calling while Georgia Sue was out cold on Bryn's kitchen table. Bryn had told Astrid she couldn't come over. And when she'd wheedled her way onto his property, he'd put her in the guesthouse, away from us.

"Tamara?"

"What?"

"Come back to my house. I can't protect you from this distance."

He sounded so sincere, but then maybe he was just trying to lure me there. Maybe he'd found the note and wanted his coins back.

"We do need to talk. I'll come by soon," I said, then flipped the phone shut. "Bryn Lyons. He said Astrid's been acting strange. Told me not to trust her."

Zach rolled his eyes. "Little late to warn you."

"Yes." I chewed on my lip, trying to decide what to do. Bryn's house did seem to be the only place the werewolves didn't attack, and I needed to negotiate the return of my locket.

Some of the other deputies showed up, and Zach talked to them. I tried to figure out what to do. I didn't really want to go to Bryn's by myself, but taking Zach would be like bringing a lit match into a shed of fireworks.

"All right, it's been fun, but it's time for us to go," Zach said, sliding an arm around my shoulders. "Give Smitty the keys to Nadine's vehicle. He's going to return it for you."

"But I need to fill it up with gas and run it through a car wash for her."

"You're a real considerate thief."

"Momma raised me right."

He rolled his eyes. "You can buy Nadine a tank of gas another time. You're coming with me."

I gave Smitty the keys and walked with Zach to his prowler. I slid into the passenger seat, thinking that I'd borrowed the prowler and hadn't gassed it up or cleaned it, or had the dent fixed. And here he was always saving my life and getting bitten by werewolves for me. I was a terrible ex-wife.

He got in the car, and I leaned over and kissed him on the cheek. He looked at me.

"That the best you can do?" he said, mock serious.

"You know it's not."

"Then lay it on me. Can't think of anything I could use more right now."

We leaned together, and I kissed him for real. One of the guys banged on the roof to encourage us, startling me. I drew back. Only a man would think whooping and startling the heck out of a near-kidnap-and-murder victim was a good idea.

"You're gonna be all right," Zach said, like he could tell I was still worried. He started the car and pulled out, heading toward the station.

"You've got paperwork to do?"

"Nope. I'm putting you in protective custody. Smitty's off duty, but he's gonna drop the truck at TJ's and then come back to the station to play cards with you 'til I get back."

"I'm not five years old."

"I'm well aware of that."

The sun was setting. I definitely didn't have time to play cards in jail. "I'm refusing protective custody. If you want to, you can come with me. I'm going to ask Bryn Lyons some questions about this whole mess."

"I don't need you to help me question Lyons," he said.

"Got a warrant?"

"Not at the moment."

"Then you won't get in to see him without me."

"The sheriff's working on the warrant."

"Feel like twiddling your thumbs until then?"

"When did you get such a smart mouth? You used to be sweet."

I folded my arms across my chest and frowned. I didn't like to get ugly, but I couldn't afford to be too sweet under the circumstances.

We drove to Bryn's property, and there was a big delay at the gate while security cleared things with him. Finally, the gate slid open, and we drove inside.

Mr. Jenson was waiting for us in the foyer, and he scrutinized my face with an expression like he'd just found some renegade ants making a run for the pantry.

"Mr. Lyons is in the living room," he said, holding out a hand to point the way. The house shook slightly, and Zach and I both looked up.

"Another quake," Zach mumbled.

I bet it wasn't Bryn casting spells while we were a room away, so who did that leave? Astrid? Hadn't seen her car and bet she was on her way back to whatever rock she lived under. Lennox maybe.

I heard Bryn curse from down the hall, which surprised me since nothing seemed to rattle him much. I led the way to the living room, only pausing when I first stepped in because Mercutio jumped down from the top of a secretary to greet me. I hugged him and kissed the top of his head.

"It's rare that I envy a cat," Bryn commented as he sat on his sofa.

Zach stood in the doorway, arms akimbo, stance wide.

"I need to talk to you," I said, straightening up.

"It's mutual." Bryn's tone sounded like he wasn't too happy about it. I guess he'd been in his closet since we'd last talked.

"Ladies first," I added quickly.

"That is the house policy," he said, his cobalt blue eyes mocking and sexy at the same time.

Bryn was too darn smart not to realize that he was taunting Zach, and Zach was too darn smart not to realize he was being taunted. If I didn't play my cards right, I was going to find myself right square in the middle of a fistfight.

I cleared my throat and cast a glance at Zach. He frowned slightly but stood totally still. Of course, he'd looked relaxed holding a twelve-gauge on a trio of wolven murderers, too. Who knew how long he'd keep up the pose?

"When the gang came to the actors' meeting, I thought you were an innocent bystander, like me, but now I think they probably came looking for you or Lennox or both."

Bryn raised his eyebrows. "Interesting theory, but without merit."

"It was no accident that you were at Georgia Sue's Halloween party instead of the mayor's, was it? You were there because you knew what was going to happen."

"Are you accusing me of something?" His gaze slid to Zach, then back to me.

I knew I would never get the truth out of him in front of a cop, but it wouldn't have mattered if I'd told Zach to take a tour of the house, he wasn't going anywhere.

Mr. Jenson reappeared with a hand towel wrapped around something. He held it out.

"Ice," he said.

"Thank you." I put the ice to my cheek and sat down on a thick-cushioned ottoman across from Bryn. "Astrid turned me over to the gang. One of them cracked me across the face before Zach got there and saved me." I held up the icepack for a second as illustration.

"I'm sorry I didn't warn you sooner." His voice was even and very formal. This was getting us nowhere.

I sighed. "Is there anything that you can tell Zach to help him catch them?"

"Regrettably, no."

I frowned and shook my head. "Look, if I don't—"

A phone rang, startling me, and I looked around trying to place it. Bryn moved quickly to the opposite wall and slid a painting aside, reaching into a cubbyhole.

He pulled a security phone loose and answered it.

"I understand. I'm sending Jenson to you with Ms. Trask. Lock yourselves in the vault."

Chapter 27

* * * * *

I stood, staring at Bryn, but he didn't look at me. He turned to Zach instead.

"Feel like being a cowboy?" Bryn asked as he walked to the couch he'd been sitting on and reached behind it.

He yanked a shotgun free and tossed it to Zach, who caught it one-handed.

"I've got guns," Zach said.

"Not like these," Bryn said, tossing him a pistol. Then he got a couple guns for himself.

"I'm a good shot," I said. "I can help."

"No," Zach and Bryn said in unison.

"Jenson!" Bryn called out, yanking a small pack from behind the couch. I could hear the bullets rattle as he walked to the door.

"Sir?" Jenson said, materializing.

"Take her to Steve and follow his instructions."

I grabbed Bryn's arm and lowered my voice to a whisper. "No, I should stay and help. You might need to siphon power or something!" I said, my heart racing at the thought of my two favorite men getting slaughtered.

Bryn flashed me a smile. "I wish there was time for that. I'll hope for a rain check on the offer."

I stepped back, shaking my head.

Zach pumped his gun, then leaned over and planted a kiss on my trembling mouth. "Go on now." He looked at Jenson and said, "Carry her if you have to."

"Yes, Jenson, get her out of here," Bryn commanded him and walked out, waving Zach to follow him.

Mercutio bounded after them. *Of course, he's going to play. That cat likes fighting entirely too much.*

"We need to help them," I said.

"Mr. Lyons is the most excellent strategist I have ever had the occasion to meet," Jenson said, extending a hand to indicate that I should precede him from the room. "If he feels that he and the officer can handle the difficulties, I'm sure they will be able to."

"Then why do we have to get locked in a vault?" I asked, walking out of the room.

"The vault is a terrible idea," Lennox Lyons said, appearing from around a corner in the hallway. "And, as it happens, I am in need of Ms. Trask's assistance with another matter." Lennox looked like he needed the teaspoon of sugar and lumberjack breakfast I'd started the day with. He was pale and sweaty and even from where I was standing I could see the dark spot on his black shirt. His wound was bleeding.

"Sir, there seems to be rather considerable trouble. It would be best if you joined us in the vault."

Lennox looked like he was considering it, then stepped forward suddenly and clocked Jenson in the head. The elderly butler went down like a sinker in a pond.

"Oh!" I gasped, dropping to my knees. His pulse was steady in his throat. "With the exception of some werewolves, I can't remember when I've *ever* disliked anybody as much as you," I said, trying to keep myself from screaming curses at him.

Lennox grabbed my arm in a steely grip, making me wince. I was already bruised from the darn wolves.

"Let go of me," I snapped, trying to yank free.

A second later, I was staring into the barrel of a gun. My mouth dropped open in surprise.

"I've got no patience left and no time. Come with me or I'll shoot you," he said.

"What the heck are you talking about?"

"Let's go," he said, waving the gun to emphasize that he was in a hurry. I stood, glancing around. I hoped Steve was catching all this on one of those security cameras because I was *so* going to press charges if I lived through it.

I went with Lennox deep into the house, then out a back door through a fabulous-smelling garden to a path where a golf cart waited for us.

"You'll drive," Lennox said, sitting in the passenger seat.

"Does it interest you to know that your son needs help fighting werewolves right now?"

"He can take care of himself. I raised him," Lennox said, his voice weary.

"You've lost a lot of blood, haven't you?"

"Just drive."

My mind raced as I drove the cart down the cobbled path. Lennox had been sick before the witch's meeting. Maybe he hadn't gotten his bad wound that night. Maybe it was just covered up and had reopened during the fight there.

"Why did you kill Diego, the werewolf?" I asked, taking a stab.

He ignored me. I noticed he didn't deny it.

"Well? I have a right to know! I've nearly been witch tartare more than once, and now men I care about are going to be in a shootout over all this trouble you caused."

"Quiet down, Nancy Shrew," he said. "We can talk after."

"After what?"

"After I've washed this blood off, and you've helped me cast a spell."

"What spell?" When he didn't speak up, I added, "I want answers, and I want them right now."

"To quote Jagger: 'You can't always get what you want.' "

I pursed my lips together. Yep, I definitely hated him. I wished we were on the tor. Consequences be damned, I'd have made a crack in the earth and shoved him in it.

We parked the cart in front of the biggest pole barn I'd ever seen. Easily three thousand square feet. I followed him inside, stunned to see a huge aquarium full of murky water. The place stank of fish, and the tank took up two-thirds of the barn. It was incredible. The tank walls stretched up to about eight feet tall, and there were ladders leading to five-foot platforms. I wondered what in the world they needed such a big fish tank for.

Lennox hit a button, and I heard gears turn, but couldn't tell what he'd done. He walked over to a ladder and pointed to it.

"Get in the tank."

"I don't—"

He grabbed my arm roughly, giving me an impatient yank.

I hissed in pain and climbed up the ladder, looking down into the grayish water.

"Get in the water now."

I pinched my nose and jumped in. The salt water stung my eyes, but it wasn't as cold as I'd expected. I treaded water, sputtering in aggravation.

A moment later, a set of bars slid overhead.

"What are you doing?" I screamed. He'd trapped me.

"I don't want you wandering off while I'm occupied."

"Let me out!"

"You'll be fine. Just keep away from the bars."

The bars were about three feet above my head. What the hell did I look like? A porpoise?

I heard a splash and knew he'd gotten in some other part of the tank.

"What in the Sam Houston?" I mumbled, swimming toward the sound of him grunting in pain. I reached another set of bars. So the tank was partitioned in sections, like underwater jail cells.

Something in the next part grabbed my leg, but I didn't have time to scream before it dragged me down. I thrashed and fought, but whatever had snatched my leg yanked it partway through the bars.

My pulse hammered through me as the thing tried to pull my leg out of joint. My chest squeezed tight. I needed air, but I didn't have to worry about drowning. I was going to have a heart attack before that.

I pretended to relax, not thrashing, then I pressed my free foot against a bar and shoved with all my might. I guess all that Tae Bo three years ago really worked because I got free and broke through the surface of the water, sputtering and shrieking.

I treaded water, thinking that I was pretty damn tired of having the life nearly scared out of me all the time. My legs cramped, and I wasn't sure how much longer I could stay above water.

Then the thing's head emerged. A ferocious face with slimy hair plastered around it and needlelike teeth. It shrieked, hurting my ears, and then, with a swish of its scaly, greenish tail, it disappeared.

I stayed silent in the water for what must have been five minutes before the bars overhead retracted and I saw Lennox, soaked to the bone on the ladder.

"I specifically told you to stay away from the bars."

I made a nasty face at him.

"Would you like to swim a few laps or are you coming out of there?" he asked.

"What was that thing?" I asked.

"Merrow, from a very nasty tribe," he said, glancing at the tank as he climbed down.

"Merrow?"

"Merman. His race is especially vicious. Also, he's angry that I've had him trapped in a tank almost a month."

"Why do you have him in the tank?"

"The scales from their tails have special rejuvenative properties. Fresh scales in salt water, ocean water, heal the most stubborn wounds. It's the only reason I'm still alive."

"So you plan to keep him in that tank for the rest of your life?" I asked, shocked.

"No, I'd rather be dead than continue this much longer. Do you know what it feels like to soak an open wound in salt water? And to be too weak to spell-cast properly? It's no way for a Class Six wizard to live. No, this was a temporary solution."

"Until you found a cure for a werewolf bite?"

"Precisely."

"And have you?"

"Perhaps." Lennox walked over to a button and hit it. "I open the partitions to give him more room to swim when I'm not in the tank." He turned to me. "How is Zach, by the way?"

"He seems fine."

"Yes, the scales work very well at first, but it's just temporary."

My eyes darted around the place, then back to him. "What do you want me to do?" I asked.

"Despite the accent, you're fairly clever." He reached inside his shirt and produced my locket. "I want to meet your ghost."

I gasped. Just like that, there it was. "Give it to me," I said, reaching. He lifted the chain from around his neck and handed it to me.

"You put a binding spell on it, but I stole the bundle and protected the locket with counterspells," he said.

So he'd been the one who'd broken into my house. Bastard. And that's when he'd probably marked my house with the werewolf blood and put them on my trail. Bastard! Lying, thieving, bring-the-town-under-siege bastard!

". . . but she hasn't come out."

"What?"

"I've done a lot of spells for calling ghosts. She won't appear. It makes me believe she's very stubborn and quite powerful. What spell do you use to call her? One of your family's own creation, I suppose?"

I shivered. Even with the crazy heat wave, it was too cold to stand around soaking wet in a cool dark barn. "We don't call her. Edie appears when she feels like it."

He looked surprised for a moment, then tipped his head back and laughed. "Are you serious? You people can't even bring a ghost to heel? How your family has survived all these years, I'll never know."

He sat down on a white marble bench up against the wall.

"We can't wait for her to make an appearance. I expect she's at least got a soul connection to you. When she realizes you're in distress, she'll come."

I didn't like the sound of "in distress," but Lennox was the last person I felt like helping.

"Sit," he said, nodding to the bench. "We'll try some spells together."

I didn't move. He took the gun from his belt and pointed it right at my heart.

"We're out of time. I've been spell-casting here today, so the wolves have tracked me to this place. Bryn won't be able to contain them for long. I need to talk to your ghost so that I can get out of here. Then you can be on your way, too. When my full power is restored, Bryn and I will be able to defeat the wolves."

"Why should I trust you?"

"Because I have a gun pointed at your chest?"

"If you just wanted to talk to her, you could have asked for my help without stealing my locket. No, I don't know why you want her, but I'm not going to help you call her."

"If I'd asked you and you'd said no and then your locket disappeared, who would have been at the top of Sutton's list of suspects? Now, sit here. I want you to think about the first time you ever talked to her."

I tried not to let any memories pop into my head, but there Edie was telling me to cut all the Barbie dolls' hair into bobs, including the Collector's Edition Snow White that was supposed to be Georgia Sue's birthday present. I'd gotten in so much trouble.

He murmured something and lurched forward and grabbed my sore wrist and squeezed.

"Ouch!"

He looked around. "She's not here. I'll need you to recite the verse with me."

I'd always sworn I wouldn't betray my family or friends. Not if terrorists took me hostage. Not if someone offered me two million dollars and a free lifetime subscription to *In Style* magazine. Edie was family, and Lennox couldn't be trusted. I wasn't going to help him.

"No," I said.

He moved the gun and pressed it to my forehead. I squinched my eyes shut, my pulse pattering. Bravery is kind of overrated, and I hoped I wouldn't need to be this brave in the afterlife.

Chapter 28

After a few seconds of not losing consciousness from a bullet breaking into my head, I opened my eyes. Lennox had leaned back on the bench with the gun sitting next to him.

"You were bluffing about shooting me," I said.

He nodded curtly.

"Good for you. Maybe you won't go to hell after all."

"Too late." He took a few short gasping breaths and pointed at the gun. "Take it. They're coming. Get out."

He tipped his head back to rest.

"This isn't the time to pass out," I said, taking the gun into my right hand with the locket and tugging on him with the left. "Get up."

Blood seeped through his wet shirt. "C'mon, have a dip in the smelly water and then we'll go. Edie will be showing up in a little while, and we'll ask her if she knows a cure for werewolf bites."

"That's not the question to ask her," he said. Sweat sprang up on his forehead, and he slumped over.

"Dang it," I mumbled, trying to get him upright.

Mercutio darted in, meowing wildly, and I knew wolves were chasing him. I ran to the door, pushed it shut and bolted it.

"C'mon, let's get you in the water," I said to Lennox. I grabbed him and the locket fell to the floor. Mercutio snatched it, playing with the chain.

Lennox swayed, but pulled himself upright, leaning heavily on the bench. Something crashed into the door.

"Too late." He sagged, but I grabbed him and squeezed his arms.

"Zach and Bryn will come rescue us. And we've got to be ready to walk out of here, maybe even to run. Now we're getting in the tank. Show some grit."

He didn't say anything, but he let me lead him to the ladder.

He shook his head at the rungs. Mercutio scaled it easily and sat looking down at us, the locket hanging from his neck like he was some king cat on a throne.

"Gee, thanks for the help," I said, shoving at Lennox, who climbed wearily.

The doors groaned under the blows, and Mercutio swiped at the air and then bent and grabbed Lennox's shirt with his teeth and pulled.

A couple moments later, Lennox lay on the platform, panting. "Hurry," I said, trying to roll him into the tank.

"Wait. You've got to raise the inner bars." He coughed and there was a little bright blood at the corner of his mouth.

I scrambled down the ladder just as the bolt snapped and the doors flung open. Three snarling wolves rushed in. Merc roared, and I screamed.

Two ran, leaping in the air toward the platform. I fired at them. Lennox, who looked dead, moved a leg at the last moment and kicked one, causing him to vault into the tank, while Mercutio fought with the other. They rolled, snarling into the tank, too.

"No, Merc! Get out of there," I yelled.

The last wolf changed into Samuel, and his yellow eyes narrowed. "My wolves have your friends surrounded. When their ammunition runs out, they'll be ripped to shreds."

My gaze darted to the open door and in an instant Samuel was on me, knocking me back, the gun flying from my hand. He ripped my clothes, and I screamed, struggling.

Water splashed over the edge of the tank as the animals in the tank battled. Suddenly a wolf broke the surface, howling in rage and fear. Samuel looked up at the sound.

We heard another wolven howl of pain along with the merman's shriek.

"Ahh!" came the growling scream from the tank. Samuel leapt up, running to the tank. He jumped, clearing the wall, and plunged in.

I stood up on shaky legs, biting my lip. There was more splashing and screams, and the water turned a murky maroon.

"Mercutio," I cried, racing to retrieve the gun. I snatched it up and ran to the ladder. I climbed up with the gun in my teeth, like a deranged pirate.

I glanced at Lennox. His eyes were closed. I couldn't tell if he was still breathing. I gripped the gun with both hands, trying to make out the wolves and the merman.

Suddenly the waves died down. The gun shook in my hands.

Samuel, in half-wolf form, broke the surface of the water and sailed up onto the platform, his jaws open wide, giant teeth ready to snap my neck.

I yelped and pulled the trigger over and over. The bullets tore into him and knocked him back into the water. Then everything was still, the bloody water settling, calm as death.

"No," I whispered.

Then there was a tiny swish, like a snake moving. And I saw the tail sweeping away from us. And Mercutio's head broke the surface as he clawed his way up the inner ladder.

"Mercutio!" I cried, throwing my arms around his neck when he got to the platform. He shook and spit out a mouthful of dog hair and green scales, coughing a bit before he settled down to lick his fur.

The bodies rose to the surface. The merman had sliced them up. I shuddered, looking away.

"Tamara!" Bryn shouted, running into the barn.

"Here." I said, bending down to check Lennox. "Where's Zach?" I asked, feeling a faint pulse.

"He's okay. Bleeding some, and it slowed him down. Are you all right?"

I nodded. "Lennox isn't doing very good though."

Bryn's pace slowed, and his face creased with sorrow. "I know." He came up the ladder with an expression that made my chest hurt.

"Tammy Jo?" Zach called.

I looked up to see Zach shuffle to the doorway and lean heavily on it. I could see the blood soaking his shirt even from twenty feet away.

"I'm here," I said, hurrying down the ladder. I was almost to him when he crumpled to the ground.

"Oh!" I dropped to my knees next to him. He had a second wound now, a slash to his side, and both wounds streamed blood. I shoved my hand over the chest wound and pressed down as hard as I could.

He winced a little and opened his eyes. His tongue touched his dry lips as if to wet them, but there wasn't enough moisture.

"Hey there," I whispered.

"Hey, darlin', you all right?"

I nodded.

"Good. A couple got past us. I thought . . ." His eyes were unnaturally bright. "Hell, you're still the prettiest thing I ever saw." He paused, his lids drifting down before he forced them back up. "I wasn't all I should have been to you, but I loved you. You'll always remember that for me, won't you?"

Tears spilled from my eyes. I leaned down and kissed his lips. "Don't go," I whispered against his mouth, crying harder.

"No help for it." I felt his hand rub my back and then fall away.

I sobbed over him.

"Don't cry, darlin'." His voice was so weak.

"What have you all been up to?"

I looked up through blurry eyes and found Edie bending to examine Mercutio.

"Zach's been bitten by a werewolf. He needs help!"

"Oh," she said grimly. She drifted toward us and curled down to have a closer look. "I'm so sorry," she said.

"He's dying. Do you know anything? Any spell?"

She shook her head sadly. "My poor darling," she said, brushing a phantom finger along my cheek. "Don't worry. He's very capable. He'll find his way to the other side straight away. And maybe

I'll walk with him partway. I've wanted to have a chat with him for such a long time."

Zach was staring directly at the spot near my shoulder where Edie's face was.

"What?" I asked.

"Nothing," he said, closing his eyes.

"*You* had her locket all this time?" Bryn asked, his voice a combination of surprise and anger. I looked over my shoulder and found that he'd carried Lennox down from the platform and set him on the nearby bench.

"She can dance on my grave when I'm dead, and you can watch if you wish," Lennox said, putting the focus right back on his own trouble, which I couldn't blame him for.

Bryn sighed, frowning, then spoke a few words in their foreign language. Lennox answered, and Bryn looked over to me.

"My father says there's a legend of healing water, Leon's Spring. He thought your family ghost might know the location. Another ghost told him she did."

I looked expectantly at Edie.

"It's not pronounced *lee-on*. It's pronounced *lay-own*. And I do know where it is. It's along the second northeast ley line. About seven miles outside the town."

I told Bryn what Edie had said.

"I'll get the car," Bryn said, hurrying out.

A few minutes later, Steve from security was helping Bryn load Lennox and Zach onto the bench seats in the back of the limo. I sat on the floor between them, applying pressure to their wounds. Edie sat on the floor, too, with Mercutio curled up near her.

Bryn jerked the car out of the driveway and sped out of town. I gave him directions via Edie through the open partition.

"Hurry," I whispered as Zach's breathing got more uneven, and I could hardly feel a pulsation from Lennox's wound anymore.

After about ten minutes, Edie announced, "We're here."

"Stop the car!" I said.

She floated out through the roof. Bryn and Steve yanked the doors open. Steve pulled Zach out and hauled him over his shoulder in the same fireman's carry Bryn used.

"Which way?" Bryn asked. The light from the headlights petered out a few feet into the blackness, and I couldn't see anything farther ahead.

"Follow me," Edie said.

"This way," I said to the men. "Follow my voice." I stumbled forward over the rough ground and then after a few feet, tripped and pitched forward. I put my arms out, but didn't hit the ground. I plunged underwater, thrashing from the shock. When I surfaced, I could hear the others. They'd all fallen in. We were up to our necks in water.

"Steve, dunk him all the way under a few times and pull him back out," Bryn said.

We all took a bath in the cool, fresh water. I swam a few feet, then crawled out on a bank that Edie led me to.

"I'll meet you at the car," Edie said.

"I can't see where I'm going."

"Follow your ears," she said, but the only sound I could hear was the noise the men were making, dragging Lennox and Zach out.

A few seconds later, I heard the car stereo. Some a.m. station was playing old jazz. I was amazed we could pick up the signal.

When I got to the car, I found Edie lying on the roof, looking at the night sky. Merc was sitting next to her, licking his paws.

"How did you turn on the radio?"

"Mercutio turned it on for me."

"Mercutio?"

"Our cat."

"I know he's our cat. How did you know his name?"

"It's on his collar."

"Oh," I said.

"Don't sound so disappointed. Just because he can't talk doesn't mean we don't understand each other."

I heard the men over my shoulder. I turned. "How are they?"

"Let's see," Bryn said, lowering Lennox to the hood of the car and yanking his shirt open. He laughed that gorgeous laugh. I turned from them and hurried over to where Steve was lowering Zach into the back of the limo. I pulled his shirt up and stared down at the skin, perfectly sealed with small white scars.

"Ha!" I shouted, bending to squeeze his cool chest in a makeshift hug.

"Am I dead?" he mumbled.

"No," I said.

"Sure feels like Heaven."

Chapter 29

*

I woke early and found out my body didn't ache nearly as bad as it should have. The scratches on my legs had been healed in that spring, and my wrist only throbbed if I cocked it all the way back.

Bryn and Zach had both tried to convince me to sleep in a bedroom with them, but I slept on the living room couch with Mercutio instead.

It turned out we'd skipped fall and headed from our freak heat wave right into winter. A cold snap, the weatherman called it. Darn chilly, I called it, and was glad I was inside making a black raspberry torte using Bryn's state-of-the art kitchen instead of outside with him talking to a team of divers who were going to put the merman back in the ocean. A big rig had just been loaded with a temporary tank.

Georgia Sue called, sounding way more cheerful than someone after a near-death experience ought to have. She told me all about the hospital in Dallas, including its lunch menu that tasted nearly as bad as the squirrel stew her momma made once with curry. Then Georgia went on for two full minutes about how Parkland should invest in some Downey fabric softener for its stiff cotton hospital gowns. The thing she barely mentioned was what happened to get her there. She couldn't remember a thing about the park that night. And she seemed totally unconcerned about it, too. Well, that's Georgia Sue, I guess.

I glanced over at Mr. Jenson. He had a very neat, white bandage on his head and, looking as undisturbed as Georgia Sue sounded, he went about his business. He poured a small bowl of cream for Mercutio, who tap danced in anticipation like he didn't have a million scratches and stitches on his body.

Mr. Jenson arranged fancy china on a silver tray and then set a pot of tea on it. He poured a bit of expensive Scotch whiskey into each of the two cups and then a tiny drizzle of honey. It looked so nice I wanted to take its picture instead of taking it down the hall to our recovering wolf-bite victims.

"You want some arsenic to put in that cup?" I asked.

"Arsenic?" he asked, setting down linen napkins while I cut slices of dessert, including one for Mr. Jenson.

"Yeah, for Lennox's cup. Don't guess we'll use enough to kill him since I went to some trouble to save his life, but enough to teach him a lesson for knocking you in the head."

"The circumstances were most extraordinary yesterday. It doesn't seem worth dwelling on them."

"That's right kind of you." I know it's unchristian to hold grudges, but in my genes I'm part pagan, and I couldn't help but be annoyed on Jenson's behalf. He could've broken a hip or his head when he fell.

Jenson laid an iron pill on each of two small dishes, and I decided I want Jenson to stay with me next time I get the flu.

"I shall take the tray," he said.

"Oh no you don't." I slid the tray to me. "You'll serve Lennox Lyons tea and torte today over my dead body. Kick your feet up and rest."

He might have wanted to protest, but I was quicker and was halfway down the hall before he could answer.

Lennox lay in bed, reading a magazine called *WitchWeek*. It sure looked interesting, but I pretended not to care. I was gonna try to go back to being a pastry chef again, so I didn't need to know what happened at the last Conclave meeting.

I set the tray down and poured tea into one of the cups. "Why'd you kill Diego, the werewolf?"

"That is none of your business."

"You want cake and tea or not?"

He rolled his eyes and lifted his magazine again. "If you're not going to serve it to me, please remove it."

I clenched my teeth. He was still the king of the bastards.

"Fine, you don't want Jenson's whiskey-honey tea, that's your business, not mine." I lifted the tray and was halfway to the door.

"Tamara?"

"What?" I asked without turning around.

"The wolf was holding a weather witch hostage, a friend of mine as it happened. When I tried to liberate her, he attacked us. She died, leaving a rather significant heat wave in her wake. Obviously, I was bitten, but survived. That's all I'll say on the matter."

I turned and set the tray back down. "Iron to build your blood," I said, handing him a pill.

"My own personal Florence Nightingirl. I feel very fortunate," he said dryly, but he put it in his mouth and swallowed it with a mouthful of tea.

I set the dish of cake down with a napkin and started to pick the tray back up to head down the hall to check on Zach.

"I apologize," he said.

"Which thing are you sorry for? 'Cause the list of stuff you could be apologizing for is kind of long."

He smiled. "When I went to your home and when I counter-spelled your family locket, I tangled our magicks together—so far as the werewolves' tracking was concerned. It wasn't intentionally done, but I suppose I owe you an apology."

Darn right.

"Well, I suppose I accept your apology for that." I waited, but he didn't say any more. "Do you think the wolves could've tracked my magical energy to someone else who cast a spell using my blood to power it?"

Lennox took a bite of cake. I held my breath waiting for his reaction. "This dessert is the most important reason that I'm pleased you didn't end up dead during our little adventure."

I decided that the only compliments the man knows how to give are the backhanded kind. Whoever Bryn had learned to be charming from, it sure wasn't his father.

Unfortunately, I was just dumb enough to care that he liked it. He took another bite and closed his eyes to savor it.

"And yes to your question," he added.

Hmm. So the werewolves probably had torn up Doc Barnaby's house looking for me after he'd used power stolen from me to cast his ill-fated wife-raising spell.

I took my tray and knocked gently on Zach's guest room door.

"C'mon in," he called.

I opened the door. Mr. Jenson had laundered Zach's pants as best he could, but there were still a few bloodstains on them. His shirt couldn't be saved, so he wore a borrowed white T-shirt that was too tight. It looked good on him, like most things do.

He stood near the bed, talking on the phone. "Yeah, I'll be there. Gimme 'bout half an hour." He hung up and smiled at me.

"You're up. Feel okay?" I asked, setting the tray down.

"Feel fine. Even better now that I'm looking at you," he said, walking around the bed.

"I brought you some tea with honey."

"You brought me the honey I want, all right," he said, pulling me to him. He felt as solid and strong as ever, and the kiss was so potent I had to sit on the edge of the bed when he let me go.

"Take this. It's an iron pill."

He popped it in his mouth and gulped down the tea with it. He looked in the empty cup. "Not bad." When he looked up, he said, "I've got to go make a report at the station."

"What will you say?"

"Gang violence," he said.

I nodded. Zach didn't mention that they'd been werewolves, so neither did I.

"Don't you want to have some cake?"

"Not right now." He yanked his boots on and walked over to the door. "Hey, that ghost of yours. What's she supposed to look like anyway?"

"Black hair. Very pretty. Delicate as this cup."

"Hmm."

"Did you—"

"Now that I'm leaving here, I'll expect you to pack your stuff and head home, too. I'll call you there in an hour."

Just like that, he was back to calling the shots. "I've got some errands to do. I might not be there when you call," I said.

"Errands around town?"

I nodded.

"That's all right, so long as you clear out of here. And I told TJ and Nadine we'd have dinner with them and the kids tonight. To make up for the car business. Maybe you could make a pie or something," he said on his way out the door.

I looked down at the cake I had already spent several hours making and gritted my teeth. Sure, I would make Nadine a pie, but if Zach thought everything was just going to go back to the way it was, we were sure headed for some trouble. Turns out taking on a werewolf pack changes a person.

I took a few bites of torte, letting the buttercream melt on my tongue. Delicious. It was good to be alive. I reloaded the tray and returned to the kitchen with it. All the pots and pans were rinsed and already soaking in soapy water. Yep, I love that Jenson.

I sat down at the table and watched Mercutio lick cream off his whiskers.

"Any dessert left?" Bryn asked.

I glanced over my shoulder to see him stroll into the room. He sat next to me at the table. I lifted one of the pretty white china dishes and put a slice of the torte on it for him with a silver spoon.

Bryn took a bite, then licked his lips. "This is incredible."

"Thank you."

We sat quietly considering each other for a few moments. I didn't know how I felt about him siphoning power from me every time he got the chance, but I guessed he had mostly helped me over the past few days, giving me Mercutio, getting me out of jail, saving my life. I supposed that kind of made us friends, even if I couldn't totally trust him.

"I put your gold coins back in your room. On the bench at the foot of the bed."

"I saw. Thank you."

"Sorry about the door. I'll pay for the damage as soon as I get on my feet money-wise."

He waved away the offer. "The door was flimsy. I needed a reminder to replace it."

Bryn's pretty darn generous. I wondered if that might have been because he had a guilty conscience. I kept asking myself, how much had he known and when?

"So, that night that Georgia got bit, Lennox said that he owed Kenny a favor. Do you know why?" I asked.

"Kenny makes his own bullets. My father commissioned him to make several boxes of silver bullets. On his way to meet my father, the sheriff pulled Kenny over for speeding and spotted the ammunition that had been sitting in the passenger seat. The sheriff wanted to know what was going on, but Kenny wouldn't tell him who he'd made them for or why, so Hobbs confiscated the boxes of bullets."

"Is that why the burglars broke into the sheriff's safe? To get the silver bullets?"

Bryn nodded. "And to keep the sheriff distracted by the break-in at his own house, so Hobbs wouldn't focus on the other things that were happening in town."

"How involved were you in the break-ins?"

"I wasn't. I suspected my father might have orchestrated things when I cast a spell to find my watch, and it was repelled, but he didn't admit to everything until this morning."

"Then why'd you come to Georgia Sue's party?"

"To see you." He smiled. "I had a premonition, of sorts, involving a beautiful girl and some incredible sensory details of a night of—"

"I get the idea," I blurted, holding out a hand to stop him.

"My seer cards have shown me more than usual lately. A red witch kept coming up, often with a lion. At first, I thought the lion meant courage. But then Mercutio came down the Amanos River on a raft, like a feline Huck Finn. The current brought him right to the landing. I knew immediately I was supposed to introduce him to you."

"Yeah, that worked out. He and I get along." I tapped my thumb on the table. "On a raft, huh? I wonder where he came from."

Bryn shrugged.

"Well, I guess I'll go get my things together. The torte will keep fine in a cake dish or Tupperware in the fridge." I stood and started away from the table. Bryn caught my hand and held it in his.

"I want to see you. Have dinner with me this week."

"I don't—"

"We have things to discuss about our case."

"Case?"

"There will be an inquiry into this matter."

"Zach's giving a statement to the sheriff. They'll chalk it up to gang violence, I guess."

"Not that inquiry. One from the Otherworld community."

"Oh." I tilted my head. "Well, tell them whatever you want, whatever you think is best."

He went right on holding my hand, which tingled in his grasp.

"Still planning to avoid me?"

"It's just one of those things." I wasn't sure if the impending theft of the locket had been the reason we were supposed to stay away from the Lyons family. Now that it had been returned safe, maybe they could come off Lenore's list, but I'd have to wait to talk to Momma and Aunt Mel about it when they got back. I tugged, and he let my hand go reluctantly.

"Sutton doesn't have the market cornered on tenacity."

"What's that mean?"

"It means, I won't give up easily on the idea of you and me having some sort of relationship."

"I sure wish you would. It would make things a heck of a lot easier for me."

He smiled. "Sorry. No."

"Well, anyway, I can be all tenacious-like too when I set my mind to it. So I wouldn't get your hopes up."

He continued to smile at me, looking as smugly happy as Mercutio with that bowl of cream.

"Merc, you ready or what?" I demanded.

Mercutio looked up lazily.

"Okay, stay here for all I care. I'm going." I was out the door and halfway down the hall when I felt Mercutio bound up next to me.

I bent down and ran a hand over his sleek head. "You were tempted to stay in that kitchen with him and all that cream, huh?" I glanced around to be sure no one was listening. "I can't say as I blame you."

He meowed, and I smiled.

"Yeah, you're my favorite, too." I said, hugging his neck and adding in a whisper, "But it's probably best if you don't tell the men I said that."

* * *

I just had one thing left to do before I could go home and see about getting my doors fixed. I'd decided to let Zach loan me some money until I got a new job, so Merc and I drove to Macon Hill, and I retrieved Earl's .38 from the roof.

Johnny Nguyen called while I cleaned it. I reassured him that I'd gotten the locket back and Edie was safe and sound. He asked how I was feeling emotionally because Rollie's coven had called to tell him about how gruesome the attack at the witch meeting had been.

My lip did tremble a little when I thought about all the dead people. I filled him in on the details of the past couple days, and my voice sort of choked up as I did. Johnny told me I'd done a good job protecting the town. I wished I could have helped more at the meeting.

In the background, I heard Rollie say, "Hey, these things happen. Tell her there's no point crying over spilled blood."

I shook my head, but couldn't help smiling a little.

"Rollie say, listen to relaxation tape and get sleep. You feel better."

For not being a native English speaker, Johnny's sure got the translation thing down pat. "You're sure a good friend, Johnny. I'm sorry I thought—"

"Oh, that all behind us. Come for haircut and scalp massage. We talk about happy things."

"Thanks."

I pulled up to Earl's pawnshop and tried not to be nervous. Mercutio slept in the passenger seat, which was good. I didn't think Earl'd be too happy to see me, let alone Merc.

I went in and was surprised when he didn't glare at me.

"Hey, Earl."

"Tammy Jo," he said evenly. I noticed Jenna Reitgarten standing near a big mirror next to an original Elvis Presley Vegas polyester jumpsuit that I didn't think anyone but the king could really pull off.

I shifted uncomfortably, not wanting Jenna to hear my conversation with Earl, but there wasn't any help for that I guessed.

I set the gun and the four hundred dollars on top of the glass case he was standing at.

"I brought back what I borrowed. I'd like my jewelry, please."

He grinned, and my heart pounded in alarm.

"Too late. Jenna bought the lot of it about five minutes ago."

"What?"

"Yep. She likes to get a good deal, so I called her this morning to let her know I got some nice jewelry in stock."

Only a former friend knows how to really hurt a person deep. And Earl definitely fell in the "former" category when it came to friends.

"Well, I guess we don't have anything else to say to each other then." I picked up the money, but left the gun where it lay. Just as well. I didn't think I should have a gun in hand when I talked to Jenna.

I walked over to the mirror and saw that she was holding up her hair to check out how Aunt Mel's emerald earrings looked on her. My stomach churned, and I swallowed hard.

"Morning, Jenna."

She smiled, smug as can be. "Good morning, Tammy Jo."

"I'll be wanting that jewelry back."

Her grin got wider. "Not a chance."

My blood started to boil. "You really plan to wear my family's jewelry?"

"Well, it could be a little better quality, but it'll do for regular occasions."

My heart hammered from the effort of not screaming my head off at her. "Name your price. You can make a profit and buy something that suits you better."

She turned and looked me up and down. "First of all, you couldn't afford it." She paused, turning her nose up. "And second, lately you've been acting a lot higher and mightier than you are. It's time someone taught you a lesson. That's going to be my fall project."

I clenched my fists, tempted to hex her, and tried not to give her a four-letter piece of my mind, but I couldn't help it. I opened my mouth to holler that I didn't deserve this kind of treatment the morning after the most traumatic day of my life. Then she hiccupped.

"Well, I'll see you around," she said, hiccupping again.

Uh-oh.

She rolled her eyes at me, then strolled to the shop door. "Darn hiccups," she muttered after she hiccupped again.

I watched her walk to her car, her shoulders jerking every few seconds from a new hiccup.

Earl ignored me, until I started giggling.

"Something else I can help you with? Otherwise, you can go on and get out of my store."

"Earl, you turned into a real nasty person, and temporarily losing my jewelry was a small price to pay to find that out."

He frowned.

"You know, I was just thinking that the universe and the good Lord have ways of seeing that things work out. Better watch yourself, Earl."

I hurried out and hopped in the car. Mercutio woke when I slammed my door shut, which was real convenient since then I could tell him about what happened.

I pulled out of the parking space as I said, "And having the hiccups gets old pretty darn quick."

As usual, Merc didn't disagree.